QUEEN OF HEARTS

by
Dahlia Schweitzer

THE BAO HOUSE
TORONTO * LOS ANGELES * NEW YORK CITY

Queen Of Hearts
By Dahlia Schweitzer

Copyright © 2013 Dahlia Schweitzer

Contents

Chapter One	7
Chapter Two	19
Chapter Three	33
Chapter Four	45
Chapter Five	63
Chapter Six	69
Chapter Seven	75
Chapter Eight	81
Chapter Nine	89
Chapter Ten	99
Chapter Eleven	119
Chapter Twelve	129
Chapter Thirteen	145
Chapter Fourteen	153
Chapter Fifteen	165
Chapter Sixteen	177
Chapter Seventeen	187
Chapter Eighteen	201
Chapter Nineteen	207
Chapter Twenty	215
Chapter Twenty-One	227
Chapter Twenty-Two	235
Chapter Twenty-Three	247
Chapter Twenty-Four	277
Chapter Twenty-Five	283

"When the performance ends and the climax is reached, one of the most divine emotions can be enjoyed: that created by the experience of the impossible."

- Roberto Giobbi

CHAPTER ONE

I held Mark's hand as we walked in to the theater. The room was small, seating forty-five people, maximum, including the ten who had to stand behind the back row. We were in the famous Peller Theater, in the basement of the even more famous Magic Castle, located in Hollywood, California. The chill of the air conditioning drew me close to him, and I pressed my body against his as we found our seats. My short dress left a lot of flesh exposed, and I wished I had worn tights.

Once we were seated—front row, center, because that was Mark's style—I took his hand and rested it on my bare thigh. The air conditioning was so strong that I could feel goose bumps running over my skin. I was grateful for his hand, the warmth of his body sending a necessary heat, and I wished his hand could cover more than that small patch of thigh.

I studied Mark's profile as he read the show's playbill. His face was dimly lit in the darkened theater. This was my first time at the Magic Castle, an exclusive members-only club devoted to magicians and lovers of magic. I had driven by it many times, its roost up a winding driveway above Franklin Avenue, just off the 101 Freeway near the Hollywood Bowl, not far from my house. But in my six years in Los Angeles, I had only gone to the Hollywood Bowl once, and I had never been to the Castle. Its Victorian architecture seemed dated amongst the glitz of the Hollywood, and its perch so far above street level made it seem even more exclusive and isolated.

Why would I go?

Who went to magic shows, anyway?

There were a few times I had almost gone, but it never felt worth the effort, visions of awkward magicians playing with cards and coins filling my head. The members-only admission policy was just one more deterrent on the list of reasons to go elsewhere, like the multiplex down the street.

And yet, here we were, thanks to Mark's friend Ryan, who had gotten us on the list, insisting that Mark and I *had* to see this particular magic show. Apparently, or so Ryan told me, Rafael Delgado and Peter Mills, celebrated magicians in their own right, had joined forces and were doing a show together which was basically reinventing magic. I took Ryan's word for all this, not knowing who either magician was or that magic even needed to be reinvented. I had been to a Copperfield show once when I was twelve, and that was the extent of my magic experience.

Not only did magic feel dated to me, but The Magic Castle, too, felt like a relic from another era. It was a Victorian mansion inside as well as out. The entire place was carpeted in a lush deep red that not only silenced the sound of footsteps, but also made the place feel like an embracing womb of refined elegance. Making our way from the entrance to the Peller Theater necessitated navigating a labyrinth of stairs and hallways, all covered with the same deep red carpeting, and walking past countless bars and numerous other theaters. It felt dizzying and surreal.

To add to my dizziness, there were at least five magic shows happening at once. There were, for example, the Parlour, the Close-Up Gallery, and the Palace, each one varied in size and ambiance. The Palace was the big one, with the headlining acts and the Vegas glitz. The Close-Up was tiny, full at twenty people. The Parlour was somewhere between the

Peller and the Close-Up, a little bigger than the Close-Up but lacking the Peller's technical capabilities. In other words, if Vegas glitz and showmanship was not your thing, the Peller was really the best theater in the place. It was small enough to feel intimate without the claustrophobia of the Close-Up, and the fact that the magicians were able to control light and sound often led to more thrilling performances than you could find at the Parlour.

While all these scheduled shows were taking place, there were also countless informal performances happening throughout the Castle. Magician members would set up stations impromptu at various locations, in the endless nooks and crannies the Castle offered, or sometimes just at a bar. They would pull out a deck of cards, and that would be enough of a signal for people to gather. These magicians would do tricks for free, sometimes for just a few minutes, sometimes for as long as half an hour. All this led to an atmosphere of wonder throughout the venue. Cards were literally disappearing everywhere you turned, met with exclamations of amazement and sounds of laughter and joy. It was an incredible experience, and I could not stop staring, trying to take it all in.

Since it was our first time at the Castle, we had to be escorted to the Peller because we would never have found it on our own. From the main entrance, we had to climb up a winding flight of stairs, go through the restaurant, up some more stairs, past the Palace and then past the Parlour, around a corner and down a narrow flight of stairs into what felt like the catacombs of the Magic Castle, a basement area with no cell reception and a floating fish tank with some Houdini artifact inside. The room was lined with a winding red couch, predestined for the crowds waiting to see this show. People were driving in from Vegas, flying in from New York, sitting on the couch for over three hours to get a spot in the Peller Theater for the coveted Rafael and Peter show. It did not matter how hard it was to find this room, or how difficult to get in to the Castle itself, show after show was sold out.

We, however, did not have to wait long. Mark would not have had the patience for that. Ryan knew the house manager, and so we were able to be seated first, which was how we ended up front and center, with me staring at Mark's dimly lit profile, holding his hand against my cold thigh, the room filling up with people and anticipation.

The deep red carpeting and the décor that felt like it had not been updated this century, combined with a strict dress code that resulted in a room full of suits and evening dresses, made me feel as though I had been transported not only out of Hollywood but also to another century. I loved it. The night felt full of magic and possibility, and the show had not even started. I had no idea what to expect. The endless lines outside the Peller Theater and the excited buzzing around us just enhanced my anticipation. It would be a night full of illusions, only I had no idea just how spectacular they would be.

The room went dark. Music started to play. I squeezed Mark's hand in excitement, and we smiled at each other. I had never been a big fan of magic, not even after the Copperfield show, but when the spotlight switched on, centered on the two men sitting across from each other on the stage, I could not tear my eyes away. They began dealing cards, matching each other move for move, with perfect choreography and in total silence.

They both wore gray suits and were equidistant from where I was sitting, but my attention centered on one of the two men as if by magnetic pull. Rafael was smaller, with delicate features and curly dark brown hair that was a little too long. His suit was rumpled, the shirt pulled out of the waistband, the tie slightly askew. Peter, with his short dark hair, perfectly pressed suit, and Abercrombie model cheekbones, was unquestionably the more conventionally attractive one, but he did not hold my interest.

My eyes were mesmerized by the first magician, by the way the cards flowed through his fingers like water, by the way his glasses slid down his nose, by the piercing grey-blue of his eyes, the squareness of his jaw, and the casual way his shirt wrinkled. The fluid motions of his hand seemed more flexible, more dexterous, than a hand had a right to be. The artfully askew nature of his clothing, the shirt tails sticking out behind his suit jacket, made me envision those clothes on the floor of my room, torn off his body by my greedy hands.

I had a sudden flash of his hand stroking the side of my face, his lips kissing mine, and I had to shake my head to lose the image. I was on a date with the love of my life. What was I thinking? What was I doing? My cheeks flushed with guilt, and I was grateful that Mark was riveted by the show and did not notice.

Despite my lack of focus, the cards were still being dealt and selected, vanishing and reappearing at appropriate moments with stunning precision. Every revelation was more spectacular than the one before, as the deck of cards was pushed back and forth across the table, each magician pulling out exactly the card he had predicted.

I was as mesmerized by the seeming impossibility of the performance as by the action happening in my head. I tried desperately to block it out, embarrassed as if everyone could see it and would know what I was thinking. I crossed my legs, as if that would somehow make the scene in my head fade to black, but my face still flushed with a guilty shame. Mark remained oblivious while I imagined those cards falling down upon my skin, my body reclining on the soft green velvet of their table, aces and clubs covering my naked body as Rafael's delicate fingers shuffled and reshuffled the deck, all fifty-two cards landing across my body, before those fingers found a different task between my thighs.

When I crossed my legs, Mark's hand was knocked off my thigh, but he did not notice, and I did not care. He did not notice because he was too busy watching the magic, and I did not care because I did not need his hand anymore. A heat of an entirely different sort was running through my body.

The next trick required audience participation. I sat, riveted, as the two magicians scanned the crowd for the right volunteer. I could not take my eyes off Rafael's face as his eyes roved the crowd. Despite my focus, it was still shocking when he looked straight at me, as if he had read my mind.

"What card do you want?" he asked.

I looked around, the classic clueless audience "who me?" maneuver. He just kept looking at me and smiling, nodding as if to say yes, *you.*

"I want you" is what I almost said.

But I stopped myself just in time. My face flushed a deep shade of red. I could not look away from him. I could not look at Mark. I felt mortified and infatuated. The magician's eyes locked onto mine, and the entire room disappeared.

Only it was not that kind of magic show. Peter and Mark were still there, unfortunately. As was everyone else in the full theater. And they were all staring at me, waiting for my answer.

"Name a card," he repeated, and I realized I was holding everything up.

"Queen of hearts."

He smiled, his straight white teeth contrasting with the scruff of several days worth of dark beard. He understood the subtext, or, at least, I imagined he did. I smiled back, my skin feeling red and hot, the rest of the room a million miles away. My brain felt wiped clean. I could not think of anything else. I just stared at him. I was consumed by this man I had not even really met and by my crazy desire to tear off his rumpled clothes.

"Queen of hearts," the other magician repeated, a reminder that he was there, that he existed, that Rafael and I were not alone, and that we were not naked despite the brilliant detail of the images in my mind.

The show continued.

Everything that happened next was a blur. I could only focus on the moment that had just transpired, our brief but significant exchange, and the vivid X-rated scenario in my head. All I could think about were his hands on me, his eyes staring into mine, and that persistent image of cards showering down on my naked body. On stage, cards were being selected, concealed and then revealed, there was something involving a box and a blindfold, but I only noticed two things: one, that when my beloved magician was blindfolded, I suddenly realized I had a kidnapping fetish, and I wanted to grab him, make off with him, throw him into my car, and tie him down to my bed, and two, that at the end of the trick, my queen of hearts appeared in a box, and I got to take her home with me.

I may not have been able to kidnap Rafael Delgado, but, when he handed me my queen of hearts, there was a moment when his fingers—oh my god, those fingers—brushed against mine, and I knew I would be bringing home a piece of him with that signed playing card. We stared at each other, and the room disappeared for the second time that night. My heart pounding, I took that card and slipped it carefully into my bag. I would not lose the one thing I had that he had touched.

For their final trick, the two magicians performed a signed card-to-pocket routine. They divided the room in two, each half selecting its own card. A volunteer from each side signed the card, which then got put back into the deck. The unexpected part was when the cards crossed physical barriers and space—the right side's card showing up in the left side's magician's pocket and vice versa. When the magician pulled the card out from his pocket, everyone gasped—because it was the wrong card. Then, when they realized that the *other* magician had *their* side's card, they gasped again.

I could not have cared less about the card, or where it turned up. All I could think about was having my hand in Rafael's pocket and his hand between my legs. I watched that hand as it slipped into his pocket to retrieve the card, imagining it was my own palm, my own fingers, feeling the warmth of his skin as it penetrated the thin fabric of his suit.

The room may have been cold at the beginning of the

show, I may have needed the small expanse of Mark's hand then to keep from shivering, but that was the least of my problems now. All I could do was shift in my seat and hope that the flush in my cheeks was not as conspicuous as the shame and embarrassment I felt at my inability to keep my imagination under control. My skirt felt shorter, somehow, and I tried inconspicuously to pull it down, ignoring the wetness that had seeped into my underwear, hoping that I was not staining the seat. At least I had worn black, and the room was dark.

When the show was over, and the magicians had retreated behind the curtain after thunderous applause, I felt dazed. I fumbled to grab my purse off the floor, tugging my dress back into place, pulling myself together, acting as if nothing unusual had happened.

I pretended to listen to Mark as he raved about the show, about how he thought they had done the box trick, but I was not hearing a word. I wanted more, far more, than I was going to get out of that evening, and there was nothing Mark could give me that I wanted. I wanted my magician. I wanted his body in my bed with that blindfold lovingly wrapped around his head. I wanted him to shuffle cards for me. I wanted to be the sole recipient of his dexterity. I wanted to taste his mouth, to feel his lips, and, more than anything, I wanted to feel those hands on my body, those fingers *in* my body.

I was no longer impressed with Mark, or with his suit, or the fact that I got to go home with him. In fact, one thing I knew for sure was that I did *not* want to go home with him. I wanted to go home to my house, alone. I wanted to think about everything that had just happened in my mind and on that stage.

And I wanted Mark to be nowhere near that picture.

I kept nodding as he went on and on about the show, animated with his enthusiasm about some slip he was sure he had seen, about how there must have been a third person behind the curtain, about where they could have hidden that box. I let him talk all the way up the stairs, past the Parlour and the Palace, through the restaurant, down the other stairs, and out to the valet. I let him talk all the way until we had hit Franklin Avenue, and then I told him I was exhausted, and that I needed to call it a night.

He was so thoroughly distracted by his determination to unravel the secrets of the show that he barely seemed to notice. He dropped me off with just a quick kiss, for which I was grateful, since I would never have been able to fake any sort of genuine desire, and we made vague plans for another date the next night.

I rushed home to the quiet sanctuary of my own apartment. Finally, I thought, as I dropped all my belongings by the door. Finally, I thought, as I collapsed in front of my laptop, my dog Miles panting happily beside me. Finally, I could begin my own research into the magician who had just stolen my heart. Finally, I could be as alone with him as I could manage.

Twenty minutes later, I was not even close to satisfied. I had watched some of his videos, I had found his Facebook page, I had read his bio—but all these bits of Internet trivia just left me hungry for more. Knowing he was down the street, performing at the Castle's late show a mere ten minutes from my doorstep, made the Internet feel even more superficial and inadequate than normal.

I thought about that pocket, the warmth of his skin penetrating the suit, and what it would be like to have my hand in there, separated from his thigh only by a thin piece of fabric. I imagined him in the blindfold. I imagined him in that blindfold and nothing else, lying on my bed, strips of fabric tying his hands together above his head, his entire body before me like a meal ready for consumption. I ached to feel his skin, to be in the same room as him, his breath on my cheek, touching those fingers and being touched by them in return. I wanted those hands.

I stared at the clock and debated what to do.

15

At this hour, it would take me fewer than ten minutes to get back to the Castle. My name was still on the list from when I had entered earlier, so ideally they would allow me re-entry. The performance had been forty minutes long, so if I left right now, that would get me to the Castle just as Rafael's last show would be wrapping up. And then what? What would I do then?

I had no idea, but I did not have time to figure it out. I needed to leave right away if I hoped to get there before he left. I did not know what would happen, I just knew that I had to see him while I still could.

I tugged my heels back on and ran out the door. Even though it was a Friday night, Franklin was clear, and it took me no time at all to race to the Castle, valet my car, and make it down to the Peller just as the late show was streaming out. I stood nervously against the bar, watching the crowd disperse, their faces all sharing that same level of dazzled astonishment I had seen on Mark. I felt a temporary pang at how many people had gotten the opportunity to see my magician, to marvel at his hands and quiet charm, to be seduced by the sultriness of his accent and charmed by the rumpled suit and tousled hair. I did not want to share him. Especially when I did not have him myself.

But all that evaporated the instant Rafael walked out of the Peller. He was talking to someone, some older man with a gray beard. They seemed serious, a conversation of peers more than fan and performer. I studied Rafael with a fixation I allowed myself because of how oblivious he was to me.

I was physically standing farther away from him than I had been during the show, when I had been seated a mere four to six feet from him, but I still felt closer to him. It was as if the fact that he was no longer on stage rendered him more accessible, as if the spotlight had been a barrier, and now, with us all bathed in the same dim light, we were on more equal footing. I used this sensation to propel me forward when he and the man shook hands, and the man stepped away.

"Hi," I said, as Rafael turned back to re-enter the theater.

"Hi," he said, startled by my interception.

"I saw your ten p.m. show," I told him. "Front row. Queen of hearts."

He nodded, memory jogged. "Of course!" He seemed nervous and uncertain, awkward without the protection of the stage.

Somehow I faked poise as I reached forward to take his hand. It was a handshake, but not like the handshake he had just shared with the bearded man. This was a handshake that lasted, his fingers wrapped around my hand, the soft tips of fingers warm against my flesh, electricity coursing from palm to palm.

I did not let go. Neither did he. We smiled at each other.

"It was a great show," I said.

"Thank you. And who are you?"

"I'm Adrian. Adrian Harper. A fan."

"And I'm Rafael. Rafael Delgado. A magician."

There was more I could say, there was more I *wanted* to say, but I left it at that, and he seemed to understand. We just looked at each other, hand clasping hand, and then Peter came out, and Rafael fumbled, our hands dropping to our sides. I lost my nerve, and the moment was over. I nodded at Peter as I turned to leave.

When I turned the corner, I paused, leaning against the wall, my face too flushed to walk past the crowded bar beside the Palace. That was when I heard Rafael say to Peter, "She's cute." I smiled. I beamed, in fact, as if I had been showered in diamonds or in magic cards by a certain Spanish magician whose body, hands, and mouth I could not stop thinking about.

I kept smiling the whole way home. It may have meant nothing, but that night, those two words meant everything.

CHAPTER TWO

Well-educated, literary, successful, Mark was charming and knew how to fuck, valuable talents in a city built on charm and sex. Since Los Angeles was also a city of unfinished screenplays, it was only fitting that our story never seemed to end, despite breakup after breakup. Over the last three years, Mark and I had established a pattern of heartbreak (always mine) and repentance (always his), and, as self-conscious as I was about the absurdity of it all, I could not stop. I really did think he was "the one," even after every effort he made to prove otherwise.

I would brush my teeth in the morning before leaving for work while he was in the shower and imagine doing it as little kids ran around underfoot. He always slept later than I did, and I would stare at him as I dressed, at the way his hair curled behind his ears, at the length of his lashes, at the perfection of his cheekbones, and I would imagine what those kids would look like. When we sat on the couch together, watching television, and my head fit perfectly in the dip of his shoulder, I would imagine how my head would still fit there forty years later.

Mark loved routine, and I loved establishing routines with him. Sundays, we went to Trader Joe's for our weekly groceries. Saturdays, we did yoga and took Miles to the dog park. Wednesdays, Mark always had his writers' group, and I stayed home, wearing a facemask and catching up on all my trashy television. The relationship worked. It felt like home.

We had met three days before my twenty-eighth birthday. Birthdays are always a little awkward in new relationships, so I told him he did not have to acknowledge my birthday at all, but he showed up with a bag full of gifts, anyway. Rather than get me something expensive yet impersonal, or even something inexpensive and impersonal, Mark had spent the day driving around Los Angeles, collecting odds and ends that he felt reflected me. A little Buddha since I loved yoga. A book of words that made you sound smart, since I was a writer. A necklace with my name on it. And a little stuffed dog that looked exactly like Miles. Three days into meeting me, and he seemed to know me better than anyone else.

After that, nothing else mattered. He was the person I wanted to marry. And that night, when he fucked me against my refrigerator, and it was the most amazing sex I had ever had, I knew it for sure.

Until two years later, when we decided to visit a couple's therapist to improve our communication skills. He suggested it, but I agreed. It seemed like a good idea. I was a fan of therapy and self-improvement. How could it hurt?

But as I was getting ready that morning, I started feeling uneasy. I watched him, pouring his soy milk into his coffee, and, even though this was the same as every other day, something felt different. I looked at Miles in his dog bed under the kitchen table and then down at my uneaten bagel.

One of my favorite things about my life with Mark was our Spanish-style apartment in Los Feliz. Complete with terracotta floors, curved archways, and an outdoor terrace I had commandeered with jasmine and bougainvillea plants, the apartment was always warm and full of Southern California sunlight. But today it felt cold.

"Honey…should we drive there in separate cars?" I asked, knowing how strange that question sounded. My voice did not sound like mine.

He looked over at me, puzzled by my hesitation, spoon circling through his coffee, but he did not miss a beat. It was obvious nothing was bothering him, or at least the innocent expression on his face conveyed as much. "Why would we do that?"

"I don't know," I said, and I really did not. I just had this strange feeling in my gut.

"That doesn't make sense," Mark said, giving me a reassuring squeeze on the arm, before putting the lid on his travel mug. "Plus, we've got to have lunch at that Middle Eastern place! Come on, let's go."

Right. We were going to have lunch after our appointment. How could I have forgotten? One of our favorite restaurants happened to be near the therapist's office. So why did I feel so weird? We were going to strengthen our relationship, and then we were going to eat. It would be stupid to take two cars. Shaking my head at my own paranoia, I tossed my uneaten bagel into Miles' food bowl, grabbed my coat, and followed Mark out of the house.

The drive to the therapist was short. Early Saturday morning was one of the best times to drive anywhere in Los Angeles. Most people were still in bed, not quite ready to head off to the Americana or Target or the beach or whatever else L.A. people do on Saturday afternoons that clogs up the freeways sometimes worse than rush hour. But now the freeways were all green on my traffic map, and it only took fifteen minutes to get from our house in Los Feliz up the 101 to Encino and the therapist's office.

As soon as I got out of the car, that strange feeling of uncertainty rushed over me again, and I shivered, pulling my jacket tighter.

"You okay?" Mark asked, giving me a "what's-with-you" look.

"I'm fine. All good."

I slammed the car door behind me as if to emphasize that I was okay, following Mark into the average, three-story office building at the end of the parking lot. Despite my insistence, all I felt was dread.

Martha McAllister, L.C.S.W., was waiting for us with her door open. I suspected we might have been the first appointment of the day. She sat us down in her tidy and nondescript office, decorated discreetly in muted brown and beige tones. I took the armchair and let Mark have the loveseat. I figured it would be better to face him rather than be beside him, craning my neck. And my nerves were still insisting that I needed space.

Ms. McAllister looked at both Mark and me. With her muddy brown hair cropped neatly around her face, she looked as inoffensively neutral as her office.

"So? What brings you here today?" she asked, smiling, turning her head to make conspicuous eye contact with each of us.

I looked at Mark, uncertain where to start or how to explain the situation, but he would not look back at me. His behavior, his physical posture, seemed different, more aloof than just a few minutes prior. I was confused by the change. I watched him, curious as to what he would say. It did not take him long to explain the reason for his distance—or the uneasiness I had felt all morning. In fact, it took about five seconds.

"I don't love her anymore."

I stared at him, then at the therapist, then back at him. This I had not predicted. The therapist blinked. Clearly she had not predicted this, either. She had only just met us, after all, and most people do not go to therapy to break up. They go to therapy to fix things. She looked at me, as if I would have some explanation. As if I would be able to tell her what was going on, what he meant, and what I had done to cause it.

Only I had no idea what to say or think or even do. I tried to swallow, but my mouth was too dry. I felt nauseous. I could not speak. My mind was frantically spinning, trying to process what had just happened.

"Do you want to say more about that?" Ms. McAllister asked, giving up on me and turning her gaze back to Mark.

About "*that*"? As if we were talking about the weather or last night's bad dream? This was a bombshell exploding all over my life. I squeezed my fists together, struggling not to cry, not to exhale, not to let anything out. I was shocked. I was furious. I had no idea what was going on anymore. We had only just arrived. He had hauled me all the way to Encino to tell me this?

Mark swallowed more successfully than I had, continuing to avoid eye contact with me. Leaning forward, with his palms on his knees, he moved closer to the therapist as if to block me out. As if somehow I would not hear what he said next.

"I'm just over it. *This*."

He gestured as if he meant the room, but I knew he meant me. Our relationship. My life as I knew it. My vision narrowed, the entire room going out of focus except for a very small window around those damn hands. He was gesturing as if about a business deal, or the sandwich he had gotten for lunch at Subway. Casual, light, and easy. Not as if he were tearing my heart apart.

Martha McAllister looked at me again, either to gauge my reaction or wait for me to fill in more information. She was drowning, out of her element. Her brown eyes were wide-open and helpless. Five minutes in, she had already lost control. How could she resolve something she did not understand?

I sympathized with her situation but not enough to help her out. Not only had I also lost control of this session, but I had lost control of my relationship and my life, and it was not even noon. I did not know what to say. Ms. McAllister and I both stared at Mark.

"I can't do this anymore" was all he had to say.

And, as if that was the last word on the topic, he leaned back against the couch, arms crossed, seemingly relaxed and satisfied. I knew him enough to guess that it was probably an act, as much of his "public" behavior often was, but that knowledge did not make me feel any better. I alternated between wanting to leave long bloody trails with my fingernails across his skin and wanting to die. I mentally calculated how much Xanax I had at home. At my soon-to-be former home.

In my armchair by the window, with considerable less room than him to move around even if I had wanted to, I did not move. I felt frozen. I remembered the time my parents had sat me down on the living room couch to tell me they were getting a divorce and that my dad was moving to Florida. Later, I would find out he was moving there with some woman named Linda whom he would marry a few months after the divorce went through, but I never met Linda because my father stopped talking to me after he left for Florida.

I was not thinking about my father or Linda then, however. I was just remembering what it felt like to long for the ability to make myself invisible, to be able to inhale so tightly that my ribs folded in among themselves, my body disappearing so that the two people talking at me would be forced to turn their attention elsewhere. I did not want to be here. I did not want to be seen. I did not want to exist. I did not want this to be happening.

The therapist tried to smile at me, but it came off as forced, weak, and ineffectual—much like her skills as a therapist. I stared at the simple gold wedding band on the fourth finger of her left hand. Even her, this useless and average-looking woman, with her soft, doughy figure and generic hairstyle, was loved by someone, someone who wanted to spend his life with her. Who was Mr. McAllister? Did he cook her dinner when she had to work late? Did he kiss her goodbye in the mornings? Did he remind her to take an umbrella when the forecast called for rain? All I wanted was someone to cook for me, someone to love me, someone to hold me as I fell asleep at night. Did Mr. McAllister love Martha McAllister?

I failed to prevent myself from crying. The first couple tears jolted Ms. McAllister into action, and she passed me a box of tissues. I grabbed them, unable to look at Mark. I looked only at her, down at the tissues, and then back at her.

"Did you know this was coming?" she asked me gently, realizing that I was about to lose it completely.

I could not open my mouth or everything would fall out, so I just shook my head, clenching my lips together, struggling to maintain some level of control.

The therapist looked back at Mark. "Could you tell Adrian why you've made this decision?"

Finally, he started to talk, and the therapy session started to feel more like a therapy session, only we were not really working on *fixing* any problems. Mark just told her all the reasons why he was done with me as if I was not even there. All I could do was struggle not to cry, clenching a tissue in my right hand as if it would give me the strength to listen to him tell her that he did not feel like being in a relationship anymore, that he needed to focus on his job at this stage in his career, that he did not know if he even wanted kids, and that, basically, our relationship was a rock around his leg he had been dragging around for far too long, and it was time to cut it (and me) loose.

I listened to the stream of words coming out of his mouth and longed for a hole to open up in the middle of the floor so that I could disappear. This was the man I had loved, the one with whom I shared what felt like the first real home of my adult life, the person I had planned to marry, and he was ending everything without even looking me in the eye.

After what felt like an eternity of Mark spelling out the end of our future together with the calm detachment one would discuss the assembly of IKEA furniture, he finally stopped talking. By this point, I had stopped hearing him, my mind drifting back to that moment of me on the couch, facing my parents, feeling my life crumble then like it was crumbling now. I did not know what he had just said when the therapist turned to me for my response. I could only stare back at her blankly.

"What are you going to do?" she asked.

Maybe Martha McAllister, L.C.S.W., thought I had had some magical insight during the last few minutes. I shook my head, tears running down my face against my best efforts. I had no control over the situation, much like I had no control over my parents' divorce or my dad's affair. I hoped she would turn back to Mark, that he would start talking again, that I could steal a minute to pull myself together, but she just kept looking at me with that empathetic compassion that made me want to hit her. As if she knew what I was going through. As if she knew me well enough to feel sorry for me. As if she had any right to be looking so placid while my life was collapsing.

I managed to shake my head one more time, afraid to open my mouth because I did not know if I would be able to control what came out of it. Unfortunately, she would not let me off the hook. She kept staring at me with that helpful expression they probably taught in therapy school, with those wide-open brown eyes that gave me nothing but an illusion of convenient compassion. I could not look at Mark.

"What will you do next?" she asked again, louder, more insistent.

Was she kidding me? I was supposed to have a battle plan in place? An emergency kit ready to go for when your boyfriend drops the bomb out of nowhere? Right. Sure. Let me just grab my Lara bar, my back-up supply of water, and fire up my battery-powered radio. We can head over to the bunker reserved for fucked-over ex-girlfriends.

Seriously? What was I supposed to say?

She seemed oblivious to my turmoil, perhaps complacent because at least *she* had a gold ring around her finger. Or maybe she thought talking about the situation, forcing an answer out of me, would somehow distract from a therapy session run straight off the rails.

"What will you do next?" she asked a third time, with a little more emphasis.

"I don't know." My tone, unlike hers, was totally flat. I shook my head. "I don't know," I repeated. And then I cried some more.

She looked at me with more of that useless compassion. I

thought I detected a critical glance over at Mark, but that could have been wishful thinking. Obviously, I had been blindsided. Obviously, this was not my fault. *Obviously*, I had done nothing wrong. I was sure she had picked up on all that, even knowing us as briefly as she did.

Mark stayed silent. He was done for the day. Maybe he was realizing the full enormity of what he had done. Or maybe he did not give a fuck. I did not know. I could not think about him. All I could think about was that I had to get away, and that I had to do it fast.

"I have to move out," I said, as if saying the words would make it real, easier, somehow more manageable. But they did not. I cried into an already soaked tissue.

"Do you know where you will go?"

I shook my head. Martha McAllister had to stop expecting me to be MacGyver, to pull some duct tape and a safety pin out of my bag and rig myself an escape hatch. I did not know where to go or what to do. How could I? This was all happening so fast. I could not get enough air.

By the time the therapy session dragged to its painful close, I was practically in a paralyzed stupor. I ran down the hall to the bathroom while Mark finished up the insurance and billing paperwork. I locked myself into a stall and tried to pull myself together. *I would not fall apart*, I repeated, like a mantra. I had to keep moving. I had to get my stuff and Miles out of the apartment as soon as humanly possible.

I texted my friend Tyler, my fingers barely able to punch the keys on my phone, leaning against the cold wall of the bathroom stall—the first secure source of support I had felt all morning. "Mark broke up with me," I typed. "I have to move out. What do I do?"

"I will get boxes and meet you at your place in an hour. You can stay with me," was his rapid response. I heaved a sigh of relief. Thank god he was there. Thank god someone could think clearly.

I stared at myself in the bathroom mirror, willing myself

to maintain strength for at least a couple more hours. I had a lot I needed to accomplish before I could let myself break down properly. My eyes looked hollow and red, hidden behind puffy eyelids. My blonde hair seemed uncombed and scraggly even though I remembered running a brush through it this morning.

This morning felt like a million years ago. I was a hot mess. I sniffed, blowing my nose one last time. I splashed some cold water on myself and walked out of the bathroom with my jaw clenched. I could do this.

The ride home was silent. Mark and I stared straight ahead; the damp tissues clenched in my hand my only recourse at maintaining composure. I had no dry tissues left, so I could not cry anymore.

When we got back to our apartment, he dropped me off and made himself scarce, leaving me to meet Tyler and pack.

"I'm sorry," Tyler said, when he got there.

He was tall, lanky, and when he stood in my doorway, folded boxes under each arm, he looked like a godsend. I smiled at him, through my teary eyes, and grabbed the boxes. He gave me a big hug and then, when he felt like I had had enough, he leaned back to give me one of his penetrating gazes.

"I'm sorry," he repeated. "But he's a douchebag. Let's get you and Miles out of here."

I could not argue with that. Armed with packing tape and a pile of boxes, Tyler prepped the boxes as I threw my worldly possessions into first one box and then another and then another. We crammed my car and Tyler's car full of boxes, and, to my surprise, everything fit except for my books. My books could stay with Mark until I had a more permanent home. But for now, several hours after that painful session with Ms. McAllister, my life had shifted from a home into two cars full of badly packed boxes. At least, I had someplace to take those boxes.

Full of gratitude for Tyler, Miles and I squeezed

ourselves into what space remained in my little hatchback and followed Tyler to his downtown loft, where we would spend the next two weeks.

Miles was my little rock, during this traumatic period and through every traumatic period. Even during the non-traumatic periods. I had never considered myself a dog person, and then one day when I was walking the Silver Lake Reservoir with Mark's friend Ryan, we stopped by the dog park, because Ryan loved to look at the dogs. This guy with scruffy hair—but without the right clothes to be a proper hipster—approached us and asked if we wanted a dog. He had two dogs with him, a yappy Chihuahua and a sad red-haired Spaniel. I looked at Ryan and then back at the two dogs.

"Which one?" I asked.

"That one." He pointed at the red one before launching into some sob story about how he had rescued the little guy from the streets of Echo Park, how he had flyered the neighborhood for two weeks, and called the local shelters, and checked for a microchip, but I had stopped listening. It was love at first sight. I looked into those big brown eyes and knew that there was no way I was leaving this dog behind.

Miles was my first dog, but, more than that, he became my best friend, the source of unconditional love I had never gotten from my family. I was not sure who was more obsessed with whom. Miles always seemed eternally grateful to be rescued from whatever shithole he had been born into, and I was eternally grateful for the love this little guy showered on me. Waking up with him every morning, coming home to him every evening, day trips to the beach, long hikes in Griffith Park—everything felt more complete with Miles. And during this breakup, I felt more grateful for him than ever.

After two weeks with Tyler, home shifted to my friend Corinna's office, where Miles and I shared a twin bed, and my life became neatly organized into piles beside her bookshelves and on top of her printer, as I tried to figure out what to do next. Stay in Los Angeles? Leave Los Angeles? Get a new apartment? Corinna, thoughtfully, did not seem to care. What she did mind was that, four weeks later, Mark changed his opinion about the break-up.

"Are you fucking kidding me?" were her exact words.

Part of me knew she was right, but I did not want to listen to her. I wanted to listen to the part of me that told me that romance, when it was worth having, did not come easy. That good things were worth fighting for—and every other cliché I could rally to my defense. Corinna kept her mouth shut, bless her, but she sighed a lot when she saw me getting ready for a date with him, and she sighed even more when she saw me packing up my things.

When I moved back in to our old apartment (yes, I was that stupid), it lasted two months, after which we broke up *again*, when he decided he did not want kids after all, possibly ever. And definitely for at least not "eight years." I did not know where eight came from, and I did not really care. All I knew was that this time I was a little more prepared. I was stronger. I had done this before. I insisted on staying in our old place until I had found a new apartment. If he wanted to be a dick, that was his prerogative, but I would not be homeless again. I found a cute one bedroom a couple streets over, and Miles and I moved out two weeks later.

Six months after I moved into my new home, Mark began, once again, a campaign to get me back, and, after about a month of romance, I succumbed. *Again.*

And so it went. I was a fool, but an optimistic fool whose buttons he knew how to press, in the bedroom and out of it. Our cycle of heartbreak and seduction. On and off. Highs and lows. An embarrassing weakness of mine was my willingness to trust him when he told me he loved me.

So now, once more, despite my best efforts to the contrary, despite my attempts to move on and date other people and sever contact with my biggest guilty pleasure, here I was, back on a date with him. Mark had seduced me in that way that only successful Hollywood sociopaths can, telling me exactly what I wanted to hear, making promises so genuine that I believed that this time, *this* time, he really meant it, promises so vast and determined that they could not possibly be inauthentic (right?).

He really wanted to marry me, to buy me a ring and then a house, and we were going to have children together. Zoe, if it was a girl. Ethan, if it was a boy. He was good. He could play me. He could feed into all my fears and promise to assuage them. Who could make this stuff up? Who would want to? He could feed into all my desires and promise to satisfy them.

So I fell back into dating him and ignoring Corinna's sighs, hoping that this was the final round, that this time (but who was counting?) would prove the charm. After all, Justin Timberlake and Jessica Biel broke up who knows how many times before getting married. It could happen. Or that was what I told myself because I needed to believe it. After all, what was love but a need to believe that the impossible was possible?

CHAPTER THREE

The day after my visit to the Magic Castle, I woke up to an email from Rafael. I rubbed my eyes as I stared at the phone.

"Hello from Rafael" was the subject line. That was not possible. I had not given him my email address. I must be reading it wrong.

I rushed across the room and grabbed my glasses. Putting them on, I sat on the edge of my bed and squinted at my phone. No, this *really* was an email from Rafael. There was no explanation for how he had tracked down my contact info. In fact, there were only two sentences.

So, you're a writer and you don't tell me. Hiding secrets should be a privilege only for magicians.

I fell back on the bed and closed my eyes, images from last night swimming across the backs of my eyelids like a film projected on my personal movie screen. I saw his face, the tousled hair, the rumpled suit, the blindfold, the tortoiseshell glasses, the untucked shirt, and those hands. Those hands. I was obsessed with *those hands* and with the way the cards swam from one hand to the next like water.

Had I made the whole thing up? But when I reopened my eyes, the message was still there, staring at me. I grinned. I read it again. And again. This meant he had left the Magic Castle the night before thinking of me. He had sat in front of his computer and figured out who I was and searched for me. He was thinking about me, and maybe I would get to see him again.

I had to write a response. And the quicker I did it, the quicker I would hear back from him.

Haha. I have many secrets. :) It will take as long for you to discover them as for me to figure out your tricks!

I pressed send and lay back on the bed to start a new Google image search for my magician. I needed my fix. But before the browser had fully loaded the first batch of images, I had a new email. I scrambled to open it. There was no way it would be from him so soon. But it was.

Well, I am really good at figuring out secrets... So, do not push me. :) Thanks once again for seeing the show.

I blinked. A response so quickly? I got out of bed and made a cup of tea. Was it too early to call Corinna and Tyler? I needed to rally the troops. I needed advice. Pacing back and forth in my kitchen, I tried to decipher the subtext of the situation. He could not possibly write to all his fans. It had to mean something that he had made the effort to track me down.

There had to be more to this, but what? Was it a platonic respect? Did he even know enough about me to respect me? Or did he sense the undercurrent that had consumed me the night before?

My phone buzzed, and I glanced at it. Phone call from Mark. I pressed ignore. I was not ready for him. I had to deal with this first. I had to figure out what "this" even was.

Tea in hand, I sat down in front of my computer.

Your show was amazing. I can't stop thinking about it.

I pressed send and waited a moment. I stared at my email interface. I pressed refresh. Refresh again. I was jittery even without caffeine. The third refresh gave me a new message in my inbox.

Why can't you stop thinking? I will not be mad at you if you don't want to answer.

I smiled. So charming, even via email. I could imagine him sitting on the other side of his computer. Was he wearing pajamas? A t-shirt and boxers? His hair was probably even more tousled in the morning. I ached to run my fingers through it, to feel his fingers on my skin. I cleared my head and tried to focus. I composed my reply.

Oh, I can't stop thinking about the show because it was

amazing, on so many levels. The dexterity with which you flip, grab, shuffle the cards is like watching an incredible ballet performance. I have no idea how you do your tricks—they are totally dumbfounding. Absolutely amazing. The theatrical elements of the show are sophisticated, precise, and again, like watching a well-choreographed dance performance. And the dialogue is so well written. Your chemistry perfect. The comedic timing brilliant. I want to see it again!

I pressed send and went to walk Miles. It would surely take Rafael some time to respond. But just in case, I took my phone along. It took him less than a minute.

Probably, next time, we will do something new. So, there is a possibility that you will never see that exact show again. Some parts, for sure. But not the same exact show. :) Thanks for all the good comments.

It took me the whole way around the block to figure out what to say in response. He was not inviting me to see another show, he was not asking a question. By all rights, this should have been the end of the email exchange, but I could not let go of the slim line of contact I had with him. I decided to reveal, indirectly, that I had researched him, too.

Should I buy one of your books?

The direct question would force him to respond. And it would also show him that he had made enough of an impression on me that I had looked him up, too. This time, it took him two minutes to write me back.

No, you shouldn't. They are boring stuff for magicians. Nothing spectacular. I am actually drafting a book about things everyone should learn from the experience of being a magician. There is a lot of psychology involved in magic, in learning how to control the attention and focus that attention in the right places to create a mystery, playing with expectations and other similar aspects, are very interesting topics to discuss openly, without revealing any secret at the same time.

When I have this one out, you can read it. Until then,

you'll have to wait. :)

I was hooked on Rafael, and I was now hooked on magic. I had gone from not even thinking about either the day before to being completely obsessed. I wanted to know Rafael, I wanted to understand his mind, and I wanted to understand this world of illusion and artifice like nothing I had wanted in a very long time.

Wow. That book sounds amazing. And it's all about exactly the kinds of things that fascinate me.

Before Saturday, my idea of magic shows was old men with cards and disappearing quarters and David Copperfield-type illusions. I had no idea it could be like what you do. I think that's why I was so blown away.

His response only served to make me fall further for him.

I understand. That's what most people think about magic. It's good to know that my work made a difference in your perception of magic. I will keep doing my best to impress you (or, at least, surprise you), although I don't know if I can handle the pressure.

He was flirting. Or maybe it was his European charm. Whatever it was, I was eating it up. I could not stop smiling. The phone fumbled slightly in my hands as I typed, perched on the edge of my couch. I had gotten absolutely nothing done this morning other than walk the dog around the block. The rest of the time had been spent hitting refresh on my email window, pacing around my apartment, and sending him messages.

Haha. I think you will do just fine. You seem to work well under pressure!

His answer came quickly.

Why do you think that? Just because I go on stage? :)

My response was just as fast.

Because you go on stage and because of what you do on stage!

For some reason, his response turned me on.

I actually only perform well under pressure on a stage.

Other than that, I am very ridiculous when under pressure.

Now all I wanted was to put him under pressure. I wanted to see this charming European sweat. But it only took one more email from him to crush my over-inflated expectations.

My girlfriend is leaving town tomorrow. I will have much more time after she leaves. Would you like to go to the Castle together on Friday?

I should have known. Of *course* he had a girlfriend. It took a minute before I remembered that I had a boyfriend. Mark had called twice that morning. I still had not listened to his voicemails. I felt guilty, but, most of all, I felt disappointed. Had I read too much into Rafael's emails? Had I projected an interest that was not actually there? Obviously, I had misunderstood something about our dynamic. Either that or he was a player, but if he were a player, why would he have told me about the girlfriend at all? That seemed like a fact easily left out of the conversation, at least until after he had gotten me into bed.

A knock at the door interrupted my downward spiral of self-doubt and dejection. It was Mark.

"Why aren't you answering your phone?" he asked when I opened the door.

"Oh. Sorry. I didn't realize it was on silent." I glanced down at the phone that was clearly in my hand. I could not claim ignorance. "I just saw that you called. Sorry. I didn't have a chance to listen to your message."

I may have been a bad liar, but Mark did not care. He lay down on my bed, arms behind his head, oblivious to the fact that my morning had been spent obsessing over another guy.

"Want to go to brunch?"

"Sure. Okay." I might as well. That sounded good, and I was not getting any work done at home. I should probably get out of the house and stop thinking about Spanish magicians. "Oh, hey, do you want to go to the Castle on Friday?"

"The Castle? Of course. How'd you swing that? Is Ryan getting us in?"

"Oh. No. But good idea. I should invite Ryan. Rafael is getting us in."

"Rafael? Wait—what?" Sitting up, he stared at me. "How did that happen?"

Shit. I hadn't thought this through. How not to incriminate myself?

"I emailed him last night to get on his mailing list. He wrote me back, and we exchanged a couple emails."

That was partly true. I could not be held responsible for downplaying what might have been a totally innocent exchange. Rafael had a girlfriend, after all. My charade felt justified.

"And he invited you to the Castle?"

Mark was still trying to figure out how this had happened, how I had gotten a contact he did not have.

"Uh…yeah. I told him we had a good time last night, and so, uh, he invited us."

Mark seemed convinced. I exhaled. One of the perks of dating a narcissist was that it did not occur to him that it would be possible for me to be interested in someone else while he and I were together. Now all I had to do was clear it with Rafael, who, if he had a girlfriend, had no right to complain if I showed up with my boyfriend.

I rattled off a quick email to Rafael.

Is it okay if I bring my friends Mark and Ryan with me on Friday to the Castle?

It was not until I read his reply, telling me that this would be fine, that I realized I had referred to Mark as my friend rather than boyfriend. Oops. Innocent mistake, I told myself. No Freudian misadventures. Regardless, Rafael did not seem to care we were now a party of four. Satisfied with my lack of subterfuge, I closed my computer and turned my attention to Mark. It was time for brunch.

And then it would be time for a powwow. I needed some serious processing. I invited Corinna and Tyler to come over for dinner.

***

Corinna burst into my apartment first, her laughter and energy filling up the room, Tyler following her, his arms full of two Trader Joe's bags. I may have invited them over for dinner, but both of them knew how abysmal my cooking could be, so my invites were code for me supplying wine and salad, while they took care of the more serious issues. Corinna usually made dessert, and Tyler was practically a gourmet chef, having spent summers working for his mother's catering service when he was in high school and college.

"Dollface!" she exclaimed, kissing me on the cheek. "It's good to see you!"

I smiled at her. With her dark hair and almond-shaped brown eyes, it was always good to see her, but what I loved most about Corinna was her warmth. She was like the mother I never had. My mother had been distant when I was a kid, but when my dad left, she seemed to retreat even further into herself. She was never outwardly negligent—dinner was always on the table at a reasonable hour—but for any real emotional support, she was the last person to ask. Which was all the more reason why I gave Corinna a huge hug every time I saw her. I was thrilled she was in my life and seeing her made me feel taken care of.

When I first met Tyler, I did not like him. He seemed quiet and reserved during the times I stumbled into him at yoga practice. But then we ended up at a birthday party together for a shared acquaintance, and he was the only person I knew there, other than the birthday boy, and I was the only person *he* knew, so we had no choice but to speak with each other. And that was when I found out that he was only quiet and reserved with strangers. Once he got to know you, he never shut up.

So between him and Corinna, there was not much need for me to say anything. I usually just sat back and let them run the show, their exuberant monologues fusing into dialogues that ran circles around the room, bouncing from conversation topic to conversation topic often faster than made sense. But the more wine we drank, the less sense mattered, anyway.

Tyler had brought marinated chicken with broccoli. He cooked the chicken in my one frying pan as I heated up the broccoli (I could manage simple tasks like that), while Corinna stirred up my salad and made a custom dressing using ingredients I did not even know I had, regaling us with tales of auditions she had had that week. Corinna was an actress, which meant that every story could not simply be told. Everything had to be performed and performed *well*.

Tyler and I could not stop laughing at her anecdotes, and by the time the food was prepared, and we had all had at least one glass of wine each, the mood was excellent. You could tell Tyler did not want to spoil the mood, but he also could not resist asking, so he whispered his question, as if that would somehow keep the mood intact.

"Where's Mark?"

Corinna looked horrified. She hated Mark, and she hated hearing about him.

"Tyler!" she admonished. "I was hoping we could pretend he didn't exist!"

I laughed. "Yes, Corinna, I know. You hate my boyfriend."

"Ugh." She cringed. "Do you have to call him that?"

"I do, but I try not to do it around you."

"And so...?" Tyler prodded.

"And so I might have met someone else."

There was a stunned silence. Then Tyler and Corinna looked at each other, as if to coordinate reactions, and then they both raised their glasses into the air.

"That, my dear, deserves a toast," Corinna declared, and we all clinked glasses.

"That, also, deserves a story," Tyler added. "And we're waiting to hear it."

The two of them turned their chairs so as to face me better, and I launched into the story. Neither of them had been to the Castle, so I had to set the scene, describing my outfit (Corinna wanted to know) and the décor (Tyler was curious), and then I got to the magic show itself. The two of them sat in stunned silence as I told them about returning to the Castle that night to meet Rafael. That was not my usual mode of behavior, and I could see in their reactions how shocked they were that I would do something so forward.

"So wait, where was Mark when you went back?" Corinna asked.

"He was at home."

"You ditched him?" Tyler seemed pleased.

I nodded. "I told him I wanted to go to bed."

"Naughty girl." Corinna grinned. "I love it. Is there more?"

"Yes."

"Oh my god, are you serious? Wait. I need another glass. Tyler, would you open another bottle? None of us are drunk enough to process all this."

Tyler pulled another bottle of white wine out of my fridge and refilled all our glasses. Adequately fortified, I finished up the story by detailing the email exchange and concluding with the plans to go to the Castle on Friday.

"Okay. Wait. I need a recap. You have a date with Rafael on Friday?" Corinna asked, giving me one of her looks.

"I'm meeting him at the Castle, but it's not a date."

She shook her head, as if to disregard what I had just said. "You have a date. Right, Tyler? It's a date."

"It *was* a date. Until you invited your boyfriend along." Tyler seemed positively judgmental.

"Guys! It is not a date. He has a girlfriend."

Tyler shrugged. "In another country. That doesn't mean anything."

"What do you mean, that doesn't mean anything? It means everything. It means he has a girlfriend."

"In. Another. Country." Corinna liked to add dramatic pauses for emphasis, as if that somehow changed everything.

"Guys. He has a girlfriend. I have a boyfriend. We are just friends."

Tyler and Corinna both gave a simultaneous "hah" of contempt and disbelief.

"Back to my recap," Corinna continued. "So you have a date with Rafael on Friday and you *invited your boyfriend*? Why would you do something so ridiculous?"

"Because, as I keep saying, I have a boyfriend, and he has a girlfriend."

"We'll see how long that lasts," Tyler muttered under his breath.

"What was that, Tyler?"

He just shook his head and grinned. "Nothing. I didn't say a thing."

He and Corinna looked at each other and raised their wine glasses in a private toast.

"To love," Corinna said, winking at me.

I sighed dramatically. The more time I spent around Corinna, the more dramatic I got.

"Alright, you guys. You haven't been a lot of help."

Tyler laughed. "You don't need our help. You're doing just fine, you sly minx."

"It's true," Corinna added. "You've got a magician wrapped around your finger, and it hasn't even been twenty-four hours."

"So this isn't a mistake then?" I asked.

"What would be a mistake? Inviting Mark on your date? Yes, that was a mistake," Corinna said.

I shook my head. "Okay. Fine. I get what you're trying to say. But so neither of you thinks that hanging out with Rafael is a bad idea? What with the girlfriend and all?"

"Just be careful," Tyler replied.

"I agree with Tyler. Just be careful and if things get serious, then you can tell Rafael it's all you or nothing." Corrinna smiled. "But have fun. And stop inviting Mark to tag along."

"Okay, okay." I smiled back at her. "Now where's your dessert?"

CHAPTER FOUR

Dressing for the Castle Friday night was difficult. Not because I did not have anything to wear, but because I wanted to wear the perfect dress. I wanted to look amazing. I wanted Rafael to be unable to take his eyes off me. Even if he had a girlfriend, and even if I was totally content with the notion of a platonic friendship (or so I had convinced myself), I still wanted to make an impression. I wanted to make one hell of an impression.

I spent a good hour trying on every cocktail dress in my closet. My bed started to look like a Culture Club album cover—bright yellow on top of turquoise on top of pink. I owned the little black dress, of course, but it was so much easier to make an impression in bright, vibrant color.

The final verdict was the turquoise, a dress so tight it was hardly worth wearing anything at all. You could see with perfect precision the shape of my pelvis, the curve of my waist, the outline of my ribs, and, most importantly, the dress was short enough that my legs looked endlessly long, especially in the right pair of heels. At the very least, I would prove to be a distraction, even to a man who was unavailable.

By the time Mark and Ryan picked me up, the heels were on, the dress was tight, and the teeny tiny jacket barely covered anything, providing just enough warmth on my upper arms to get me through the night, which, really, was all I needed. The heat from being close to Rafael would be enough to keep me warm. Plus, being cold was a small price to pay for sex appeal.

Mark may have complimented me on my dress as I got into the car, but I did not notice. My head was already somewhere else. I was glad that Ryan was with us, because it meant I did not have to fake my way through another conversation. As the week had inched closer to Friday, it had not only grown harder for me to fake it with Mark, but it had grown increasingly difficult for me to think about anything but the diminishing hours until Friday evening.

And now it was finally Friday.

I had had minimal contact with Rafael all week, just enough to confirm the details for the evening. I did not want to come off as desperate or needy, so I kept reminding myself that he did have a girlfriend. We were barely even friends. We had only exchanged a couple of emails and a handshake. I had no right to expect anything from him.

Rather than helping me contain my excitement, this logic only served to emphasize how important tonight was. Tonight was my first night hanging out with Rafael. Not only would tonight legitimize our friendship, but, if I made enough of an impression, I might convince him to think about leaving his girlfriend.

No. No, I did not mean that. I did not mean that at all. I was determined to respect the girlfriend presence. Staring at the buildings whirring by on Franklin Avenue, at the approaching lights of Hollywood, I took a deep breath. This was a totally safe and responsible situation.

Almost.

"Stop it, Adrian!" I told myself.

I looked over at Mark. He was sexy. He had a really great nose and the kind of cheekbones that could get you a modeling gig. He was the kind of boyfriend a girl would be proud of having. I needed to focus on what I had and stop being so ridiculously fixated on some stupid crush. Who dates magicians, anyway? I wanted a good guy who was going to buy me a house and give me a baby and a family. I needed a guy with a real job and a real career. Not some international playboy with a deck of playing cards.

By the time we got to the Castle, I had talked my excitement about seeing Rafael down to a manageable level. I even reached out and slid my hand into Mark's as we walked through the main entrance. I felt his reassuring warmth, our predictable chemistry. "This is good," I thought, as I smiled at him and Ryan. It would be a fun night.

Mark looked amazing in his sleek charcoal suit with a red tie. Ryan looked pretty awesome, too, with his brown suit and tan tie. Ryan was one of Mark's better-looking friends and definitely his nicest. He was the only friend of Mark's I hung out with alone, without Mark. If he had not been gay, I could even have imagined having a crush on him.

To enter the Castle, you first have to give your name to the lovely girls at the front desk who check if you are on "the list." If you are a member, I assume you do not have to do this, but since I have never been a member, my experience has always been the same. Tonight, we had the privilege of saying we were guests of Rafael's, which got us an extra nod of respect and an even more obsequious wave toward the fake library wall.

The threshold of your Castle experience may be initially guarded by the front desk girls, but it is to the owl that you must lean over and say "Open Sesame" in order for the fake library wall to slide open, allowing you entry into the hallowed halls ahead. My stomach tingling with anticipation, I squeezed Mark's hand as we walked inside.

Rafael was at the front bar waiting for us. As soon as we entered, and I saw him sitting there, shuffling a deck of cards, his coffee perched in front of him, my heart did a somersault, and all my plans of staying cool were forgotten.

"Hi," I said.

He turned around. We stared at each other for a moment.

"Hi," he said, smiling at us.

Again, there was that crazy surreal sensation where the world disappeared, the roller-coaster swirl of sensory deprivation—or, more accurately, sensory re-focus—only to shift back into reality at the sound of Mark clearing his throat.

Oh, right. I had forgotten he was here.

"Rafael, this is Mark." I gestured to my right. "And this is Ryan." I gestured to my left. The two guys reached forward and shook Rafael's hand in turn.

"Great show, man."

"Yeah, great show."

The dialogue dissolved into dude speak for a couple minutes, as both men competed with each other to kiss Rafael's ass. Each described how amazing the show had been, which tricks had been particularly thrilling, as if their enthusiasm correlated directly to the depth of their perception and, in turn, to their intelligence. It was easy to tune them out, not only because the impression Rafael had made on me at his show so superseded anything either of them had experienced, but because Rafael was standing straight in front of me, his face maybe a foot from mine. While he talked to them (to be accurate, while he *listened* to them, providing the obligatory occasional nod or expression of gratitude), I studied him with impunity.

I had not noticed, because I had never stood this close to him before, how delicate his lips were and what a particularly compelling shade of rose-red. They looked like they had been sucked on, which only made me want to suck on them even more. His eyelashes were darker and longer than I had remembered, and his eyes more green. His hair looked as soft and tousled as it had the other night. I wanted to run my fingers through it. I noticed that his shirt was tucked in this time.

"Your shirt is tucked in."

I interrupted the guys by accidentally speaking my thoughts out loud, but the conversation was stupid, anyway, and I was sure Rafael was as bored with it as I was.

He looked down, as if to confirm the fact, and laughed. "Yes, it is. I have to tuck it in. Dress code."

"Even you?" I asked.

"Yes. Even me. The only time I don't have to tuck it in is when I'm on stage. Then they don't say anything. But as soon as I'm off stage, then I have to follow the rules." He looked at me and smiled. "Well, shall we go upstairs?"

"Yes," I said. "Absolutely."

I turned and looked at the boys. They nodded.

"Let's do this," Mark said.

Rafael smiled again but not at Mark. At me.

The first show of the night was in the Peller Theater, the same place where Mark and I had seen Rafael the weekend before. This time, however, we were his guests. We were escorted in by the house manager, who knew Rafael by name, of course, whisking us ahead of the throngs waiting in line. Well, not really throngs. This show was not as hyped as Rafael and Peter's show, so there were fewer people waiting on the winding red couch, but still, it felt pretty cool to be whisked in first.

The magician performing that night was a friend of Rafael's, as were most people who performed at the Magic Castle—and, if not friends than fans. As we had made our way to the Peller, along the route that was already starting to feel familiar, up the stairs, down the stairs, past the Palace, past the Parlour, around the corner, down more stairs, all single-file to facilitate navigation through the Friday night crowd, it really did feel like anyone who was anyone knew Rafael. It felt like we were trailing a royal dignitary or Kanye West. I loved it. I felt myself glowing.

It was not that I loved feeling famous or important (although that may have played a small role), it was that I loved feeling part of something with *him*. I loved that everyone we passed saw him with me. I loved that I was with him, that we were sharing this experience *together*. I knew Mark and Ryan were sharing it, too, but they seemed inconsequential. Maybe Corinna and Tyler had been right? Maybe this had originally been intended as a date? Was I playing by an antiquated and naïve set of expectations? Had it been a mistake to follow the rules?

When we filed into the Peller, we kept the same

sequence. Rafael entered first, followed by me, then Mark, then Ryan. It was therefore only natural that we sat in that order, as well. Rafael took the seat at the end of the row, with me between him and Mark. The Peller was not a large theater, and neither were its seats. They were small, not intended for large Midwestern American types, and cozy even for us. My thighs touched Mark's on my right and were mere inches away from Rafael's on my left.

I stared at those inches. Maybe three? Four maximum. I shifted over slightly, bringing it down to two. It was so close that I could not stand it. I looked up and over at Mark, anything to distract myself. He and Ryan were talking about an episode of *Breaking Bad*. I looked over at Rafael. We smiled at each other. Having him in such close proximity made me nervous. I did not know what to do with my hands, so I just clenched my little black purse on my lap.

The room was as cold as it had been the week before. I could see goose bumps forming on my bare thighs. I leaned toward Mark, feeling the need for his body's warmth. Without turning to look at me, he rested his left hand on my right thigh. His heat soothed me temporarily, and I turned to look back at Rafael. He was no longer looking at me. He was staring intently at the empty stage. Was he upset about Mark's hand on my thigh? I could not tell. I could not read him.

I reached forward to touch his sleeve, to get his attention, to begin a conversation about anything, but just as my fingers grazed the thin fabric of his suit jacket, the lights dimmed, and the show began. Disappointed, I brought my hand back to my lap and turned my attention to the house manager who was about to introduce the night's magician.

Every theater at the Magic Castle always had a house manager. The house manager's job was, as far as I could tell, to control the lines of people entering the theater, to make sure the room was filled to capacity but never over, to provide a few instructions and a welcome at the beginning of the show, to introduce the magician, and then to vanish until the end of the show, when he (and it was always a he) would reappear to make sure people exited in an orderly fashion through the correct door. I was not sure if the house managers were aspiring magicians, struggling actors, people with an unusual job, or a combination of all three. Nonetheless, they helped make the experience even more formal and special with their black suits, skinny ties, and official air.

Justin, our house manager that night, reminded us to turn our cell phones off or to "pleasure mode" (everyone snickered at that, and I speculated he used the same joke every time), to refrain from talking or texting during the show, to exit through the same door we came in, and then he introduced Shitako Yomaguchi, the Peller Theater's magician for the evening.

I did not know if it was merely because the Peller Theater still felt like Rafael's domain to me, or if my standards for magic were unfairly skewed by Rafael and Peter's performance the week before, but I was unimpressed by Shitako's performance. I could even see Mark stifling the occasional yawn. Shitako did a couple rope tricks—where the rope was knotted, then split, then fused together again, then reknotted, etc.—and the classic "object in the bag" trick, which, in his case, was an egg that kept disappearing and reappearing in the bag at the appropriate moments, never breaking or smashing or seemingly *there* when he smashed the bag against his fist, but I still did not care. There was no intellectual sophistication or elegance. There was no narrative. There was no psychological suspense. And, most significantly, I did not want to fuck him.

I snuck a glance at Rafael. He was staring straight ahead at Shitako. There was no way Rafael could be riveted by this performance. If I felt like I had seen it all before, I was sure he had seen it a *million* times before. But his gaze was fixed intently on Shitako, so I took the liberty of staring at Rafael out of the corner of my eye. His legs had not moved. Our thighs were still two inches apart. The distance seemed at once massive and miniscule. I sighed. I wanted my hand on that thigh. I wanted my hand running *up* that thigh. I could just barely smell his aftershave.

I studied the perfect crease in the center of his pant leg, a straight line running down his thigh and over his knee. I looked at Mark's pant leg. His had the same crease, but his was a lot less interesting. Who knew a crease could be interesting? I was losing my mind.

I forced myself to stop thinking about Rafael. I put my hand on top of Mark's hand, which was still on my leg, and I watched the rest of Shitako's show as well-behaved as I could be. I watched it, but I saw none of it. My mind was elsewhere. It was at home, in my bed, with Rafael's body below me and above me. It was here, in the Peller, with everyone gone, seats knocked every which way as Rafael and I wrestled each other's clothes off. It was in a bar, in a hallway, in my kitchen—anywhere Rafael could press me against a wall and run his mouth along my neck.

By the time the show finished, and we filed out in the reverse order from which we had come in—Ryan, Mark, me, and then Rafael—I felt as if Rafael and I had shared an experience, which, to be literal, obviously we had. But I also felt like we had shared an experience exclusively of our own. Our thighs, after all, had been two inches apart, and there is a limited list of people with whom you can say you have done that. And the list of people with whom you *want* to be that close is even shorter. Of course, I had also stared at him out of the corner of my eye for most of those forty minutes, so the bond was even more heightened as a result.

Whatever it was, I blissfully followed Rafael and the boys back up the stairs as we headed toward the Palace Theater for our second show of the night. As we turned the corner, toward another endlessly long line for that night's major magic show, a funny thing happened. You are not allowed to take any photos in the Castle—it is a strict policy—so the only way you can get a picture of yourself there is if you pay the official Castle photographer, who bears a striking resemblance to Morgan Freeman, to take your picture.

I had not done it myself, but I had seen people do it. I was one of those people who always forgets to take pictures of things (birthdays, reunions, baby showers, friends) until the event is over, when I would realize, to my disappointment, that there was no visual proof that any of it had happened, unless Corinna was there, and then photos would show up all over Facebook and Instagram. Even though I recognized this flaw, it had still never occurred to me to pay an official event photographer to take a picture of my friends and me. It would still not have occurred to me to document that night, memorable and significant as it was, except that the photographer approached us.

"You're such a good-looking group," he said, "I have to take your picture."

"No, no," Rafael said, shaking his head and putting his hand forward, as if to block an invasive paparazzo.

"Aw, come on, Rafael. You guys look great. Let me take a pic. It's on the house."

Of course, the photographer knew Rafael. And, of course, we would be comped. I realized, suddenly and unexpectedly, how very much I wanted a picture. I wanted nothing else at this moment more than a picture of me with Rafael.

"Come on," I chimed in, tugging on Rafael's arm, like a four year old begging for dessert. "Just one picture! It will be fun. Please...!"

Rafael sighed, smiled, and agreed. I would get my dessert. We lined up in the nook outside the Parlour Theater, and Morgan Freeman took our picture. For those brief seconds, I had full liberty to put my arm around Rafael's waist while my other arm went around Mark's. Ryan stood to the left of our group. Rafael's waist felt smaller than I had expected, narrow and slim, but his warmth was just as intoxicating as I had anticipated. I wanted to breathe him in. I wanted his aftershave to linger on my clothes, a ghostly presence that I could bring home with me.

His left arm went around my waist, and I wondered if I was making any sort of impression on him at all. Was my dress working? Was *I* working? He was inscrutable. If he had not been a magician, he could have been a poker player. His face was like a mask that occasionally flickered with warmth as though it was static interference.

I found out after the shutter had snapped that this was not one of those cases where we got our Polaroid on the spot. Oh no. The Castle, apparently, did *everything* with style. We were going to get an 8x10 in a little cardboard frame, and it would be ready for us after the Palace show.

I was pleased. I could not wait to bring that photograph home.

Once again, we got the VIP treatment at the Palace. Here the house manager was Dennis. He escorted us to our seats in the third row, center. We sat in the same sequence, with Rafael on my left and Mark and Ryan to my right. This time, in the Palace, we were going to see three magicians.

"Three magicians?" I asked Rafael. "Are they performing together?"

He shook his head. "One will be like an MC, introducing the show, doing his set first, and then coming on between the other two magicians, who will each do a fifteen or twenty minute set."

"Are you friends with any of them?"

He smiled. "I know them. But I'm not sure if I'm friends with them."

I laughed. "Really? It seems like you're friends with everyone here."

He shook his head again. "No. They just know me. We aren't friends."

This was hard for me to believe. "Really? It seems like everyone here loves you."

"No. They love my show. They don't love me. They don't even know me."

I stared at him. This was unexpected information. "So

who does know you?"

He had to think for a moment. "Peter. Peter knows me."

And then there was silence. We looked at each other. I noted that he had not mentioned his girlfriend.

Dennis bounded to the front of the theater, and Rafael and I turned our attention from each other to him. It was time for another show. I glanced over at Mark, who was staring intently forward. He felt me looking at him and turned to smile at me. I smiled back and took his hand. It was not as cold in the Palace as in the Peller, but it was still nice to hold his hand and feel the heat of his body. I rubbed his fingers, feeling how smooth they were. Growing up rich and successful before the age of twenty-five, Mark had never worked a manual labor job or cleaned a toilet in his life. I wondered what he would look like shuffling cards. I decided that it would be disappointing.

After a boisterous welcome by Dennis, and another reminder to silence our cell phones, the performance began. The first act was more comedy than magic, based around an elaborate PowerPoint presentation that broke down the basics of the "perfect" card trick. Somewhere along the way, a card disappeared, only to reappear in the wallet of an audience member, a card that was identical to the final slide of the PowerPoint presentation. The crowd laughed and oohed at all the appropriate times, but my attention was elsewhere. I wanted real magic. I wanted illusion and mystery. And this was not it.

The next performer was far more captivating, for a variety of reasons. For one, when he bounded onto the stage, his energy was infectious. After the dull click-click of the PowerPoint man, this was like a bolt of lightening. I turned to Rafael.

"What was his name again?" I whispered.

"That's Jack. Jack Ferguson."

"Is he any good?"

Rafael smiled at me. "Just watch."

It was not only that Jack had the energy of a man on a triple espresso, followed by a Red Bull chaser, but he was distracting for another reason entirely. The man was gorgeous. He could have been a movie star. Ryan Gosling or Matthew McConaughy would have been ignored if they had all been in the same room. His white-blonde hair stuck up on the top of his head, very short on the sides, a chic version of the 1950s schoolboy look. But I did not notice his hair so much as his eyes, which were a brilliant blue, and his cheekbones, which reminded me of Peter Murphy and my high school Goth days. The man was beautiful, plain and simple.

On top of that, he could do magic. And he knew how to *perform*.

It may not have been Rafael-style, it may not have been based on the same level of psychological conceptualization and theatrical narrative, but it was magic with a capital "M." He was showy, fabulous, and BIG. This was Vegas-style magic. This was illusion and spectacle thrown in with a lot of glitter and pizzazz. He even had a girl, an outrageously hot girl in a very tight, very short dress, who disappeared in a box, who locked him up in another box, and who generally showed her very long legs on cue. But I did not really care about her other than wondering how I could get her job.

I did, on the other hand, care about Jack. He was delicious to watch. He was funny and charming and, my god, that energy. He was bouncing off the walls. He even literally bounced a tennis ball off the stage and made it disappear, all while wearing an adorable green terry-cloth sweatband.

"Do you like his magic?" I asked Rafael, when Jack had finished.

Rafael shrugged. I was not surprised. Their styles were so different that it made sense that this kind of show would not be up Rafael's alley. Honestly, if Jack had not been so gorgeous, I was not positive it would have been up mine, either. But, regardless, currently feeling high on my ability to befriend charismatic magicians, I resolved to get to know

Jack.

The third and final magician was true Vegas glitz—but not the good kind.

He was much older, with tanned orange skin, and his female assistant matched him in color. He spent an excessive amount of time doing coin tricks, flipping the coins around his fingers, making them appear and disappear, and I could feel the lateness of the evening wreaking its toll on me the longer this guy's act dragged on. Jack's Vegas style was clearly the new kind, whereas everything this guy did felt dated. For his final trick, the girl went in the box, disappeared, and then reappeared in the audience. Everyone clapped politely, but they seemed as tired as I was and as unimpressed. Or maybe it was just the comedown after losing Jack's energy. Without him on stage, everything felt a little more tired.

Once Mr. Vegas's show had concluded, we all stood up and made our way out of the Palace. It was late. I did not have the stamina for any more shows. We had seen a lot that night.

As we made our way back into the bar area, Morgan Freeman was there, waiting for us.

"Here's your photo."

I had forgotten about the picture. Morgan reached forward with it in his right hand. I snatched it before any of the guys could have a chance. This photo was coming home with me.

"I'll scan it and email it to everyone," I said.

"Okay, okay," Mark said. "But let's look at it."

"Yeah, let's see it," Ryan added.

I pulled my hand away. "Nuh-uh. It's mine! Let's look at it together."

Rafael, to my disappointment, did not seem interested. He had drifted over to the bar to chat with the bartender, some woman slightly older than me with brown hair and too much eye makeup. Oh well.

I opened up the photo which was encased in a little cardboard frame for protective purposes and probably also to help justify whatever ridiculous price they charged for these images.

"Cool!" Ryan exclaimed, a sentiment that Mark echoed.

I exhaled slowly. It *was* a cool photo, but not only for the reasons Ryan and Mark liked it. It was cool because it was a glossy 8x10, and it had "The Magic Castle" printed along the bottom in an old-fashioned cursive font, and it had today's date on it, and we all looked great. But it was incredible because of something else entirely. Something that I had not realized when the photo was being taken.

The message being communicated by the body language could not have been more obvious if it had been accompanied by a blinking red neon sign. Rafael and I were standing, arms around waists, on the left side of the photo, bodies touching. We looked fused together. Several inches away from me stood Mark. In the shadow of the image, it was impossible to tell that my arm was around his waist. Mark seemed to be standing alone in the center of the image, a barrier between me and Ryan, who stood at Mark's left, but so many inches away from Mark that it was almost as if Ryan belonged in another photo entirely. This image clearly belonged to Rafael and me. Rafael and I were the couple, the focal point, with Mark an awkward third wheel, and Ryan almost a stranger. It was an amazing photo, and I was only glad that Mark, delightful narcissist that he was, probably had not looked at anyone else in the photo beside himself. Ryan was a very perceptive guy but also perceptive enough to keep his mouth shut.

Rafael was still talking to the bartender and had not even come over to look at the photo. Was he over us? What was his deal?

"Rafael!" I called to him. He turned to look back at me. "I think we're going to leave soon. It's late."

"Oh? You've had enough magic?" The creases around his eyes wrinkled as he smiled. "Did you have a good time?" His blue eyes roved all three of our faces as if anxious that we had not been fully satisfied.

Mark and Ryan nodded enthusiastically. "Oh yeah, it was awesome," Ryan said. "Thank you so much for getting us in and taking us around."

Rafael smiled again. This time he turned to look exclusively at me. "And now you're tired? You're going to go home?"

I nodded. "Yes. Thank you for everything, though."

"But you can't leave yet."

"We can't?" I asked.

"No." He shook his head. "You can't."

"Why not?" asked Mark.

"Because I can't let you leave without seeing some good magic."

"We *did* see good magic," Ryan insisted. "It was a fun night. Thank you." A good, well-trained Midwestern boy, Ryan was always polite.

Rafael shook his head again. "No. You didn't see good magic. That wasn't *good* magic."

"If that wasn't good magic, what was it?" I asked.

He shrugged. "Those were tricks."

"And what do you do?" I asked. "Don't you do tricks?"

"I don't do tricks. Dogs do tricks."

We all laughed, but Rafael was deadly serious. Not a twitch in his lips, although I was pretty sure I saw a glimmer of a laugh in his eyes.

"Ok, so if you don't do tricks, what do you do?" Mark asked.

"I do magic," Rafael said, as if it was the most obvious answer in the world. "Follow me."

We followed him back down the stairs to the bar near the front entrance. To the side of the bar were a couple armchairs and a loveseat arranged around a small card table. He motioned with his hand for us to sit. Mark and Ryan took the two armchairs, and Rafael and I shared the loveseat. I never failed to be surprised at Mark's lack of jealousy, or perhaps general oblivion, but this night, I was certainly not going to

59

complain. For the first time all evening, Rafael and I were forced, by the nature of the loveseat's narrow size, to press thigh against thigh, and *that* was all I cared about. There was prolonged physical contact for the first time. I was so distracted that I barely noticed what he was doing.

"Choose a card," Rafael requested, fanning the cards across the table. He was looking at Mark, so Mark reached forward and slid one out from the group.

"Good. Now look at it, show it to Ryan, but don't let me or Adrian see it."

Mark did as instructed.

"Now slide it back in."

Mark slipped his card back into the mix, and Rafael proceeded to shuffle the deck. His gestures were so effortless, the cards flowing seamlessly from one hand to the next, that it was easy to forget that not everyone could do this. After shuffling the cards, Rafael turned to me and held the deck up so that I could only see the backs of the cards.

"Pick one," he said.

Since all the cards looked the same from my vantage point, I reached forward and pulled out the one that was third from the left.

"Pull it out slowly," Rafael continued, "and show the front to Mark and Ryan before you look at it."

I did. Mark and Ryan both exclaimed.

"Is that the same card Mark selected?" Rafael asked.

"Absolutely!" Mark replied.

And now Rafael turned to look at me. "It's your turn. Look at the card."

I flipped the card around. It was the queen of hearts.

"Is that the same card you selected at our show?"

He knew it was. He did not even have to ask. I just nodded, speechless.

He smiled at me. I smiled at back. I felt giddy.

"You can take this one home, too. Now you have two queens."

"Thank you," I said.

"But of course. A queen deserves more queens."

I could feel myself blushing. This was shameless. I could not look at Mark. Partly because I did not want him to see the expression on my face, but also because I could not tear my eyes away from Rafael's. Luckily, Rafael broke the mood before it got weird, standing up from our cozy perch on the loveseat and turning toward Mark and Ryan. He reached forward to shake their hands.

"Thank you for coming."

Mark and Ryan practically fell over themselves to thank him for hosting us and for giving us a private magic show. Rafael just nodded and smiled. "Anytime," he said. "Anytime."

The second "anytime" was meant for me, though, as he turned and looked at me, reaching forward with one hand to help me stand up. His hand, for those brief moments, held mine, and neither of us let go, standing, facing each other, those fingers I had not been able to get out of my head wrapped around my hand.

"Thank you," I said, my voice just barely above a whisper. That was all I could manage.

My hand still held in his, I turned to face the boys. They were waiting awkwardly. I could not tell if the awkwardness came from the moment that had just transpired between me and Rafael, or if it came from their awe at having received a private magic show courtesy of one of the world's most acclaimed magicians. Whatever it was, I was aware enough to know I had to diffuse the mood.

Releasing Rafael's hand, I walked over to them. "Alright, let's go."

I turned back, one last time, to say goodbye to Rafael.

"Thank you," I said, my cheeks flushed. I never knew how to end a first date, and I definitely did not know how to end a first non-date date.

"It was my pleasure," he said. And he smiled.

I headed out into the night with Mark and Ryan to reclaim our car from the valet with three souvenirs: the photograph, the playing card, and the memory of how Rafael's hand felt in mine.

CHAPTER FIVE

In the days that followed our Magic Castle outing, my friendship with Rafael grew. We started texting instead of emailing, an exchange that felt more immediate and personal. The texts came intermittently throughout the day, with him often sending the first one shortly after he woke up and the last one usually sent by me, since I tended to go to bed earlier. Rafael kept "magician hours," which were similar to "artist hours," going to bed between one and three a.m., although he sometimes stayed up working on magic until five. He did not seem to sleep much, averaging a pretty consistent six hours a night. All of which left us with many hours in the day to send text messages.

Sometimes Mark noticed. Sometimes he complained. If I checked a message while the two of us were out together, his default crack soon became "Is that from Rafael?" even if it was not. I knew my behavior was wrong, but I could not stop. All I could do was try to be more subtle, like checking messages when I went to the bathroom or waiting until I was at home. It was not like I was cheating on Mark—or like Rafael was cheating on his girlfriend. The texts were platonic. We just liked each other. A lot. We had stuff to talk about.

And that was an understatement.

We talked about our childhoods (mine on the East Coast, his in Spain), we talked about movies, music, books, people, life, television, art, theater, and, most of all, we talked about magic. He told me about how he had performed his first magic trick when he was four years old, trained by his father, who was a hobby magician. And that he had learned English in order to understand the books on magic that were not translated into Spanish. Even the ones that were translated, he preferred to read them in their original language.

"The translations suck," he told me. "Magic can be like poetry. You need the right words."

The town where he grew up was a small one, so he would beg his father to take him on pilgrimages to the bigger towns to see magicians perform. He fell in love with Juan Tamariz and Dai Vernon. They became his idols. As soon as he was old enough, he got a car, and that was when he not only started traveling almost every weekend to see performances, but that was when he started performing professionally himself. After high school, he went straight to an engineering program in college, pressured by his father, who was an engineer by trade, but quit after the first year because his tour schedule was too demanding. At first, it was just Spain, but it quickly became all over Europe, and then Asia, and then the United States. When he was twenty-two, he won the title of best Close-Up magician in the world, and, when his parents saw him receive that award on television, they both cried. After that, his father stopped mentioning engineering school. After that, Rafael told me, they finally realized that maybe he could succeed at "card tricks." That maybe being a magician was an actual career. They stopped being disappointed in him and started being proud.

I imagined this little boy growing up alone in a small town, his best friends a stack of playing cards and some out-of-print books in a language he did not entirely understand, struggling to learn magic as he was struggling to learn English. I felt a tenderness for him that I had never felt for anyone before and a shared loneliness. Two people misunderstood by their families and their geographic locations. For Rafael, it was not that life was magic, it was that magic was life. Magic was the way an awkward kid could connect to the world.

I had become obsessed with magic after that first night at the Castle. Seeing more that second night, and realizing how bad it could be when it was done poorly, not only how amazing it could be when done well, made me want to learn more about it. Much to Rafael's surprise, I did not want to learn about technique. The last thing I wanted to know was how the magic happened. I adored the feeling of wonder I felt when I saw things disappear and reappear, when I watched the logic-defying spectacle that was a successful magic show. I wanted to preserve that. I loved the childlike amazement, and that was part of what made magic so extraordinary for me. I knew that finding out how it was done would only destroy that.

What I did want to know about was the psychological element, the way a successful magic show was structured. The trick (even though I knew Rafael hated that word, it was one I kept reverting to) was only a small kernel of the whole affair. Everything else was the packaging, the psychological component that buffered and insulated that kernel. It was the build-up to the trick that made it worth something. Beyond that, it was, really, just a trick. But with the right narrative, set-up, and delivery, the experience could be astonishing. That was when it was magic.

I asked Rafael to recommend a book for me after our night at the Castle, and I was eagerly awaiting its arrival from Amazon. I had specifically requested a book that would teach me about those aspects of magic on which I wanted more information without dwelling too much on the behind-the-scene machinations of the tricks themselves. It took him a while to figure out which book to recommend, since this kind of request was not a common one.

"*Strong Magic*, by Darwin Ortiz," was his suggestion via text message after several days of contemplation.

"It costs $50," I texted back, a little shocked.

"Magic books are expensive."

"Is it worth it?"

"If you don't enjoy it, I will buy it off you."

That satisfied me. I ordered the book. I was desperate not only to learn more about my latest obsession (Rafael), but I also wanted to learn more about magic.

Another bit of information that emerged during our almost incessant texting was that Rafael did not have a car, a pretty shocking fact in the city of Los Angeles. To be fair, he had only been in L.A. for several months, but still, it was hard to imagine.

"How do you get around?" I asked, knowing how naïve I sounded and hating it.

"I spend most of my nights at the Castle, which is across the street from where I live. And when I go elsewhere, I take the Metro, or go with Peter, or I borrow his car."

I knew Rafael lived close to the Castle, but I had not realized that he lived across the street. That seemed absurdly convenient but also a little incestuous.

"Where does Peter live?"

"Peter and I live in the same building. He's two floors above me. Dennis, the house manager, lives in the building, too."

Okay, now *that* was incestuous. It was practically a Magic Castle rooming house. But it was also kind of cute. I wanted to be part of that gang.

"Invite me over some time."

"Ok," and then there was silence. No invitation was forthcoming. Bored and needy, I kept texting.

"Do you really spend most of your nights at the Castle?" I asked.

"Yes. It's sad."

I could not tell if he was joking or not. I did not think it was sad, but I was also currently obsessed with the Castle. "Well, if you ever want to go anywhere that isn't the Castle, just let me know."

I hesitated for a second before pressing send on that message. Was it permissible to be so forward? I felt like I was playing a game for which no one had bothered to give me the instructions. I pressed send, anyway. At the very least, he could always say no, or blow me off in a discreet and polite way.

But he did not.

"That would be great," he texted back.

Wow. Okay. So what next?

My fingers hovered over the phone for a minute. I started and deleted the text message several times before sending. This was tricky. Was I doing the right thing?

"Mark and I are going to see a play this weekend. It's a one-woman show. A friend of mine. Kristina Wong. Do you want to join us?"

Before I could over-think, before I could analyze the ramifications of inviting Rafael to join me and Mark on a date, before I could think too closely about who would be the actual third wheel if this were to happen, I sent the message and stared nervously at the phone.

"Sounds good. Should I buy a ticket?"

And just like that, I might have dug myself a grave. Or, maybe I was underestimating the whole thing. Maybe it would be a delightful trip out amongst friends.

"I'll get the ticket. I just have to let Kristina know."

"Great! ☺"

He seemed so pleased that I wondered why I had waited so long to invite him out. Well, that was a stupid question, I knew exactly why, and it was exactly the reason why I was now wondering if I had made a mistake. Whatever I had done, it was too late. I hoped Mark would be okay with it and would not cause a scene.

I quickly texted him that Rafael would be joining us on Saturday. I did not ask if it was okay, I just sent the text as information. I wanted to act as if *of course* it was going to be okay, that it was not even worth asking if it would be.

Luckily, Mark was so excited to get the chance to hang out with Rafael again, and seemingly pleased that I was finally sharing Rafael, that it was a non-issue, so I emailed Kristina to request a third ticket for her show. It would be an interesting night.

CHAPTER SIX

Saturday *was* an interesting night, but not for the reasons I had anticipated.

The night before the play, Mark and I had made plans to go to an art opening. It was, like many art openings, happening between five and eight p.m., so we had not set a specific time to meet. I got in the shower around five to get ready. When I got out of the shower, I saw that I had missed a call from him. No voicemail, just a missed call. I called right back, standing there in my towel, dripping water on the floor. No answer. Weird. I shrugged and left a message.

"Hey. Saw I just missed your call. I'm getting ready now. I figure we can leave around six. Or later if you'd prefer. We don't really need to be there before seven. Just let me know."

I hung up the phone and went back to getting ready. I dried my hair, put on a little eyeliner and mascara, and slipped on a pair of black jeans and a striped black and white sweater. I glanced at the clock. It was now almost six. Nothing from Mark. I tried calling again. No answer. This was strange.

I put on some lipstick and walked Miles. 6:30. Still nothing. I tried calling a third time. No answer. Now I was starting to get worried. He knew we had plans. He had *just* called me when I had called him back the first time. I paced around my apartment, looking back and forth at the clock and then at my phone. I was tempted to go to the art opening by myself, but the Jewish mother in my head would not shut up. "What if something happened to him?" she kept asking, in an endless loop. Mark had a bad back. I had visions of him slipping and falling in the bathtub, unable to get up, unable to reach the phone, perhaps unconscious, perhaps paralyzed. I looked at the clock again. It was now seven. I called Corinna and Tyler, but neither of them answered.

"Fuck it," I thought.

I got in the car to drive over to his apartment. I felt a little stalkerish, but this whole thing was just too weird. We had made plans. If he was going to cancel them, you think he would have, well, *canceled* them. What the hell was this nonsense? If I had not been so worried, I would have been livid. But as it was, I was starting to freak out that something serious had happened to him. Maybe he had been in a car accident? Maybe he was in a hospital somewhere? My brain started to cycle through all the horrible reasons why someone would disappear.

I texted Ryan. "Hey, do you know where Mark is? He and I had plans for tonight, and he's not answering."

Ryan texted back right away, "No. No clue. Want me to call him?"

That had not even occurred to me. What if Mark was perfectly okay but just not answering my calls? That did not make much sense, since he *had* just called me, but what could have happened in those few minutes between when he called me and when I called him back? Maybe he had found something out about Rafael and me? Okay, now I was getting paranoid.

"Yes, please. Call him."

Twenty seconds later, Ryan texted, "Nope, no answer."

Fuck. Where was he? I pulled up outside Mark's apartment. I had worked myself into a total state. I left the hazards blinking on my car and rushed out to the back of the building. Mark lived in the rear apartment on the first floor, so it would be easy to see if he was home. I could literally circle the building and walk past his living room, kitchen, bathroom, and bedroom. If he had gotten knocked out in the shower, for instance, the lights would be on in the apartment. If something had happened, it would be easy to tell if he had been home when it had.

Unfortunately (or maybe fortunately because it meant

Mark was not paralyzed in his bathtub), all the lights were off. The apartment was in total darkness. I peered through the living room windows (okay, yes, this was stalkerish!), but I could not see anything. It was pitch black in there.

I texted his mother to ask if she knew where he was. She did not. I asked her to let me know if she heard from him and told her I would do the same. And then I went home. I could not think of anything else to do. It seemed too soon to call the hospitals or the police or anything that people do on T.V. shows, so I just went back to my apartment and paced back and forth. I tried to read an old yoga magazine. I walked Miles around the neighborhood, but I was too busy checking my phone to appreciate the lovely sunset or the summer flowers. I watched some *Daily Show*. I looked at the clock. I looked at my phone. I called Corinna again. This time she picked up.

"Hey."

"Hey, lady. What's wrong?" She could tell from the sound of my voice that something was going on.

"I don't know if Mark is being a dick again."

She snorted. "Knowing Mark, he's *always* being a dick. Why? What did he do now?"

"I don't know. That's the weird thing. I don't know if he's *done* anything. He's just kind of disappeared."

"Disappeared? What do you mean?"

"Well, we had plans for tonight...and he called me when I was in the shower...but now I can't reach him. And he's not calling me back. It's unlike him. I even went by his apartment."

"You did WHAT?"

"Is that crazy? Does that sound crazy? Am I crazy? I just went by his apartment to see if he was there, to see if he was a right..."

Corinna sighed. "Yes. That's crazy. And then what happened?"

"Nothing. Lights off. Totally dark. Not there."

"That's strange. So he's not at home, he's not answering

his phone, and you guys had plans?"

"Yeah. I even texted his mom."

"Adrian, seriously?"

"Was that bad?"

She sighed again. "You like this guy too much. You spend way too much energy on him. It's a drain for you and, frankly, for me. I like you better when you guys aren't together. Next time, don't text his mom. If he blows you off, just call me. We'll go out for drinks and good riddance. Okay?"

"Yeah. Okay."

Corinna was not convinced. "I'm serious, lady. You've got to stop letting this guy string you along."

"I don't know that he's stringing me along. What if something happened to him?"

She laughed. "I bet you good money he's fine and just being a dick somewhere."

"Maybe..."

"Adrian. You're too good for him. I would drag you out for cocktails now, but I'm tied up with some work stuff. Will you check in with me later or tomorrow and let me know what ended up happening?"

"Yeah, okay."

"And stop letting him jerk you around! Watch a movie or go meet Tyler for a drink or something! Get yourself out of the house. Stop thinking about him."

"Okay."

"*Okay*?" she repeated, for emphasis.

I laughed. "Yes, yes, okay."

But I did not want to meet Tyler for a drink. Tyler had never liked Mark, and I knew he would just give me a tough love talking-to that I was not prepared to handle. I knew both he and Corinna wanted me to dump Mark *yesterday*, and I was not in the mood to hear that. And getting myself out of the house felt like too much effort. I did not think anything could distract me from what was going on, so why bother? I got in bed with Miles and tried to watch television.

Finally, at eleven p.m., Mark texted me.

"What's your problem?"

I did a total double take. I confirmed that the text came from him. I read it three times, and then I called him. He did not answer. I was starting to feel hysterical. Since he would not answer my call, I texted him back.

"What are you talking about? Where have you been all evening? Are you okay? Why aren't you answering the phone?"

"I'm fine. I fell asleep on the couch."

Was he joking? Was this for real?

"You fell asleep on the couch? For the last six hours?"

"Yes."

"We had plans tonight."

"No, we didn't."

Okay, now I felt like I was losing my mind. Was this an episode of *The Twilight Zone*?

"Uh. Yes. We did. The art opening."

"No. That is tomorrow."

"Tomorrow is the play."

"Oh."

OH? Was he fucking kidding me?

"Why didn't you call me? Why won't you answer the phone?" I asked, so angry I could barely type the words on my tiny phone keypad.

"Because I don't want to talk to you."

Holy fuck. I felt ice cold when I read those words. And then I wanted to rip his eyes out. But I tried to stay very, very calm.

"You don't want to talk to me? Did I do something wrong?"

"Yes, you're crazy. You texted my mom. And Ryan. And you called me like a million times."

"I texted your mom and Ryan and called you because we had plans, and you weren't answering, and I didn't know where you were, and I thought something happened to you."

"I told you, nothing happened to me. I fell asleep."

"Yeah, I know that now. But I didn't know that then. And I thought maybe you were dead."

"I'm not dead."

Wow, he was for real with this. I was incredulous. I was furious. And I still wanted to throw up.

"I spent the entire night worrying about you, convinced something terrible had happened, and you can't even apologize for standing me up?"

"I didn't stand you up. I told you, I thought the plans were for tomorrow."

"Fuck you," I texted back. "And forget about tomorrow."

I turned my phone off before he could text back. I did not want to see his response. I did not even want to know *if* he responded. I certainly did not want to let Corinna know that she had been right. I did not want to talk to anyone. I slid the phone across the floor hard enough that it banged against the far wall of my bedroom. I wanted that horrible device contaminated with his nastiness as far away from me as possible. I pulled the blankets over my head and cried. Miles pawed at me and whimpered. I brought him under the blankets with me, and that was how we both fell asleep.

CHAPTER SEVEN

The next day, I crawled out of bed. I had slept fitfully, for obvious reasons, finally resorting to a Xanax around three a.m. At this point, I was more depressed and drained than emotional. I did not want to talk to Mark, and I certainly did not want to think about him, but I braced myself for the worst as I turned my phone back on. I went to brush my teeth and wash my face as it rebooted. I was afraid to look and see what awaited me.

What awaited me were sixteen text messages, five missed calls, and two voicemails from Mark, two text messages from Corinna, and one text message from Rafael. I clicked on the text message from Rafael. I would deal with everything else later.

"What time should I be ready?"

Oh, right. The play. I had forgotten that was tonight. I glanced at the clock. It was now noon. The play was at five p m. The odds of me resolving things with Mark within the next five hours were slim to none, primarily because I doubted I would have even listed to his voicemails by then. I had zero interest in plowing through his text messages, which, if I knew him at all, would run the range from pure asshole to apologetic to hysterically emotional.

I resolved not to think about him for now. I would revisit the issue later, once I felt up to it and the grogginess had worn off. I vaguely remembered telling Mark to forget about the play the night before, which probably meant he was not expecting to come, anyway. I doubted he had even wanted to come. He was probably indulging me, using it as leverage to get me to go see an improv show or something with him. He had been more excited about the prospect of Rafael joining us than for the play itself. So whatever. He was out. Which meant, to my growing pleasure, that it was just going to be Rafael and me.

Maybe this was working out after all? I was going to hang out alone with Rafael, and there was zero reason for me to feel guilty about it. Mark had brought this on himself. I knew both Corinna and Tyler would approve.

I texted Rafael back. "I'll pick you up at four. What's your address?"

Rafael sent me his address, and we were all set. That left me about three and a half hours to get myself presentable and functional. Not hearing from Mark during that time helped, as did a Cardio Barre dance class with Corinna (during which I filled her in on all the different ways she had been right about *everything*), a hot bath, a dog walk, and a huge salad. By the time I left the house, I had shed all the anxiety of the night before. I was ready for my "date" with Rafael.

I knew that I should wear something sensational, something jaw-droppingly fabulous, but I felt too shitty. I needed something that felt more protective. I was not up for heels and a short skirt. It took every ounce of motivation not to leave the house in sweatpants, so I settled for a pair of slim pink pants and a loose fitting white top. With the right heels and jacket, it looked chic while still feeling comfortable.

When I picked him up outside his apartment building (which really was across the street from the Castle), I realized it was the first time I had seen him in casual clothes. The other two times he had been in a suit. He was wearing a striped cotton Rugby style shirt and khakis. He looked cute. I also realized, as we drove off, that he seemed much more relaxed. I mentioned this to him.

He thought about it for a second. "Yes, I probably am. When I'm at the Castle, I'm working, even if I'm not performing."

Before I could have a chance to respond, Rafael glanced toward the back seat. "Where's Mark?"

Oh. Yeah. *That*. Awkward topic. "We had a fight."

I hoped Rafael would not ask for more information, and he did not. Satisfied with my response, he gave me a quizzical look, said "Sorry," and turned to face front. I could not tell, but he might have been relieved. I was not sure how I felt other than nervous. It would have been nice to have Mark there as a buffer, but at the same time, Mark required a lot of attention, and it was easier to focus all my attention on Rafael. And I definitely preferred having all of Rafael's attention focused on me.

On the way to the play, the energy in the car was light. For our first time alone together, there was surprisingly little awkwardness or tension. In fact, I kind of wished there had been more tension—of the sexual kind. But no, we felt like old friends. I guess our platonic vibe had solidified. Maybe I had imagined the tension I had felt at the Castle? Or maybe it had just evaporated in the week following? The whole situation was weird. I had been telling my friends all week not to worry, that the dynamic was strictly platonic, trying to convince them as well as myself, and maybe I was right. Maybe now that we were more peers rather than fan and artist, things were more stable?

When we got to the theater, there had been so little traffic that we were half an hour early. I felt awkward around Rafael, uncertain of what (and how) our dynamic should be, so I proposed giving him a tour of the neighborhood before I parked. The last thing I wanted was to stand outside the theater, waiting for doors to open, making nervous conversation. Unfortunately, the theater was in a grungy part of Echo Park, so other than driving by Echo Park Lake, there was not a hell of a lot to see, and soon we were back, parked, and still early.

I was relieved when they finally let us in to grab our seats. I had been trying to come up with interesting trivia about Los Angeles and Echo Park with which to regale Rafael but was running on empty, much like the lake itself, which had been recently drained for cleaning and refurbishment. For someone who had lived in L.A. for the past six years, I had surprisingly little to say about the neighborhood.

Luckily, the play started on time, and the focus was taken off me. Rafael, for someone with such a mesmerizing mind, could sometimes be hard to engage in dialogue. He was obviously a reserved and private person. I felt as though I had to take a hammer to the walls with which he fortified himself.

I snuck looks at him during the show, wondering if he was enjoying it, taking pleasure in the moments when he laughed, studying his face discreetly. Some of the jokes were kind of raunchy, but he seemed to take it all in stride. It appeared as though he was enjoying himself, but it was hard to tell. It was, in fact, hard to tell much of anything about what was going through his head. His text messages were much more open than the words that actually came out of his mouth or the facial expressions that drifted across his face.

The whole experience was so uneventful that, when I dropped Rafael back off at his house, I felt a little disappointed. We had merely sat beside each other at the play, no contact of any kind, no flirting, no teasing, not even any relevant or real conversation. We had just enjoyed the performance with total detachment like casual friends, not like people who texted each other all day, day after day.

I did not know what I wanted, but I wanted more of *something*. Maybe I wanted to compensate for Mark's behavior the night before. Maybe my stupid fantasy was getting in the way of what was becoming a very real friendship. Maybe I was just too tired to drag Rafael out of his shell. When I pulled up outside his house, he asked me if I wanted to go grab coffee or some food, but I said no. I needed to go home. I needed a break from having to work so hard to keep the conversation flowing, from having to pretend this was so easy and effortless. I gave Rafael a platonic hug goodbye and drove away feeling deflated.

A few minutes down Franklin Avenue, my phone beeped

with a new text message. Fuck, I thought. I had successfully avoided dealing with Mark all day. This was probably him nagging me to address the issue. Keeping my eyes on the road, I pulled my phone out of my bag and glanced down at it.

It was not a message from Mark. It was a message from Rafael. I had to swerve off the road to read it properly. And then I read it again. And again.

"You look even more beautiful in the daylight."

I leaned back in the car seat and stared out the window. Metric was blasting through my car stereo. I felt like I was in a movie, and this was my soundtrack: "Everybody, everybody just wanna fall in love. Everybody, everybody just wanna play the lead. Everybody, everybody just wanna fall in love."

I looked at my phone again. I looked up at the traffic streaming by. I stared at the whiter than white clouds drifting through a trademark L.A. blue sky. It was gorgeous out. Everything felt Technicolor. And yet I did not feel alive. I felt like I was in a dream. Or in a movie. I was playing myself. This was not real, was it? I looked back at my phone. The message was still there.

I clicked on the little white iMessage bar with my left thumb. I watched the blinking cursor as if the reply would write itself. What should I say? What should I do? I knew I wanted to drive back to see him, but I also knew that he would never have made that comment, or any others like it, in person.

So instead, I settled for sending a text message. A text message that I typed hesitantly but then sent quickly once it had been written. I did not want to over-think. I did not want to doubt.

"Thank you," I started off with, since that seemed polite and appropriate. And then, "you look beautiful at every time."

It was heavy, I knew, and I cringed after I had sent it. It was too much. I felt as though I had fucked up. But whatever. I had not crossed any more of a line than he had. He had no right to judge me. I tossed the phone to the passenger seat and drove the rest of the way home. I did not let myself look at my phone until I had parked. By which point, of course, there was another message from him.

"Be careful. If you are too nice to me, I will grow cocky, and no one wants that."

I laughed.

"This is a real danger," I replied, "since I think I can only be too nice to you."

"You will have to learn how not to be nice."

"Or what?"

"Or I will get cocky, fall in love with you, gain an addiction to heroin, and destroy my life. I don't think that's good."

Hilarious. "Heroin, eh? Wow. I guess I am a gateway drug."

"LOL. No, you're awesome," he texted back.

"Thank you. And thank you for coming to the play with me."

"Thank you for inviting me. It's good to go places other than the Castle. And I enjoy spending time with you."

Smiling, I got out of the car and walked toward my apartment. It had been such a good evening that I did not want to tarnish it by listening to the voicemails Mark had left me. I scrolled through his texts, skimming them for general content. As I had predicted, it was the usual stream of emotional ups and downs. He started off accusatory. Then, when I did not answer, he got meaner, and then when I still did not respond (since my phone was off and my head under the blanket), his tone shifted, and he began to claim responsibility, to apologize, and then to plead for forgiveness.

Sigh. Here we were again. Mark's little routine. Only this time, I did not feel like I was getting sucked back in. This time, I did not have the patience to deal with him. I just got in bed and turned on the television. He could wait another day. Tonight belonged to Rafael.

CHAPTER EIGHT

I was unreasonably exhausted the next morning. I felt like I had come down with something. Either that or I had accidentally swallowed razor blades in my sleep. It could be strep. I gingerly drank some tea and confirmed that yes, this was far more than a regular sore throat. I threw on some sweatpants and a sweatshirt. I had to visit the Urgent Care center in Hollywood. If this was strep, I needed antibiotics immediately.

As I was lacing on my sneakers, there was a knock at the door. It was Mark. I still had not called or texted him back. He was the least of my concerns.

"Hey," he said.

"Hey," I croaked. It was the first word out of my mouth that morning. If there was any doubt left, I was definitely sick.

"Whoa. What's wrong with you?"

"I'm sick," I replied, stating the obvious.

"I can hear." His voice was tender, caring, and I was grateful for that.

"What's that?" I asked, pointing at a white paper bag in his hand.

"I brought breakfast."

He was trying to atone. Mark did not do flowers. He thought whatever points they garnered were immediately canceled out by the lack of originality. So today breakfast was the metaphorical flowers.

"Aw, thanks, but I've got to go to the Hollywood Walk-in Clinic. I think I need antibiotics." I was feeling sicker by the second.

"I'll go with you."

"Really?" Now he was really being uncharacteristically

nice. He must have realized how badly he had fucked up. Either that or his mom had told him.

"Sure. Sometimes you have to wait an hour for an appointment over there. I'll keep you company. We'll have breakfast while we wait for your turn."

Even though I could see what he was doing, I still melted. Mark was so good at this stuff. When it was not too much effort, Mark was the best caretaker I had ever had. It made it easier for me to ignore his jerk tendencies. In my weak and infirm state, it meant the world to me that he was going to drive me to the doctor, hold my hand in the waiting room, and feed me croissants, orange juice, and sweet potato fries. Because, yes, I loved sweet potato fries. Even for breakfast.

We did, in fact, have to wait about an hour for my turn with the doctor, but the croissants and fries and handholding were all sweet enough that the time went by at a respectable speed. Mark came in with me to the examination room, where the doctor confirmed that I did, in fact, have strep, and then Mark drove me to the drugstore, where he waited in line to pick up my prescription while I read trashy tabloids in the magazine aisle.

By the time we had picked up tea and ingredients for chicken soup, which Mark cooked for me as I lay in bed, I felt myself falling for him again. Few things made a quicker entry into my heart than being cooked and cared for. The fact that I did not hear from Rafael all day only made it easier to feel love for and be loved by Mark. I was quickly forgetting what had transpired two days before, already formulating the excuses I would give Corinna to justify Mark's behavior.

The next day, I had to call in sick to work. This was not the greatest thing I could have done, partly because the very gay and very high-strung Creative Director, Alfredo, hated it when anyone was out of physical reach, but also because I was supposed to be writing copy for an online feature about hair color. I reassured him that I would work from home, would not miss any deadlines, and that I would stay logged into

Gchat the whole time I was in front of my computer, so that he could reach me whenever. I could handle all that, but the prospect of having to get dressed, much less talk to other people, was beyond me.

I was lying in bed, restlessly surfing the Internet, trying to figure out what to say about a new line of copper tones, my brain a casualty of illness and antibiotics, when Rafael popped up on Gchat around mid-afternoon and said hello.

"Hey," I typed back.

"How are you?"

"I'm sick. ☹ I'm in bed with a bad sore throat. How are you?"

"I'm in Australia."

"WHAT? You're in Australia?" I was pretty sure he had not mentioned that when we saw each other.

"Yes. I just arrived. I'm performing at a show."

"They flew you all the way to Australia for a show?"

"Yes. ☺ I'm doing a couple workshops, too."

"When are you back?"

"I'm back on Friday. Want to go to the Castle with me that night?"

Wow. Alone with Rafael at the Castle. "Won't you be tired? Jet lagged?"

"Sleep is for pussies."

I laughed.

"Okay. We can go if you want. Are you sure?"

"Of course I'm sure. It's strange to say this, but I miss you when you aren't there."

Wait, what? I had to confirm this ridiculous statement.

"You miss me when I'm not at the Castle?"

"That's right."

"I only went with you that one time."

"That's not true. You were there twice with me."

Ha. "I was there once WITH you. I was there another time to SEE you."

"It's all the same. So are you coming?"

83

"Yes. I'd love to."

"Good. It's not the same without you."

I waited to respond, digesting the exchange that had just transpired, but before I could write anything, he wrapped up the conversation.

"I have to go meet the show's producer. Have a good day. Feel better."

"Bye."

He signed off, but I stayed logged on—just in case Alfredo needed me. In an act of semi-defiance, however, I put my laptop on the floor and lay back on the bed. I had to process this unexpected turn of events. I really should not have been so surprised that he and I were going to hang out again. We *were* friends, after all. The weirdest part of the conversation was the part about the Castle being better with me there. That might have been the nicest thing he had said to me yet. The Castle, after all, was his home away from home. He was there almost every night. And yet he missed me when I was not there.

I felt flattered and slightly giddy. I also still felt really sick. It was time for a nap before Corinna showed up with Tom Yum soup from Thai Town, her time-honored remedy for illness. I was going to do everything to make sure I was fully recovered by Friday.

***

Corinna and I had met years ago when I first moved to Los Angeles. I was a struggling freelance writer, she was a struggling actress, and we happened to be neighbors in the same decrepit apartment building in the not-so-charming (then) neighborhood of Highland Park. Highland Park may have gentrified over the years, but no amount of gentrification has made it beautiful (in my opinion), and in those days, there were no trendy bars or Fresh & Easy supermarkets to distract from the lack of beauty. There were also no scruffy hot hipsters to savor while spending hours at hip coffee shops. Those all existed there *now*, much like they had all sprung up in Williamsburg, Brooklyn a couple years after I had given up and moved into the East Village. Apparently, my presence somewhere was a virtual guarantee that it would be awesome and cool after I was no longer there.

I was still not convinced that Highland Park was awesome and cool now, despite what the scruffy hipsters said, but it was definitely not awesome and cool then, which meant there were no coffee shops for Corinna and I to hang out in, while she waited nervously to hear about an audition, and I waited nervously to find out about my next job (if there would be one). So all this meant that we hung out at my apartment or hers, which, in a way, made us better friends. We were lonely out in Highland Park, hipster-less, so we clung to each other for support and companionship.

I had just moved to Los Angeles from New York, convinced that the lower rents would somehow make my freelance writing existence manageable, and she had just moved to Los Angeles from Dallas, because who wants to be an actress in Dallas? We made other friends over the years, but the two of us had forged a bond during those tough beginnings that made our friendship unshakeable—even though Corinna had a habit of telling me how wrong I was about things most of the time.

The thing about Corinna that made her especially infuriating was that she was often right. You would think that I would have figured this out and decided to save time by always following her advice, but no. We would argue religiously, and then, inevitably, life (or men) would demonstrate that she had been right all along, at which point I would usually slump my way over to Corinna's kitchen, where she would make me tea and/or gluten-free cupcakes, her sympathy for me only barely glossing over her triumph at being right yet again. I did not mind the gloating because there was always so much love and concern behind it that it felt okay. It felt justified. After all, I was usually the deluded fool. And, unfortunately, it was often Mark about whom I was deluded.

But today, Corinna did not want to talk about Mark. She was bored with trying to convince me that he was a waste of my time. She simply knew that he was, and that time would prove it to me, yet again, and then I would have to admit she was right, yet again. So rather than try to convince me, she just decided to sit this argument out.

Despite my incessant belief that *this* time would be different, she felt irritatingly confident that this time would be like all the others, and, in which case, it was just a matter of time until Mark came around and showed his true colors. Arguing about him was now officially beneath her. When Corinna was bored with something, she simply could not be bothered. Which was a relief for me because I did not want to talk about Mark either. I, like Corinna, wanted to talk about Rafael.

"So?" she asked, holding the Thai soup in front of her. "How do you feel? You're not contagious, are you?'

I grabbed the Thai soup out of her hand and brought it to the kitchen. "I feel like crap. But no, I'm not contagious."

I looked in the bag. "There's only soup in here for one. You're not eating?"

She grinned and pulled her other hand out from behind her back. She was holding a small pink box.

"Cupcakes?"

She nodded.

"Corinna! You're the best!"

"It's true," she said, grinning some more. "I'm having cupcakes for dinner. Maybe I'll steal some of your soup."

"Yes. Let's split the soup, and then we'll eat the cupcakes."

"Perfect."

I poured the Thai soup into two bowls and set out some water and silverware for us. Napkins were already on the table.

"Is there anything missing? Do you need something?"

Corinna shook her head. "Just come sit, sick girl, and tell me about this Rafael guy. Is it serious?"

"It can't possibly be serious. He has a girlfriend."

She squinted skeptically. "He *still* has a girlfriend? Have you seen her?"

"No. I haven't seen her. She's in Spain. I told you."

"But she definitely exists?"

I laughed. "I guess he could have made her up, but why would he do that?"

"Hmm..." Corinna stared pensively into her soup. "Has he tried to sleep with you?"

"Nope. Nothing like that. If that was all he wanted, I figure he could have just lied about the girlfriend. That's why I don't get it. I don't know what he wants."

Scooping up a big spoonful of chicken and vegetables, Corinna chewed for a minute. I watched her, waiting, eating my own soup.

"This girlfriend thing is a problem."

"Well, yes, of course. I know that." Did Corinna think this was new information?

"But there's no reason you should stop hanging out with him just because he has some imaginary girlfriend."

"Corinna. I'm not going to stop hanging out with him. I'm *obsessed* with him."

"Obsessed? I'm not sure I like the sound of that."

"What do you mean?" I asked.

"I'm just worried you're going to get hurt. You're not, well, you're not always the most sensible when it comes to these guys."

"Hey, we're not talking about Mark here."

"I know we're not talking about Mark here. But you still have a habit of going for these guys you think are going to treat you a certain way—you *hope* are going to treat you a certain way—and then they never do, and then you get disappointed and hurt, and I just hate to see that happen."

"I promise to be careful."

I debated whether to tell her about Friday. Was she judging me? But then I figured Corinna was always judging me, and I had to tell someone.

"I'm going to the Castle alone with him on Friday."

"You are?" She sounded surprised.

"Yes. He invited me. And what's even crazier is that he said he missed me when I wasn't there."

"You're not going to invite Mark to tag along this time, are you?"

As soon as she asked, I realized that the thought had not even occurred to me. I shook my head.

"Good," she said, with a big smile. "Now let's have cupcakes, and then I want you to tell me how sexy he is. And then we're going to figure out what you're wearing on Friday. Because you *know* it's a date."

That sounded good to me. The cupcakes were chocolate, and Corinna always knew what dress I should wear. I was feeling better already.

CHAPTER NINE

Wednesday mornings, Mark had his therapy session with Dr Fred Grayson. I knew this because I used to go to those sessions with him. During one of the times when we were broken up, Mark called me out of the blue to tell me that he was checking himself into UCLA's mental hospital. I was too shocked by that information to ask him why he was bothering to let me know, since we had not had any contact for months. I was too busy asking why. Turns out that he had been depressed and suicidal, and he had decided he needed to go on anti-depressants.

"Ok, and, so, UCLA?"

"My doctor says that the first week on anti-depressants might actually make me feel worse, so I need to be monitored twenty-four hours a day."

"By make you feel worse, you mean that you might feel even more suicidal?"

"Yeah, it's a combination of feeling suicidal but then having the inertia to do something about it. So you can't be alone."

I had never heard that before, but then my experience with these kinds of drugs was very limited, so I had no choice but to believe him.

"And so why UCLA? You can't stay with your mom or a friend or something?"

"No. I need to be with someone that I can be with twenty-four hours a day for a week. I can't ask anyone for that."

That made no sense to me, but I was not going to ask any more questions. "Well, that's just stupid. You shouldn't go to UCLA. You don't belong in a mental ward. Just come stay with me for a week. You can come to work with me. You'll sleep on the couch. It will be fine."

I may have been foolish to offer this, much like I was foolish with most of the decisions I made regarding Mark, but it was more of a reflex than a well-considered plan. I just could not imagine him in a mental hospital, in one of those places where they take all personal effects and probably your shoelaces. He was not crazy enough for that.

He took me up on my offer, and the rest was probably predictable to everyone but me. He stayed for the week, but only the first couple days were on the couch. Then he moved to the bed. I still insisted that we were not dating; after all, he was an emotional wreck. He needed love and care and support, and I was willing to give him all three. After the meds helped stabilize him, the psychiatrist who had written the prescription referred him to Dr. Grayson for regular sessions. These sessions would, ideally, help sort out his issues at the same time as the medication was balancing the chemicals in his brain. It seemed like a good plan.

Since Mark was a typical guy, he was not the most proficient at talking about his feelings. He initially asked me to come to the first session to discuss how the meds had affected his personality, to provide an outsider's perspective on the before and during of his treatment. But I proved to be such a useful resource, not only with my outsider perspective but also at coaxing important emotional revelations out of Mark, that he and Dr. Grayson agreed I was valuable enough to come every week, at least for a month or two. I ended up going consistently for about two months because, as Corinna reminded me weekly, I was a sucker.

After I finally stopped going, I knew Mark had kept up with Dr. Grayson. Dr. Grayson may have been the most consistent relationship in Mark's life.

I did not hear from Mark at all on Wednesday. I had also not heard from him at all on Tuesday. Sunday had been the doctor's visit, and everything was good then. Monday, he had come over and brought magazines and stayed for a little while to keep me company before leaving to go swimming with his friend Robert. So when I did not hear from him on Tuesday, I just assumed he was busy, although I thought it was a little strange and heartless that he did not at least text to find out how I was doing. When I did not hear him on Wednesday— that was more than a little strange. I did not know if I should text him or give him the space he clearly needed. We had only been dating such a short time this current go-round, that, even with his protestations of marriage and engagement rings and houses, I still felt timid, insecure, and uncertain about how to proceed.

Finally, Wednesday night, after three whole days of lying in bed sick, bored and restless, when my main and only excitement was the occasional message from Rafael in Australia, I broke down and sent Mark a text.

"Hey, how's it going?" Non-committal. Casual. Easy.

It took him an hour to respond. I had actually fallen asleep before I got his message.

"You're right," was all he said.

"Huh?" I was in a strep throat, half-asleep kind of daze, but I doubted that message would have made any sense even if I were awake.

"I can't do this."

Okay, I *still* had no idea what he was talking about.

"Can you explain?" I texted back.

"I talked with Dr. Grayson today. And you're right. I can't do this. I'm not ready to get married."

Now I was starting to wonder if I was crazy—or if he was. I had no idea what was going on.

"What are you talking about? Where is this coming from?"

"I just realized this isn't what I want."

"What don't you want? I'm not asking you to get married." I sat up in bed and turned on the light. I was feeling clammy.

"No, but I know that's what you want. And I can't give

91

that to you."

"You can't give that to me…ever?"

"I don't know. Maybe not."

"Where is this coming from? I have no idea what's going on." Maybe it was the strep, maybe the meds, or maybe it was him, but I was lost.

"It's just you being needy right now. It's made me realize I don't want a relationship."

"Me being needy? I'm not needy. I'm SICK."

"I just can't do this right now. I'm sorry."

Now I was definitely hysterical. I tried calling him, but, of course, he did not answer. I tried calling him a second time.

"Why won't you answer the phone?"

"I can't talk to you right now."

"Are you serious? You're not answering your calls? Is this a joke? When have I been needy? When did I ask you for anything?"

"You made me feel bad on Monday for going swimming with Robert."

"That's a joke. You're not serious."

He did not respond. My phone was frustratingly silent.

"Are you serious?" I texted again.

He still did not respond.

"I was JOKING when I complained that you were going. I was just jealous because I wanted to go swimming. Because I have strep and feel miserable."

No response.

"You are breaking up with me AGAIN because I made a joke?"

"I just can't worry about someone else right now."

I stared at my phone. Was he kidding me? Was this really happening? I did not know if I was more angry or sad, if I wanted to punch him and beat him or crawl into a ball and sob. I knew I should have been relieved that he had finally shown his true colors (again), but I just felt angry and abandoned.

"You can add this to the list of times I have fucked you over," he wrote.

"How are you even human?" I asked him. In times like these, I was convinced Mark was a sociopath with zero empathy for mankind.

"I'm just trying to make light of a terrible situation."

"Oh, fuck you."

I was furious at him and furious at me for letting him do this to me—*again*. I was determined not to let it devastate me, even though I knew that it would. Even though I knew I had fallen for his lies and his promises, for the charm and the act, he was and would *always* be an asshole. No matter how badly I wanted a guy to want me, no matter how wonderful it felt to be pursued, to hear promises about forever and diamonds and houses and future children, I knew that nothing was worth this.

After so much time trying to make it work, I finally realized—clearly very late to the game—that Mark was full of shit. Our relationship had really been one of convenience: him telling me lies that were easy for him to tell and convenient for me to believe.

In some weird way, just knowing Rafael was out there, knowing that there was a guy like him who cared for me, made me need those lies less. I realized, thinking about Mark seriously and clearly for what felt like the first time ever, how empty our relationship had been. Like most things in his life, it had just been posturing and emptiness, a stage set that looked nice on the outside but was just some bare scaffolding on the inside. We were playing at being some couple we had never been and would never be. I also realized, to my surprise, that Mark and I had not had sex since before that night at the Castle. Rafael had really eclipsed Mark far more than I had appreciated.

And for that I was grateful. Good riddance, I thought. It was time to downsize, to get rid of excess weight. I had learned my lesson, and I was never going back.

I went into my kitchen and opened up the cupboard to the left of the kitchen sink. On the bottom shelf of that cupboard, in a large plastic bag, was every note and card Mark had ever given me. Every knickknack and little memento. All the little things, the relics of sentimentality and romance. I had kept the little post-its on which he told me loved me, I had kept the Valentine's Day cards and the love notes, the postcards he sent when he was out of town for work. It was a pretty large bag. I should probably double-bag it, I told myself. Which is exactly what I did before carrying it out of my apartment and putting it in the passenger seat of my car. Which is where it sat as I drove over to Mark's house, at which point I tossed it onto his front porch.

I did not leave a note. There were enough notes in the bag. Fuck him and fuck all that shit, I thought. This time I was done and done for good.

I may have been an idiot too many times before, but now he had crossed the line. He had exhausted my tolerance at long last. Maybe it was Rafael. Maybe Mark had done this to me one time too many. Maybe Corinna's words had finally sunk in. Whatever it was, I was free.

I drove back home and got into bed. I was too angry to cry and too angry to fall asleep. I was angry with him but mostly angry with myself for wasting so much time on a douchebag. Was Corinna right? Did I build these men up in my imagination, refusing to see them (and their lies) for what they were? I stared at the ceiling. I contemplated my life. I was single again. But at least I was off the Mark merry-go-round. I had wasted too much time on that fucker. That heartless sociopathic fucker. Who breaks up with someone because they have strep throat? Unbelievable.

I tried calling Corinna, but she did not pick up. I texted Tyler to see if he was around, but then I remembered he was at some sex expo in Vegas with his new stripper girlfriend.

I turned on the television. I was still so upset that I was practically shaking. What time was it in Australia, I wondered? I checked online. It was seven p.m. Would Rafael be around? I texted him. He was. He had just gotten back to his hotel room after his final show.

"How are you?" he asked.

I debated for a minute what to tell him. We had become close, but were we close enough to dump relationship drama on him? Did I want to make things complicated? Should I tell him? Or should I keep it clean and neat? After all, he rarely talked about his girlfriend with me.

Clean and neat were over-rated, I decided. And I was too emotional to play it cool.

"Mark and I just broke up."

I had not realized how truly sad I was about this turn of events until I typed them, as if typing them had made them real. I could feel the emotions welling up in my stomach.

"I'm so sorry."

I did not know what to say. I just stared at my phone. The little iMessage word bubble was blinking. He was typing something.

"I know it hurts, but you deserve better."

I smiled. Rafael was sweet.

"Can you text with me a little while, just to keep me company? Or do you have to go?"

"I can text with you all night," he answered. "I just have to leave for the airport in the morning."

"Really? Are you sure?"

"Of course. If you keep me up, it will just make me tired, but then I will sleep better on the plane."

"Thank you. That's so nice of you."

"It's what friends do. I do not have many friends. You are important to me. And loyalty is important to me too."

"Aww....that's so not L.A. of you. Sometimes it feels like everyone in L.A. is just out for themselves." He really did feel like he was from another planet sometimes, if not from another era.

"I'm not a Hollywood guy. I just live there."

I laughed. "Well, I'm glad to hear that. And I'm glad we're friends."

"Of course. I'm glad we're friends, too. You are a very interesting person."

"So are you!"

"No, you're more. Not only that, you're a woman, you're beautiful, you're sexy, and you can do many things."

Rafael really was the best. And he always knew exactly what to say to me.

"You just cheered me up," I told him.

"I am telling you, you're amazing. And I have said this to only three or four other people in my life."

"Wow."

"Wow for you, too."

"You are too cute."

"No, you are. And you are awesome. I have never wanted to get married, but if I ever was to get married, it would be to a woman like you."

This was a lot to process. My brain could not keep up. My heart was fluttering in my chest, my skin sending tingles of electric shock. What was going on? Where was this flattery coming from? I had no idea. I felt like this whole day was lost to a combination of delirium and drama. I was falling head over heels for a Spanish magician named Rafael Delgado who was currently texting me from his hotel room in Australia.

"That's a really nice thing to say. But I'm just me."

"No, you are a very special person, that's all. The problem is that 'all' is a lot."

"I don't think that's a problem, is it?"

"It's a small problem. To my eyes, you are the closest I have ever seen to the perfect woman. You do everything, you are interesting, you are funny...and you are still normal in all the right ways. ☺"

"How do you manage to say so many nice things? I don't know what to say. You leave me speechless."

He really was the most charming man alive. I was riveted

by my phone and the messages popping up on it. I had completely forgotten about Mark.

"I am a philosopher and a poet. Both without drinking."

I laughed. "You're funny AND sweet."

"I am a rock star at heart, a comedian by birth, a philosopher by mind, and a magician by trade."

"You should write that down somewhere. You should use that again, that's good."

"I don't need to. My best lines are only for you."

I was starting to feel delirious, either from the lack of sleep, the antibiotics, the strep, the break-up, or the fact that Rafael was being so direct with me. My brain felt overloaded.

"Thank you for talking to me, but it's really late here. And I'm still sick. I should go to bed."

"Of course. Anytime. I hope you feel better by Friday."

"I definitely will. Even if I'm still sick, I'll be able to do a couple hours at the Castle. I can't wait to go with you."

"Good. See you Friday."

"Yes, see you Friday. Have a safe flight."

"Good night. Thank you."

"Good night."

I switched my phone to silent and placed it on my bedside table. I was too tired to think straight. But even if I had been wide-awake, I doubted that I would have known what to make of what had just transpired. What *had* just transpired? I had no idea. I buried myself into bed, Miles against the backs of my knees. I was determined not to overthink or obsess. Friday would hopefully add some clarity to this mess. Whatever that night had in store, I knew I could not wait for it to arrive.

CHAPTER TEN

All day Friday, I could think of nothing else but counting down the hours until I met with Rafael. Unfortunately, I still had to go into work. After four days without me, Alfredo was having a meltdown, and I was afraid of what would happen if I called in sick for the fifth day in a row. So I hauled my sick and antibioticized ass into work.

Alfredo seemed satisfied enough just to have my physical presence back in the office, and luckily for me, he kept a reasonable distance. He was distracted by a client who had requested an excessive number of revisions, so he left me to sit quietly at my desk, musing about the fact that I had not heard from Rafael, or Mark, all day Thursday. Rafael was in transit, doing the ridiculous trip back to L.A. from Australia, and Mark was off feeling either triumphant or miserable. Whatever it was, I did not care. I did not want to hear from him ever again.

I managed to put some half-ass project concepts together, proposing variations of copy for the "copper reds and ashy blondes" hair color project while my brain was very much elsewhere. Getting text messages from Rafael was nice, but they were just temporary distractions. I could not wait to be next to him, to look at him, to feel his warmth beside mine, to stare into his blue eyes and the beaming white of his wide smile. I yearned to run my fingers through his soft hair, but I knew that would not happen on Friday.

Or ever.

Corinna called after lunch, partly, I think, to make sure I had not contacted Mark in a moment of weakness or stupidity. She seemed relieved that I was now fixated on someone else, although she was not pleased that this someone else was still attached to a girlfriend. She kept asking if he had gotten rid of her yet.

"No. No. He's off limits and will probably always be off limits."

"And you still think it's platonic?"

"I don't know what it is." She was making me cranky.

"Maybe you should say something? Bring it up?"

Who needed a mother when you had Corinna? "I think it's better not to say anything."

"Really...?" The skepticism was dripping off her tongue. She obviously had no faith in my judgment.

"Okay. Okay. I'll say something. I just don't want to scare him off. I want to figure out some way to do it that doesn't screw things up."

"It sounds to me like things are *already* screwed up. And if they aren't yet, they will be soon."

I sighed. "Yeah. I know. That's how it sounds. But I'll be careful. I promise. I really like this guy. I don't want to lose him. Even if he is just a friend."

"Just be careful. You're too nice sometimes. You let these guys walk all over you."

"I'll be careful. I promise. And I really don't think he's going to walk all over me. I think we just like each other, and things got a little complicated. I promise I'll sort them out."

She did not sound convinced, and, honestly, I was not doing a good job of convincing myself, either. I knew that, at some point, I would have to address the issue. I would have to step back from the situation or tell him he had to, but for now, I loved his attention. More than anything, I wanted to avoid any kind of confrontation that might force him to back off. I wanted to keep him as close as I could, even if part of me knew I was playing a dangerous game. There was a very good chance I would get hurt, but it was impossible for me to walk away.

I craved his company. I was addicted to our conversations and to his presence. There was something about this situation that felt larger than either of us. I could not walk away from it, masochistic as the whole thing was.

Rafael and I had talked once about regret. I told him that I had always tried to live my life by seizing opportunities, refusing to allow myself to walk away from a situation out of fear, taking advantage of the moment so that I would regret nothing. I have an obsessive personality, so if I do not follow through with something I desire, I beat myself up over it incessantly. Life is short. The result was that there was very little in my life that I regretted.

"I can see that in you," Rafael told me.

"What do you mean? What do you see?"

"You have a very special peace in your eyes. That only means that you are where you want to be, how you want to be, and that you are surrounded by many more positive things than negatives."

How could I not want to spend time with someone who said things like that? Even if he had a girlfriend, even if I could not possess him in a physical fashion, I was in love with his mind. I could spend hours talking to him, and we often did exactly that. But tonight we would actually *be* together, and I could not wait.

One of the benefits of going to the Castle was the dress code. I was one of those routinely over-dressed people, but I still could not get away with wearing a cocktail dress to the movies or for Thai food. The Castle gave me the perfect excuse to wear the sexiest dress I could find with the tallest heels. It was infinitely easier to be sexy at the Castle than on an average date, and I took advantage of this to make sure I looked amazing.

For this evening, that meant a little red dress. It was strapless, gathered in at the waist, flared out at the hips. I felt like a ballerina. Wrapping my hair up in a bun on the top of my head to finish the look, I added a cropped black jacket and black heels. The dress may only have been from Zara, but it looked like couture, and I looked like a model. Red lips and mascara finished it off.

The plan had been to pick Rafael up at his apartment building and then to drive across the street to the Castle together. Unfortunately, I had not predicted an event at the Hollywood Bowl, combined with some film premiere at the Kodak. Traffic was a nightmare. What should have been a ten-minute drive stretched out…and out. I texted Rafael to let him know I was running late.

"Traffic is horrible. I will probably be there in another fifteen."

"That's fine. I'm just at the downstairs bar."

That was unexpected. I panicked at the sudden change of plans. "Wait, what? I thought I was picking you up at your house?"

"Oh. No. I'm already at the Castle."

For whatever reason, all my social anxiety and nervousness collided in one big rush. Maybe it was my nerves about seeing Rafael after so much had been shared and exposed via text message. Maybe it was because things felt unbalanced since I was now single, and he still had a girlfriend. Maybe it was my as-yet-undealt-with reaction to being dumped by Mark *again*. Maybe it was a reaction to going out after a week spent in bed, dosed with heavy antibiotics. Maybe it was all the traffic at a time when I had not mentally prepared for it. Maybe it was the realization that I was showing up alone at the Castle for the first time, without Mark, and that fact made our breakup—and my loneliness— all the more tangible. I had no one to walk me through the door, to pay for the valet, to keep track of the ticket in his wallet. I had no one to pretend he wanted to marry me. The wave of self-pity hit me strong, and I suddenly felt on the verge of tears.

Whatever it was that was making me emotional wreck, if it had not been for that same hellish traffic, I would have turned around and gone home. More than anything, I wanted to get back in bed with Miles. But traffic was jammed, and a

U-turn impossible, so I took a deep breath and powered through. I could not turn around. All that talk about regret, and now I was going to pussy out of something I had been looking forward to merely because I had to walk in by myself? No way. I peered into the rear view mirror, dabbing the corners of my eyes to catch the tears before my makeup ran. I could not afford to cry. I had not brought more mascara or eyeliner with me.

Taking another deep breath, I made a right turn to get off Hollywood Boulevard, and, as if on cue, the traffic let up. I had passed the Bowl, and the premiere was now south of me. The streets were mine again. I shot up Sycamore Avenue and was at the Magic Castle a few minutes later. I was starting to feel better. The brief moment of wallowing had been replaced with excitement that I was about to see Rafael.

I took one more look in the rear-view mirror to make sure my face was intact and handed the keys to the valet.

"Welcome to the Magic Castle," he said.

"Thank you," I said, as the nerves evaporated, replaced with a tingling excitement.

The excitement only intensified when I gave the girl at the desk my name and told her I was a guest of Rafael Delgado's. She did not even look down at her list. She just smiled at me and waved me toward the owl.

"Open sesame," I told it, and the door slid open. It was time for my night with Rafael. *At last.*

He was at the bar, much as he had been the last time. Only now I was alone. He and I were alone, together.

"Hi," I said, tapping him on the arm.

"Hey," he said, turning around to look at me, slipping a deck of cards into his pocket. He grinned. "You look amazing."

He said that, even though his eyes had not left mine. Even though he had not seen my dress or my shoes. We just stared at each other, not moving, our gaze unwavering.

"Thank you. So do you."

There was a silence, but it was not an awkward silence. It was the silence of two people who were enjoying one another's presence so much that words were not necessary. We stood and looked at each other, taking each other in.

"Would you like to see a show?" he asked.

I shrugged. Being with him was enough of a show for me. Everything else was superfluous. "Whatever you want."

"I want to see a show with you."

I smiled. "Okay. So let's do it."

"Great. Follow me."

We walked up the stairs, past the restaurant, down the stairs, by the Palace, and to the Parlour. This would be my first show in the Parlour.

"Who is performing tonight?" I asked. As if it mattered.

"It's Adam Dorian."

"Is he a friend of yours?"

This time it was his turn to shrug. "I know him."

I laughed. Okay, I saw how this worked.

Since I was with Rafael, and since Rafael was VIP, and since he "knew" Adam, even if they were not friends (whatever that meant), Adam had already reserved seats for us. They were in the third row, marked "Reserved." The house manager, Manny, directed us to them.

We sat down as the rest of the Castle's guests filed in around us. It was a Friday night, and Friday nights in the Castle were crowded. Friday nights in the Castle were also a bit rowdy, as people pounded back the drinks. Rafael did not drink, and I did not drink when I was with him. So I experienced everything sober. I was barely able to handle myself around him when I was in complete control. I could not imagine what I would do if I was intoxicated.

As we sat and waited for the room to fill up, Rafael noticed my watch.

"That's beautiful," he said.

"Thanks. It was my grandmother's." It *was* a beautiful watch, slim and gold, antique and delicate. I reserved it for special elegant occasions.

He leaned over to look at the watch, tracing the narrow elastic band with his finger. My heart felt as though it would jump out of my chest. His finger sent electric shocks up my arm and throughout my entire body. I could not breathe. I yanked the watch off and handed it to him.

"Here. You can look more closely."

He gave me a quizzical glance, perhaps confused by my abrupt behavior, but I did not have the energy to worry. I was too busy trying to catch my breath, trying to cool myself down. The man had a girlfriend, I told myself. I needed to get a grip. I needed to prove to Corinna that this would be okay, that I could do this.

Rafael inspected the watch with a gravity I had not expected before passing it back to me.

"It's lovely," he told me, looking at me, his blue eyes intense and penetrating.

I smiled, unable to speak. My entire body felt on fire, desperate for him. What did he see when he looked at me that way? What did he think about? I slipped the watch back on my wrist. Our chemistry was through the roof. If I was so intensely affected by it, he must have been, too, right? That *was* how chemistry worked. If one person felt it, surely the other person was aware of it, too? But Rafael acted like he did not feel anything. He seemed totally relaxed, except for the intensity of his gaze, while I was still struggling to breathe.

As the lights dimmed, I leaned back in my chair. Maybe this show would prove enough of a distraction for me to collect myself. That was what I thought, at least, until Rafael leaned back in his chair and then, thanks to the Castle's narrow seats, our thighs touched.

Oh fuck *that*. Now I could not think of anything else. Forget about breathing. All I could feel was his leg against mine. All I could think about was his body *inside* mine. My left hand grabbed the armrest, as if it would provide some support or grounding. It did not. As long as Rafael's leg was against mine, nothing would be able to ground me. I felt the waves of sensation building in intensity, until I finally gave up and crossed my right leg over my left, pulling my body away from him and the overwhelming chemistry that ignited whenever we were beside each other.

I was going crazy. *He* was driving me crazy.

As if in marked contrast to the explosive nature of my dynamic with Rafael, the show on stage was serviceable, a pleasantly neutral diversion. It was not particularly memorable, and there were certain things that bothered me about it, but Adam's stage personality was charming, some of his jokes funny, and his tricks professional and polished. It was a decent way to spend half an hour, and if Rafael's leg had not been a few inches away from mine, it probably would have made even more of an impression.

When the show finished, we made our way out to the nearest bar, where Rafael ordered his trademark coffee with milk. I got a water, no ice.

"That coffee won't keep you up?"

He shook his head. "Never. When it's time to sleep, I can always sleep."

"But never more than six hours!"

"Right." He smiled. "So what did you think of the show?"

"You want my opinion first? Shouldn't you tell me yours? You are the expert."

"I'm not an expert. I just play with cards."

I laughed. "You're an expert. And you know you do a lot more than just *play* with cards."

"No. I just do card tricks to pick up girls."

"Very funny."

"Don't laugh. It's true." He gestured in my direction.

"You're right. It worked on me. And all your other groupies."

"See? Calling one's self a magician is no guarantee of talent, but at least I have groupies. Well, *a* groupie. And so what did my groupie think of the show she just saw?"

"I thought it was okay. There were certain things I didn't like, that I thought could have been better."

He looked at me expectantly.

"Well…" I felt self-conscious expounding to him about the flaws or strengths of a magic show. I had only been going to magic shows for a few weeks. He had been performing internationally for fifteen years.

He sensed the cause of my hesitation. "Go on. You've read more than one book. You know more about magic now than ninety percent of the people here. Trust me. I want to hear your opinion."

It was true. After plowing through the first book he had recommended, I had gone on to read another book and a handful of articles Rafael photocopied for me from the Magic Castle's private library. Even though I still felt horribly under-qualified to have an opinion, I evidently was also incapable of telling him no to anything. So I told him what I had thought of Adam's show. I said that I found certain tricks tedious, that there had been too much repetition of the "pulling coins out of the air" routine, that I was already bored with the "stuff in a bag" gimmick, that there was not a proper narrative structure to the show. It did not build up to any sort of finale, rendering the show sort of flat-lined. There was no great reveal. There was no story, no psychological purpose. It felt like a series of tricks in no particular order, without cohesion. Adam's technical capabilities were sound, but that was not enough to make the show feel well rounded, like an event or an experience.

Rafael smiled at me. I mock-punched him in the arm.

"Stop it! Stop smiling at me. Are you patronizing me?"

He shook his head. "No. You are right. You are right about everything. Why do you think a good magic show is such a satisfying experience? What was it that this show did not give its audience? What was the difference for you between this show and mine?"

I had to think about that for a moment. "I've been trying to figure that out, too. Not just tonight, but since I saw your show, since reading the book. I've been trying to figure out why your show made such an impact on me. Why magic, even when it's just average, is still so powerful."

He nodded at me to continue. He seemed fascinated by what I was saying. I felt a little self-conscious (who was I to have these ideas?), but I continued.

"I think magic organizes the chaos of our lives, even as it fills us with wonder at the impossible. The successful trick satisfies because it provides order to our lives. What is supposed to happen is what happens. You, as the magician, make it happen. You are in control. You impose order on our disorder. We do not know how you do it, so in this respect, we are like children, awed by the mystery and wonder of the world and its potential for the incredible. But, at the same time, you are in control of it, so we are reassured that, even if we are not in control, someone is. The mystery is controlled and contained."

He smiled at me. "I like that. That's good. It's obvious that you are a writer."

I blushed, looking down at the bar. "But I don't know. That's just what I think."

Then I remembered something else he had said. "Why did you say I know more about magic than ninety percent of the people here?"

"Because you read about magic. No one here," he gestured around him at the crowds milling about the Castle, "reads about magic. No one here *thinks* about magic. They just want to do the tricks. They want to make the cards disappear, to find the coins. They don't care about anything else. Like you said, they don't pay attention to the story. You may not know how to do the tricks, but the tricks are only a small part of the show. You know the rest of it. You know the important parts. You know the parts that matter. Everything else is just technique."

I felt embarrassed and flattered. I turned to my water and took a sip. I did not know what to say. He often left me speechless, with my mind spinning to keep up.

"Hey, hey, hey! Rafael, dude, what *is* up?"

I looked up and almost choked on my water. It was Jack Ferguson. Beautiful Jack Ferguson. Even more beautiful up close.

"Hi, Jack," Rafael said, giving him a quick hug and a manly pat on the shoulder. "Good show the other night. This is Adrian."

I smiled and reached out to shake his hand. "Hi, Jack. Nice to meet you. It *was* a great show the other night."

"Oh? You were there? That's cool!"

His energy was infectious, even off stage. He grinned at me, and I grinned back, feeling instantly comfortable with him.

"What are you guys up to tonight?"

"We just saw Adam's show," Rafael said.

"Oh yeah? How was it? Was it good?"

Rafael looked at me, as if it was my turn to answer.

"It was okay." I wanted to be political here. I did not know Jack's relationship with Adam, and the show *had* been okay. There was a certain safety in my response, but Jack saw through it.

"Ahhh…Not that great, huh?" Jack laughed, looking over at Rafael for confirmation.

I smiled. Rafael repeated that the show had been okay, but in his deadpan way that made his true opinion pretty obvious. When Jack turned back to me, I shrugged, offering no additional explanation. I did not want to step on anyone's toes. I did not know Castle etiquette and did not want to badmouth someone improperly.

"And now? Any more magic?"

I glanced over at Rafael. "Rafael is in charge. It's up to him."

"We might go catch Jeremy Miller in the Peller," Rafael

said.

"Really?" Jack looked shocked.

"Why 'really'?" I asked, looking back and forth between Jack and Rafael.

Jack leaned over and practically whispered in my ear, "Now *that* is a bad show." My stomach did a little flip at the feeling of his breath on his face.

"Oh yeah?" I was intrigued. I wanted to hear more.

"Yeah," Jack replied, smiling devilishly. He looked at Rafael. "Plus, I thought you guys hated each other."

This was even more interesting. I turned to Rafael. "What is that about? Why would he hate you?"

Rafael sighed. "It's a long story. But Jeremy basically hates card tricks. He thinks cards are old-fashioned. He thinks magic should be like Criss Angel and David Blaine. He likes spectacle and illusion. He says card tricks are boring."

"Even the kind of card tricks you do?" I was shocked.

"Yeah. After our latest show finished, he sent an email to me and Peter that told us congratulations on a good run, but that if we wanted to take our show to the next level, we should stop using cards."

This made no sense to me. "But cards are *what* you do. Your show was amazing *because* of what you did with the cards. I can't imagine you doing anything else."

Rafael shrugged. "Who knows? I told you, you know more about magic than most people here."

"Oh really?" Jack exclaimed, turning to stare at me. "You do magic?"

I shook my head. "Rafael doesn't know what he's talking about. I don't know anything about magic."

"That's not true. She reads books. She knows a lot about magic. Even if she doesn't know tricks." He winked at me. "Come on, let's go check out Jeremy's show. I want to see what a 'master' can do."

I laughed and turned to Jack. "Will you come, too?"

He looked back and forth between Rafael and me. "Am I

interrupting anything?"

"No, no," I said. "I'm just his groupie. Come with us. It will be fun."

I thought it was amusing (and a little satisfying) that Jack thought Rafael and I might have been on a date. I wondered if Jack had ever met Rafael's girlfriend. To my pleasure, Jack agreed to join us, following us downstairs to the Peller. I was more curious than ever to see this Jeremy guy in action. I was also pleased to have Jack added to the mix. I wanted to spend more time with him.

As we waited outside the Peller for the early show to let out, Rafael and Jack talked shop. It was not a conversation in which I could participate, so I just listened. They talked about the Castle's entertainment director and an upcoming festival he was putting together of magicians from Brazil. They talked about a recent appearance Jack had had on *Good Morning America*. Apparently, they had also invited Rafael to participate, but he was in San Francisco at the time and could not do it. But Rafael said he generally did not like performing magic on television.

"Magic loses something when it does not happen in front of you. It is a problem with bringing magic to television. It is too easy to fake it, to distract with cuts and editing. You need to be in the same room as the magician."

Jack disagreed, which made sense to me, since his style of magic was so different from Rafael's. Rafael's magic was the kind that worked best in a close-up situation. Jack's performance was more about spectacle, and his energy was so performative and dramatic that I could see him translating well to a television screen.

"Hey man, whatever happened with those writers you were talking to? The ones who were pitching T.V. show ideas to you?" Jack asked.

Rafael shook his head. "I'm not really interested."

"Why not?" I asked. "That sounds like it could be a great opportunity. Especially if you can collaborate with them on the concept."

Rafael shook his head again. "No. Magic is such a specific area that outside ideas normally do not work to create the magical atmosphere that you need to see magic."

I nodded. "That makes sense. And these writers don't get it?"

"No. Most people don't get it." Rafael smiled at me. "Come, let's go in. It's time for the show."

I followed him, Jack behind me, as we entered the Peller. Rafael nodded at the house manager, who ushered us in ahead of everyone else. I could get used to this kind of treatment, I thought, very much enjoying the company of these two gorgeous and talented magicians.

"So how do you guys know each other?" Jack asked, once we were seated.

I turned to look at Rafael, uncertain what to say. He just looked back at me, as if giving me the opportunity to answer.

"We met at the Castle," I said.

Jack still looked unsatisfied, so I added, "I'm just a groupie."

Jack laughed. "And where can I get some groupies like you?"

"I will be your groupie, too."

"Hey, hey," Rafael interjected. "I don't know that I want to share."

I glanced at him, then back at Jack, laughing. "You two will have to work it out."

Jack smiled, looking at me. "I'm sure we can figure out a way to share you."

Was that a double entendre? I did not know how to respond. I could feel the sexual tension emanating off him in waves. Rafael was still acting like our vibe was a platonic one—which, I kept reminding myself, it *was*. But, as for Jack, I did not know. My history had shown me that really attractive guys were often flirtatious just for the fun of it. I was not sure if Jack was seriously interested or just out for a good time.

Whatever his intention, he definitely seemed into me now.

The arrival of the house manager at the front of the stage silenced my internal monologue and our conversation.

"Welcome to the Magic Castle," he proclaimed dramatically, with what felt like an excessive amount of enthusiasm. "You are all very lucky to be here tonight to see a rare performance by Jeremy Miller, a veteran of the Los Angeles magic scene. Please silence your cell phones, take no pictures, and put your hands together for Jeremy Miller!"

The room provided an appropriate amount of polite clapping as a short balding man bounded onto the stage. He was wearing a suit that looked like he had borrowed it from a car salesman—from the 1970s. And by borrow, I mean not only that he looked like a car salesman, but that the suit looked like it had been made for someone with a different body. The shoulders were too large, extending beyond his small frame. The sleeves were a few inches too long, hanging loosely around his skinny wrists, and the pants were low and baggy. It was not oversized enough to seem intentional, it just felt like an ill-fitting suit. It was definitely *not* the look of someone purported to be a magician of any serious stature. One of the first rules of performance is that your clothes should fit your role. I could not take him seriously.

I still did not take him seriously after his first trick, which involved unusually large playing cards. Obviously intended for some gimmicky purpose, the cards were more than twice the size of regular playing cards. I felt like I was watching a clown. Where were the balloon animals?

"He's using cards?" I whispered to Rafael.

Rafael shrugged and grimaced, his face a mixture of horror and curiosity.

"Tonight, I want to begin with one of my favorite tricks, a classic standby, and one which I would like to dedicate to one of the world's foremost card magicians, Rafael Delgado. Rafael, would you pick a card?"

Everyone turned to find one of the world's foremost card

magicians. They all stared as Rafael squirmed in discomfort. Obviously, this kind of attention was not the kind Rafael liked. The look of distaste on his face was poorly concealed by his weak smile.

"Queen of hearts," Rafael said, winking at me.

"Queen of hearts," Jeremy repeated. "Excellent." And then he turned his attention to shuffling the deck of cards in his hands.

"What was that about?" I asked Rafael under my breath.

"Who knows?" He rolled his eyes, obviously not amused.

Jeremy's trick proceeded despite Rafael's contempt. The trick was a standard one, the only twist being that the queen of hearts was discovered, as the grand finale, in a picture frame to the right of the stage. Everyone oohed except for me, Rafael, and Jack. Jack seemed especially entertained by Rafael's displeasure.

The car salesman shtick was not limited to the suit or the oversize playing cards. It was, apparently, Jeremy's entire stage persona. I started to feel like I was at a children's birthday party. I could not help laughing when he did, in fact, begin a balloon trick. He inflated balloons and then retrieved cards from within them as I cringed. To make matters worse, this was followed by the generic "pulling quarters out of the air" trick that already bored me. The over-the-top facial expressions and general air of mockery and juvenile humor only made the show more painful to sit through. I could not believe he had had the audacity to provide advice of any kind to Rafael, whose show was on a level far above this one. Even Jack was barely able to keep a straight face.

By the time the show ended, and we had filed out to the downstairs bar, we all looked at each other with vaguely shell-shocked expressions.

"What *was* that?" Jack exclaimed.

Rafael shrugged. "I really could not say."

"What did you think?" Jack asked, turning to me.

I shook my head. "I don't know *what* that was."

"Shall we go back upstairs?" Rafael motioned toward the stairwell.

"I've actually got to run and help Michael Fontana set up for his late show tonight," Jack said. "I promised I would record the show for him."

"That's nice of you," Rafael said.

Jack smiled. "Well, you know, he's going to buy me dinner."

I laughed. "It was nice to meet you," I said to Jack, extending out my hand.

He took my right hand with both of his and held it for a moment. His hands were soft and smooth. I could feel tingling on my skin. "It was nice to meet you, too, Adrian. I hope I see you again sometime. I'll have to get your number from Rafael or find you on Facebook."

We smiled at each other. Jack gently released my hand, nodded at Rafael, and then sprinted off toward the Palace Theater.

"He's nice," I said to Rafael.

"Yes, he is."

I could not tell if there was any jealousy on his part. I could not read Rafael at all. It was driving me crazy.

"Do you want to see any more magic?" he asked.

"I think I'm good. It's hard to top what we just saw."

I was partly joking, but I also felt frustrated and deflated. The platonic energy between us was bumming me out. Even though I had not wanted to admit it, I had to acknowledge that I wanted more and not getting it, or even knowing what was going on, was frustrating.

"I'll walk you out," he said.

He led the way up the stairs and through the labyrinth of passageways until we emerged at the main exit.

"Do you want me to give you a ride home?" I asked.

He shook his head. "Peter is coming shortly. I will go hang out with him. We have some magic stuff to discuss."

"Okay. Have fun. Thank you for a nice evening."

115

He seemed sad to let me go, lingering with me as the valet went to find my car.

"I'm sorry about that last show. I knew it would be bad, but I was still curious to see it."

"That's okay." I smiled. "Bad magic isn't so bad when it's with you."

He laughed. "Bad magic is always bad. You're just easily distracted."

He gave me an awkward and quick hug goodbye as the valet stood waiting by my car. Even the feeling of his body against mine was enough to depress me further. I wanted to hold him and not let go. I inhaled his aftershave, wanting to feel his skin against mine. I wanted so much more from this guy than I was ever going to get, and I knew it, and it made me sad.

Dejected by the reality of the situation, I got in my car and drove back down the winding driveway to make my left turn onto Franklin Avenue.

I had turned the music up so loud that I almost did not hear my phone beep.

When I got to the red light at Cahuenga Boulevard, I glanced down. It was a message from Rafael.

"37."

I sent back a "?" as the light changed.

When I got to the next red light, I had a new message.

"The number of times I looked at your legs."

Whoa. That had come out of nowhere. As did the next message.

"Your legs are unbelievable."

I was speechless. I scrambled for something to say. "Thank you. That's an amazing compliment," I texted back before pulling into my parking spot.

"I would assume that you have noticed it by now."

"Noticed my legs?"

"That I find your legs very attractive and super sexy."

"How would I have noticed?"

"Because I look at them. ☺"

He was really too much. Totally cool in person and now this? "You are very subtle. No, I did not notice."

"Invisible things are normally more interesting. A rule I live by. Trust me, I look."

"But I think I would enjoy seeing you look at them, so not all things need to be invisible."

"This is true. Not all things have to be. But now that you know, seeing how invisible my looks can be will be interesting…trust me. ☺"

"Ok. I trust you."

"I know you need to go to sleep, so I will tell you more about how sexy you are tomorrow. Sleep well."

"Thank you, good night."

"Good night."

I let myself into my apartment and grabbed Miles to go for a walk. My mind was reeling. I had no idea what to make of all this. He had been so casual all night. What was he doing? He seemed so genuine with me that I found it hard to believe he was playing a game. So what *was* going on? Was he too shy to talk to me like this in person? Or did the text messages feel less inappropriate and therefore easier to justify in terms of his girlfriend? I was at a total loss.

But what I did know was that I was beaming as I got into bed. His words had lit me up, and, as I fell asleep, I felt his arms around me. Maybe I had to rely on my mind, but I could still imagine what his lips felt like, and nothing—or no one—could take that away from me. I could imagine the taste of his mouth against mine, the softness of his lips on my face. And I had these text messages to read and re-read over and over.

DAHLIA SCHWEITZER

CHAPTER ELEVEN

Rafael invited me to go to the Castle with him again a few days later. There was a particular show in the Palace that he wanted me to see. I still had no idea what was going on between us. The texting had continued, more of the same. Intermittent, conversational—him wishing me good morning, me bidding him good night, and a lot of everything else during the day. But consistently, there was no mention of the girlfriend. I did not even know her name. Despite his promise to tell me more about how sexy I was, he did not. There was no more explicit flirtation. There was just consistent messaging about everything, mundane and esoteric.

But I was not complaining. Even if I was confused by his intentions, I did not feel ready to confront him. For now, I would take what he gave me and be grateful for the friendship, however convoluted it was. I enjoyed him too much to risk losing what we had. Luckily, Corinna was temporarily preoccupied shooting an episode of *Southland*, so she was off my back for a few days.

To make matters more interesting, I had received a Facebook friend request from Jack the same night we had met at the Castle. I had not seen him since, as he was down in San Diego doing a series of magic shows, but we had exchanged a couple messages online. I enjoyed our limited contact, however basic it was. He was sweet and kind.

But I *adored* the contact I had with Rafael. I was hungry to know more about him, to understand his brain, to get inside his ideas. He was the most fascinating man I had ever met— and I, as he reminded me on more than one occasion, was the most fascinating woman he had ever met. We could not get enough of each other—platonically.

But whatever was happening between us, I made sure I looked amazing as I dressed to meet him at the Castle. I was going for chic and sophisticated, wearing a small black dress with a lace pattern and strappy red heels. I would have preferred to pick him up and drive there with him for the security of a companion and to save money on valet fees (members paid less than guests), but he liked to meet me there for reasons he did not explain. So as was becoming our usual pattern, I drove solo and met him at the downstairs bar.

He gave me a quick hug and a kiss on the cheek when he saw me. As always, it was great to see him, even if it was also torturous. But he was like a drug; I could not walk away.

This night was just the two of us. Since it was a weekday night, the Castle was significantly mellower than a weekend. Rafael actually told me that Wednesdays were the nights magicians usually came to see shows. Monday nights started the run for the weekly shows, and so they were often cursed with technical failures or sloppiness. By Wednesday, the performers would have had two nights of performances under their belts, so everything would be smoother. By Thursdays, the weekend crowds started to intensify, and weekends were generally to be avoided whenever possible. There were simply too many people, and the lines to get into shows were too long. I preferred fewer people—because that meant fewer people demanding Rafael's attention, fewer people he had to greet, and fewer people distracting him from me.

The only show Rafael wanted me to see was in the Palace, and, as he explained, he wanted me to see it primarily because it was so outrageous. It was not so much that it was an example of magical mastery, but that the performer was unlike any other.

His name was Oberon. He had long crazy purple dreadlocks, and his face was painted completely white, with elaborate eyebrows drawn on and lips outlined in a deep red. I was not a fan. He, like Jeremy Miller, felt more suited to a children's party than a night for adults. His tricks revolved almost exclusively around balloons, but, unlike Jeremy's balloons, these were massive balloons, balloons he would trap himself inside. He would then roll around the stage inside the balloon, filling it up with smoke, before making a dramatic exit. It was more of a spectacle than magic, and I was not entirely sure why he had even been booked at the Castle. I kept waiting for the juggling and fire spinning to start.

Rafael found Oberon both mesmerizing and horrifying, like an accident on the freeway, and he seemed to enjoy watching me watch the show. I was more preoccupied, however, with the fact that our thighs were touching during the whole performance. I would not move my leg away, and neither did he. He had to know we were touching, right?

After the show, we adjourned to the bar just outside the Palace, where we continued to sit. I made sure to keep my knee against his leg, taking pleasure in the fact that he did not shift his leg away. Our conversation was platonic, entirely harmless, two friends discussing magic and culture and art, seemingly unaware that the current running between our bodies felt like unharnessed electricity. But I was very much aware, and I was sure he felt it, too. When Rafael touched me, I felt alive. Everything tingled. When I was with him, life seemed brighter, colors more vivid. I needed him beside me. I was addicted.

We sat at the bar this way, legs touching, for over two hours. Rafael had no interest in seeing any other magic show that night, and all I cared about was being with him and feeling his body against mine. When it got late enough that I had to leave, it felt traumatizing to rip myself away from him, to separate our legs. I desperately wanted to bring him home with me, to not let go. I could not imagine the luxury of sleeping beside him, waking up next to him, much less feeling his skin against mine, but it was all I wanted.

When we said goodbye, once again at the valet station, we hugged, and this time felt longer than the time before. It was still awkward, in full view of Castle folk streaming in and out as the valet waited with my keys, but I relished the moment, imprinted it on my psyche, so that I could take it home with me like a souvenir from an exotic vacation.

As soon as I got in the car, I put my phone on the seat beside me. This time I would be ready. It was as if the whole night had been foreplay, and this, this was the real thing, the moment worth waiting for. I glanced over every few seconds, not trusting it to beep when the message came through, *if* a message came through.

But I should not have doubted. He texted me before I had even made it down the driveway.

"Don't take this the wrong way, but your eyes are so beautiful and dangerous at the same time that it is a deadly combination."

"How could I take that the wrong way?" I texted back, flattered even if I did not entirely understand what he meant.

"I don't know. Just saying that before I piss you off."

There was a pause. I could see the iMessage cursor blinking, so I waited, watching the road as I headed down Franklin.

The next message came quickly.

"They are so magical and mysterious that I would put them against any magic in the world, knowing that they will probably win."

Even if I had not been driving, I would not have texted back. I had no idea what to say. These messages were like grenades decimating my defenses. What was he doing? What was he thinking? What was I supposed to be doing? The rational part of my brain told me that I needed to confront the issue *now*. I needed to say something, to acknowledge what was happening, to bring up the girlfriend, but I could not. I was weak. I wanted Rafael so badly, in whatever form I could get him, that I was too afraid of scaring him off. I did not want to remind him that what we were doing was totally inappropriate. I did not want to risk what little I had of him. But he was driving me *crazy*.

When I got home that night, I could not sleep. I tossed and turned, the anxiety and stress eating away at me. I knew I was falling in love with this guy. I knew that I was making a hopeless mess of the situation, but I felt utterly helpless. I told myself that, the next time I saw him, I would say something. I would bring her up *somehow*. It was odd that he never mentioned her, although maybe, upon further reflection, it was not odd at all. Maybe he knew it would upset me.

I texted Tyler to see if he could have dinner soon. I needed to call in the troops. I had to admit defeat. And I wanted to hear all about Tyler's new girlfriend and the sex expo.

It was true that Rafael and I had not technically *done* anything wrong, but I still would not want my boyfriend sending these kinds of messages to another girl. It may not have been cheating, exactly, but I would have to be in massive amounts of denial to think that this was in any way okay. I knew it was not. I knew, as a rational adult, that I was playing with knives, and I was going to get hurt, but I was thoroughly sucked in. I could not bring myself to walk away. I was in love with him.

Tyler texted back that he could have dinner tomorrow. Perfect, I thought. And the next time Rafael and I hung out, I would say something. I would address the white elephant in the room. I would deal with the situation, and Tyler would tell me how to do it. Halfway reassured, I managed to fall asleep.

***

Tyler and I usually met at Home Restaurant on Hillhurst Avenue for a variety of reasons. It was really close to my house, and it was on his way home from work. It also had a full bar, and Tyler preferred proper cocktails with his meals. Considering how many Angelenos loved to drink, it always mystified me how few restaurants in Los Feliz had full bars. Tyler could make do with beer or wine, but his preference was for something a little stiffer. The main reason I loved to eat at Home—aside from the massive menu which guaranteed any food craving would be satisfied—was that the seating was outdoors, so I could bring Miles.

This night, like the others, we met at Home.

By the time Miles and I got there, having walked briskly from my house to give Miles a chance to stretch his legs after my day at work, Tyler was already ensconced in a corner booth. Tyler preferred to get to places early, not only because he was a stickler for punctuality but also because (I secretly suspected) it gave him a chance to catch up on his reading. Tyler was a junkie for books, and he seemed always to have a Nook or a Kindle or an iPhone or an iPad within arms reach. He was one of those people who managed to read five books simultaneously and to remember everything from every one. I, needless to say, did not have that kind of intellect. Tyler was always recommending books I should read, but at my more "average" pace, I knew there was no chance I would ever catch up with him. Not in this lifetime, at least.

But tonight we were not talking about books. Tonight, once we got our orders out of the way, we were talking about strippers, sex expos, and my increasingly complicated and confusing "love" life. With Miles at my feet, munching on the occasional sweet potato fry, Tyler and I got down to business.

"So? The stripper? The sex expo? Or is that the 'sex-po?'"

Tyler laughed. "I need my martini first."

I turned around to look for our server. She was heading in our direction, drinks and food on a tray.

"It's moments away. Have a fry while you wait."

I gestured toward the sweet potato fries in front of us. I should also point out that this was not Tyler's first martini. The first one had already been ordered and consumed before I got there. But if Tyler needed two martinis before he could start talking, that was fine with me.

Our server put Tyler's martini and turkey burger in front of him and my mojito and grilled vegetable chicken wrap in front of me. Tyler and I lifted our drinks and clinked them together.

"To sex-po's," I said, grinning naughtily at him.

He winked at me. "To sex-po's indeed."

And then we drank. My mojito was delicious, and the combination of it, Tyler's presence, and Miles curled at my feet was already making me feel better.

"So? The stripper?" I prodded. I was dying to know more. Tyler was always so reserved that any kind of juicy and revealing information had to be tugged out with pliers.

Tyler waved his burger in the air dramatically. "The Stripper and the Sex-Po! It sounds like a movie."

"Tyler. Stop stalling. Dish."

Tyler gave up resisting. Either my nagging or the second martini had served its purpose. "The stripper is great. The sex-po was kind of lame. But it was still something everyone should experience once in a lifetime. Have *you* been to a sex-po?"

I shook my head. "No, Tyler, I haven't. And you know I haven't. I haven't dated a stripper either. What that's like? How'd you meet? How's it all going?"

"Valerie's young. Twenty-five. From Russia. She's a classically trained ballerina. She lived in New York for two years before coming out here. She did some Broadway shows or something. She's on tour now, and they were doing an extended run at the Pantages...but then something happened with the producers, I can't remember the exact details, so the tour got put on hold for six months. She's kind of stuck, because she can't find other work, because the tour will start up again soon, so she decided to stay in L.A. since she's already here. Her manager told her he would send her on T.V. auditions, and she's gone on a few of those—for commercials and stuff—and she did land one Gap ad, but it's not a lot of money, and one of the other girls from the tour had been a stripper, so the two of them decided to do it together. Temporarily."

I nodded. "So she's not *really* a stripper. She's a 'freelance stripper'?"

Tyler laughed. "Very funny, Adrian. You can call it what you will."

"And so in six months, she goes on the road again?"

He nodded, taking another sip from his martini.

"And then what?"

"Who knows? Six months is a long time. Let's see if we get that far."

This was true. For Tyler, six months *was* a long time. Tyler was attractive, and the ladies lined up for him. He was over six feet tall, with pale skin, chiseled features, dark green eyes, and hair that always looked a little too long, but in a way that worked. His lanky body looked hot in whatever he happened to be wearing. He consistently looked so effortlessly coordinated, while yet ruggedly handsome, that he reminded me of a stylish lumberjack, with the perfect plaid shirt and the perfectly worn-through jeans. It took me twice as long to dress "effortlessly," but I knew from experience that Tyler could literally roll out of bed and look great.

If I had not grown close enough to him to think of him as a brother, I probably would have fallen prey to what every other woman seemed to fall prey to when Tyler was in the vicinity. Women threw themselves at Tyler, but Tyler, with his infuriatingly effortless style would not notice. He just moved through life looking perfect, and when he wanted a date, one seemed magically to appear.

"And the sex-po?"

Tyler snorted. "Yes. The sex-po. Valerie and her friend were offered some gig in Vegas during the sex-po. I think they made something like $2000 for a couple days of dancing."

"Two grand?!" I had to put my chicken wrap down to digest that information.

He nodded. "We should switch careers."

Tyler made good money as a content developer for Netflix, so there was no need for him to joke about switching anything, but my freelance writing career left a lot to be desired.

"Maybe I should rethink my life choices," I said, wryly. "Screw this writing crap."

"Just take a dance class or two." Tyler squinted at me. "And you might need a boob job."

"Oh shut up," I said and threw my napkin at him. "Some guys like natural."

"Some guys. But most guys tip better if they see you've made an investment."

"Okay, Tyler. Rein it in. We're getting hopelessly off track here. I need to get your advice."

"On the boob job? I say go for a D cup."

"Very funny. I need your advice on Rafael."

"Rafael? That's still going on? Tell me you've slept with him."

I shook my head. "We haven't even kissed."

"The girlfriend...?"

"Still in the picture."

Tyler grimaced. "That sucks. What are you going to do about it?"

"What am *I* going to do about it? I'm going to do what you tell me to do about it."

"Ah. I see. And what does Corinna say?"

"Nice try, Mr. Pass-the-Buck. Corinna is shooting, so I haven't talked to her about this recently."

Tyler nodded thoughtfully and took another sip of his martini. "And have you said *anything* about the girlfriend to him? Does she ever come up in conversation?"

I shook my head again. "Never. Not even in passing. I have no idea what's going on."

"And how do you feel about the whole thing?"

I had to think about that for a minute. "I didn't want to

say anything for a while because I didn't want to scare him off, but I think my feelings for him are being trumped by my increasing frustration and confusion. I want to know what the fuck is going on. I'm starting to wonder if this is ever going to go anywhere. I want to fast forward to the next scene on the DVD, know what I mean?"

"Yeah. I get it. I think it's time to force the issue. Because, honestly, your friendship is going to self-destruct if this keeps up. You aren't going to be able to handle much more of this. I'd jump the gun. Bring it up. Just ask him, hey, what's happening here? You know. Keep it casual, but like you're wondering what he wants, just to clarify. Don't get all intense about it. Don't 'we have to talk' him. Just bring it up like you almost couldn't care less what the answer is. You're just wondering."

I nodded. That made sense.

"When are you seeing him next?"

"I think Saturday, actually."

"In two days?"

"Yeah."

"Well, that's perfect then. You'll still remember all my advice by then." He grinned. "Unless you let me buy you another mojito."

I laughed. "Hey, I'm a lightweight compared to you."

"Everyone's a lightweight compared to me." Tyler sighed dramatically.

"Oh, poor you."

"Yes. Poor me. Do you want to get dessert?"

I might pass on another drink, but I could never pass on Home's apple pie. Tyler and I split dessert, he had one final martini, and then Miles and I walked home. I felt empowered. Now if I could just manage Tyler's effortless *everything*, I would be all set.

CHAPTER TWELVE

The only problem with my "effortless" planning was that Rafael canceled. We had decided to go get Thai food together at a restaurant near my house, but when I texted him to confirm the time I was picking him up, he asked if we could reschedule.

"Of course. Is everything okay?"

He had never canceled on me before. I was not sure what to make of it.

"I'm just tired. And stressed."

Rafael had never complained about being stressed before. I did not know if I should just give him space or offer to help, if I should take it personally or not.

"About work stuff?" I asked.

"No. The girlfriend. We've been arguing on Skype for the last couple hours. I just want to read and go to bed."

This was the first time he had brought up the girlfriend in ages. Now I was even more uncertain how I should respond. Should I ask for more information? Should I pry? I decided not to ask for details. Too much information might actually just upset me.

"I'm sorry. Is there anything I can do?"

"Knowing you are there makes me feel better already."

Oh man. Even though part of me felt like I should have been pleased with his response, with my ability to make him feel better through no effort of my own, I could not believe I had ended up in that clichéd situation, where I (the love interest, the other woman, the home-wrecker) was consoling a man who was not even my boyfriend after a fight with his girlfriend (the primary woman). I felt sick and disappointed in myself.

I put the phone aside and lay on the bed and stared at the ceiling. I patted the bed and Miles jumped up next to me. I petted him as I contemplated what to do next. I felt too miserable to stay at home. I kept thinking about the girlfriend back in Spain, the one he never talked about, the one he seemed to have no interest in seeing, and yet the one who possessed him. I was nothing, and yet I was the girl he texted all day long.

If our connection was as strong as it seemed, why were we not together? Was he just using me to distract himself while waiting for her to move to Los Angeles?

The situation disgusted and frustrated me. My presence *in* it disgusted and frustrated me. I looked at the clock. It was still afternoon. There would be a lot of time to kill if I just sat home the rest of the day. I grabbed my phone. I would text Jack, my alternate magician. Maybe he would be around.

"Hey, are you around tonight? Do you want to get together?"

It took him five very long minutes to respond. Five minutes during which I kept re-evaluating my decision to text him in the first place. Would Rafael mind? Should I care if he did? Did Jack really want to spend more time with me or had our "connection" just been one of those L.A. moments, where everything is fine and good at first, but then no one really cares or makes an effort afterward? Where your relationship consists of talking about how you *must* get coffee or have lunch—two things that never actually happen.

As the minutes ticked by, I grew increasingly convinced that I had messed up, which was why I was so thoroughly pleased, relieved, and almost giddy when he wrote back.

"Hey! Yes! Let's hang tonight. I'm doing karaoke with some friends. Why don't you join us?"

I had never been a huge fan of karaoke, my inhibitions usually getting in the way, but I could always decide later if I actually wanted to get on stage. And come what may, I was very much a fan of going out and spending time with Jack.

Not only because it got me out of the house, and part of me hoped Rafael would hear about it, but also because I liked Jack. I did not know him well enough to speak to a mental connection—we were not star-crossed lovers—but I had spent enough time with him to know I found him beautiful and enough time corresponding with him to know he was a good person. And he was a magician. I could never have too many of those in my life.

I was feeling better at the prospect of my replacement date, and all I needed to make me properly excited was a good long hike. I grabbed my headphones, and Miles and I hit the road. It was a two-hour hike, round-trip, from my house to the Griffith Observatory and back, and those two hours, combined with some pounding dance beats, were all I needed to clear my head and wipe away any Rafael-related cobwebs. By the time I got home, sweaty and satisfied, I was ready for my night with Jack.

I opted to keep it casual since this outing would not entail a trip to the Castle, and I did not want to stand out by being over-dressed at some dive bar in Burbank. I wore a gold top with skinny spaghetti straps, my black push-up bra, tight black jeans, and my black boots. It was definitely sexy, but seemingly effortlessly so. I felt like I had channeled some Tyler, even if it took twenty minutes of maneuvering in front of my mirror to get the effortless look down. A little eyeliner and lip-gloss finished the look, and I headed out to meet Jack and his crew.

They were gathered at one of L.A.'s many hole in the wall bars, the Corner Bar on San Fernando Boulevard at Alameda Avenue. Next to a taco restaurant and around the corner from a discount furniture shop, it was easy to miss, and I had to circle the block to make sure it was, in fact, where I thought it was.

The bar was even smaller on the inside than I had expected, but the benefit was that Jack and his friends had pretty much taken it over. Easily half the people in the bar were with him. The karaoke set-up was makeshift, a temporary feature on Thursday and Saturday nights, or so the bartender told me when I ordered my first drink. If there was even a remote possibility that I would get up there to sing a song or two, I would need some alcohol fortification.

Vodka tonic in hand, I went to find Jack. He was sitting in a booth, surrounded by a group of men and women, all in their mid to late twenties, and all dressed in casually hip clothes. I was pleased that I would fit right in.

As soon as he saw me, he got up and navigated his way through the pack to greet me.

"Hey! It's great to see you. You look fantastic!"

"Thank you," I said, flushing, suddenly awkward. It dawned on me how strange this whole set-up was. I did not know this guy at all. What was I doing here?

"I'd offer to buy you a drink, but it looks like you already have one."

"Yes. You can buy the next one, though…"

He nodded. "Absolutely. Want to sign up for a song? We've got the binder over here." He gestured to the booth behind him. "I put your name down when you said you were coming, but I didn't list a song for you."

His gorgeous face was friendly, open, and even more attractive in the dim light of the bar than I had remembered. I felt like an idiot, like the clumsy girl I had been in high school. He seemed very much out of my league. I gulped down half my drink, wondering how soon I could leave without it seeming weird.

"Sure. I will look at the songs," I said, choking slightly on alcohol that had gone down too fast, wiping a trickle off my chin. Jack was too busy escorting me through the group and into the booth to notice.

I hoped the waiting list had many names on it ahead of mine, and that maybe no one would notice I was not going up for a good long while. Perhaps never.

Sitting in the booth, sandwiched between Jack and his

friend Rosie, I nervously pawed through the big plastic binder. Every song I could possibly think of was included. There was absolutely no excuse for me not to get on stage. Fuck.

"What are you going to sing?" Rosie asked. She had just done a pretty spectacular Bon Jovi number, and now I felt even more daunted.

"I don't know," I confessed. "I'm kind of nervous about getting up there."

"Oh, don't be!" she proclaimed with the ease of the extrovert. "It's totally fun."

What did she know? She must have been able to see on my face that I was not convinced.

"Do you want to do a song together? I could get up with you. Would that make it less scary?"

I heaved a sigh of relief. "That would be great. Would you? I'd love that." At least there would be safety in numbers.

"Totally. It will be fun. I love karaoke."

She beamed at me, and I instantly felt reassured.

"Now what song should we do together?" Rosie asked. "How about Madonna? She's always great."

"Yes. I'd love Madonna. I know all the words to most of her songs... How about 'Material Girl'?"

"Done. I'll go tell the karaoke guy."

As she went to go confirm our selection, I turned to look at Jack. He was looking back at me with a penetrating gaze I could not decipher.

"What?" I asked him, self-conscious. Did I have food between my teeth or something? Had my makeup smudged?

"You and Rafael aren't dating, are you?"

Now there was a non sequitur. I shook my head. "Why do you ask?"

He shrugged. "Dunno. Just felt a bit of a vibe the other night, and so I wanted to check it out. Just curious."

"Nope. He has a girlfriend." Why did Jack care, anyway?

Jack laughed. "Yeah. In another country. Like *that* means much."

"Really?" I asked, intrigued. I wondered if Jack knew something I did not. "Does he sleep around?"

"That I don't know. I just know guys. And, well, long-distance relationships can be purely theoretical sometimes. I don't know him very well, and I definitely don't know her at all, but, well, you know, things happen."

"Got it. Well, things *haven't* happened in this case."

I felt totally entitled to leave out any additional information. In fact, I wanted to shut this conversation down, and it was true that nothing physical had happened. If Rafael was falling in love with me, or just mind-fucking me, that was not relevant for Jack. I did not want to spread gossip, and I definitely did not want Jack knowing those details. The situation was confusing enough without having to explain it to him.

"I'm happy to hear it," he said, with what sounded like genuine enthusiasm.

We smiled at each other, and there may even have been a moment there. Then Rosie slid back into the bar, bumping both of us closer together, and whatever moment there might have been was diffused by the return of her exuberant energy.

"We're all signed up," she said, grinning.

"You two doing a song together?" Jack asked.

"Yes! And it's a surprise which one we're doing, so don't even ask!"

She shook her finger at him before turning to wink conspiratorially at me. I liked Rosie and, thanks to her and my rapidly disappearing drink, I was feeling better. The second drink, courtesy of Jack, improved matters even more. I was starting to relax, so engrossed in conversation with Jack that I forgot I was supposed to go up and sing—until Rosie tugged on my arm enthusiastically.

"Adrian, come on! It's our turn! Come *on*!"

It took me a second to remember what she was even talking about. She was already pulling me to the front of the bar, to the area by the pool table where the karaoke was set up, before I realized what was going on. Oh, right. Crap. I gulped down the rest of my drink, leaving the empty glass on the bar, and trailed behind Rosie. She seemed to know what she was doing. So at least there was that.

Rosie grabbed two microphones from the guy running the karaoke and handed me one. She pulled me behind her and adjusted me so that I was standing on her left.

"Ready?" she asked, beaming with pleasure and excitement.

I could not help but smile back at her. She was cute. "I guess so."

"Awesome!"

She turned to look expectantly at the karaoke screen, waiting for our song to load, and I made the mistake of glancing out into the audience. Jack was staring at me. I flushed and looked away, feeling hopelessly awkward.

But then the song started. I had not even realized how well I remembered "Material Girl" until Rosie and I were singing it. All self-consciousness evaporated. I was too busy looking at Rosie and the karaoke monitor to think about anything or anyone else—which was a good thing. The alcohol was definitely helping, too.

By the time the song finished, I felt pumped up. I loved early Madonna. And now I loved Rosie.

"That was so much fun! Thank you!" I told her, slightly out of breath from so much shouting and singing.

"Of course! Want to do another?" She had clearly enjoyed herself at least as much as I had.

"Okay!" With enough alcohol and the right partner, karaoke could be great.

"How about a Britney song?"

"I'm all over that," I said, smiling. "You pick!"

Feeling a euphoric high from the performance and that second drink, I happily slid back into the booth and against Jack's thigh.

"You were great," he said.

"Thanks!" I was as pleased with myself as if I had just performed a full set at the Staples Center, not just one song in a dive bar in Burbank.

"You looked good up there."

I grinned and thanked him again.

We stared at each other in temporary silence before turning to look at the next karaoke performer, some friend of Jack's named Eric. He was wasted. I did not know how many drinks he had had before I got there, but he had had at least three in the time I had been there. He probably would have been a pretty funny performer sober, but drunk he was hilarious. His rendition of "Baby Got Back" was pure genius.

Even though I was laughing out loud, I was still remarkably aware when Jack rested his arm on the back of the booth and totally cognizant of the way the few inches between us magically evaporated. Without taking my attention off of Eric, without really shifting my body, I relaxed back into Jack. That slight adjustment brought us even closer together, serving as all the encouragement Jack needed to rest his hand on my thigh. I placed my hand gently on top of his, slipping my fingers between his. Just like that, without ever turning away from Eric, without any noticeable physical adjustment, our fingers were interlocked, our thighs pressing into each other, his arm around my shoulders.

It felt good. It felt *really* good. So good, in fact, that I was afraid to move, to turn to look at him, to disrupt the moment. He must have felt the same way because we sat like that, in silence, unmoving, as the next couple karaoke of performers did their thing. Everything about the experience was utterly distracting and thoroughly entertaining at the same time. The performances were consistently hilarious—and yet none of them could upstage the energy shooting back and forth between my body and Jack's, the intense warmth that enveloped us in a mini-cocoon.

I was enjoying it all so much that I was actually disappointed when Rosie bounded back to the booth to claim me for our reprise performance. I did not want to get up.

"Come on, lady! We're up next!"

She seemed unaware of my dynamic with Jack as she grabbed my hand and pulled me up. I turned to face Jack for the first time since Eric had started rapping about butts and anacondas.

"Break a leg," he said and winked.

I smiled shyly before I was yanked away by Rosie.

"You ready for this?" she asked, grinning, as she handed me a microphone.

I nodded, nerves coming back. It had been a while since that second drink. I probably should have had a third.

We stood by the amplifier as some blonde girl finished her angstful rendition of a Tori Amos song. It was way too much drama for the Corner Bar. Everyone seemed to be waiting impatiently for her to finish her emotional outpouring.

She bumped her hip against mine. "We've got to get this party started, girl."

My nerves were mixing with adrenaline. Feeling jittery, I smiled back at her. "You got it."

As if on cue, Tori Amos turned to silence and then it was our turn.

Or to be more accurate, it was Britney's turn—*bitch*.

The song started with the trademark Britney purr, and Rosie and I sang it together, bursting into full volume with the "I can't take it, take it, take no more, Never felt like, felt like this before, C'mon get me, get me on the floor, DJ what you, what you waitin' for?"

Rosie got raucous, and I was right there with her. Maybe it was the thrill of Jack's body up against mine, or maybe I was drunker than I thought, or maybe it was just the energy of the crowd, but we were jumping all over the place, shouting the "Woah oh oh oh oh oh ohhh" part at maximum volume, making faces at each other, fists pumping into the air. It was a rock show. I loved it.

And clearly so did Jack, who was watching every second

from the booth. This time I was not afraid to watch him watch me. My confidence was fueled by the adoration of the audience and the sex appeal of Britney's lyrics. By the time Rosie and I reached our climactic finish, we were both panting, and the audience was cheering.

I ran back to the booth, feeling like it was my victory lap, and Jack stood up to give me a hug.

"You guys were incredible."

"Thank you." I was still out of breath.

We grinned at each other.

"Want to get out of here?" he asked me.

"Yes. Sure. Absolutely. Let me just say goodbye to Rosie."

I grabbed my coat and my purse and went to give Rosie a goodbye hug.

"Thank you so much for those two songs. They were great."

"Aw, honey, any time!" She gave me a big kiss on the cheek. "We're karaoke partners now! You'll have to come back and do it with us again soon!"

"Totally." That sounded like a lot of fun. "Have a good night!"

Jack was waiting for me by the door.

"Are you parked nearby?" he asked.

"Yes, I'm just on Alameda."

"Perfect. Me, too. Do you want to come over to my place? I only live a few minutes from here."

"Sure, sounds fine." I did not much care where we went, I was just happy to be hanging out with him, still totally euphoric from my performance with Rosie.

"Great. Just follow me."

We walked out and, conveniently, my Ford was parked just a couple spots away from his Jeep Cherokee. We each got in our cars, and I drove behind him the ten minutes it took to get to his house.

He was right about only living a few minutes from the

Corner Bar. But what really impressed me was how nice his house was. I had never thought about how much money magicians made, and obviously there was no universal standard, but Jack clearly did well for himself because his house was gorgeous. He had seemed sort of young to me, and I had not expected much from him, but this house was the house of an adult with money and style. It made me wonder what else I had missed about him.

Not only was his house tastefully decorated, with a classy fireplace and very tall ceilings, but it had cute little magic touches throughout that gave it personality and flair. For example, there was a door in a doorframe standing in the middle of the living room. That was from a special trick he had done recently for the president of the NBC. Then there was a bowl full of tennis balls on the kitchen table. They were left over from a trick that required a new package of tennis balls every time. But on display like that, in a big open bowl, the bright green of the balls served as a striking accent in his primarily white kitchen. If I did not know where the balls came from, I would have attributed it to an interior designer with a flair for color.

"I love your place," I said, trying to keep the surprise out of my voice.

"Thanks," he said, smiling. "Want to see the doves?"

It sounds foolish, and I did not say it out loud, but for a second, I had to remind myself that the doves were alive, that they were not magical props. Of *course* they existed somewhere after he made them disappear. They were living creatures, even if he made them vanish on stage.

"Yes, I would love to!"

Taking my hand in his, he walked me out to his back porch. There, in a huge cage, were six beautiful white doves and one blue one.

He pointed at the blue dove.

"That one is a rare breed. I had to have her imported from India."

139

"Really?" I was impressed.

He shook his head. "No, silly. I just dye her blue."

I laughed. "You do?"

"Yes. Food coloring."

"Your life is so glamorous," I said, only partly joking.

"No, *you* are glamorous."

He leaned over and kissed me with lips that were soft, warm, and sweet. His mouth tasted faintly like tequila. I wrapped my arms around him, pressing my body against his, and slipped my tongue into his mouth. The kiss went through me like waves crashing on the beach, over and over, one blending into the next.

I pulled him closer. I could feel how turned on he was, and it was as if all my frustrated desire from my failed relationship with Mark, from the incessant teasing and mind-fucking with Rafael, was rushing to the surface, and I was so hungry for this guy in front of me that I could have ripped his clothes off right then and there. I may not have thought seriously about Jack before today, but now all I wanted was him. I wanted him *badly*. And I wanted him *now*.

I was not normally the kind of girl to give it up on the first date. I was not even the kind of girl to give it up on the second or third date. Despite isolated episodes of experimentation in my past, usually seen through the context of "research" and "self-exploration," I was usually traditional and old-fashioned and shy. In other words, I waited until I felt secure and emotionally connected and comfortable enough to take off my clothes, and I usually waited until after there had been a conversation about monogamy and commitment, and basically I waited until I knew the guy was still going to be there the next day and was not sleeping with anyone else and would not judge me for the extra weight that might have accumulated around my waist or my flat ass.

But tonight I was not myself.

Maybe it was the alcohol. Maybe it was the karaoke. Maybe it was Rosie rubbing off on me. Maybe it was my frustration. Maybe I wanted to get back at Rafael. Maybe it was Jack—who was, to be fair, very, *very* hot.

Whatever it was, I wanted to fuck him.

"Show me your bedroom?" I asked, taking his hand and leading him back inside.

He grabbed me around the waist, and, steering me ahead of him, he walked me through the kitchen, past the bathroom, and around the corner into his bedroom. It was as tastefully decorated as the rest of the house, all white with dark oak furniture. The bed was white, as well, covered with a tan bedspread. He threw me down on the bed playfully, tugging off my boots and then my jeans.

While I pulled my shirt over my head, he slipped out of his clothes. In a matter of seconds, I was naked on his bed, and he was naked in front of it. I stared at him in awe, his body even more beautiful naked than clothed. He leaned over and kissed me again, his tongue slipping over my lips, and I opened them, letting him into my mouth. Wrapping my legs around his waist, I pulled him down on top of me.

His hips were pressed into mine, and I could feel the heat of his skin hot against me. I always ran colder than normal body temperature, and that chill made me cling to him even harder. My arms and legs wrapped around him, and I squeezed him as close to me as possible. I was wet and hungry for him. This could not happen soon enough.

"Let me get a condom," he whispered. He fumbled in the bedside table, grabbing one. I heard the familiar sound of plastic tearing and then latex being tugged into shape.

I could not believe I was actually doing this. I knew if I stopped to think about it that I would not let myself do it, so I decided, for once in my life, not to think. I grabbed him as soon as he was ready and pulled him back on top of me, guiding him into place.

He slid inside me, and I was so wet that there was no discomfort at all. Only smooth pleasure. We both sighed in tandem, taking a moment to feel each other, warmth spreading throughout my body. His hands were on my hips, his body above mine, our panting breaths synchronized, as he pushed harder and harder into me. I pressed back into him. The tension in both our bodies built as his speed intensified. My orgasm began in the tips of my toes, rushing through my body, first in little hints and then in crushing waves. My moans only fueled his pleasure, and he, too, began to come, tensing inside me, his breath heavy in my ear, our skins sweaty against each other. Breathless, I held him close until he finished and collapsed on the bed beside me. I was tingling with post-orgasm, and the blissful look on his face meant he was feeling something similar.

We smiled at each other. It had happened so fast, and yet I remembered every second of it.

"Come over here," he said, pulling me close. I cuddled against him, my head on his shoulder.

We lay like that in silence for a while, dozing, relaxed and satisfied, until he woke me from my dazed stupor.

"Do you want to spend the night?" he asked, his voice husky, barely louder than a whisper.

"I wish I could, but I've got to go let my dog out. He's been alone a long time."

This was true, but it was also a convenient excuse. I did like Jack, and I did not regret sleeping with him, but I also wanted to avoid morning-after awkwardness. I figured, as Corinna often reminded me, that it was always better to leave them wanting more. Plus, in a weird way, even though I knew we had just had sex, sleeping together felt like way more intimacy than I was ready for.

"Are you sure?"

"Yeah. Sorry. I had a great time, though." I leaned over and kissed him one more time before getting up to put my clothes on.

He watched me get dressed, and then, when I was ready, he got up and threw a towel around his waist.

"I'll walk you out."

"Thanks." I headed back into the living room, where I grabbed my bag and coat.

He pulled me close to him for one last blissful kiss in his doorway before I said goodbye. We held each other as I soaked him in, feeling his lean limbs, his muscular arms, and the musky smell of sex, until we both leaned back to look at each other.

"Get out of here before I take off all your clothes again," he said, grinning, giving me a light slap on the ass.

I gave his beautiful naked chest one more lingering look before heading back to Los Feliz and Miles. I wanted to remember how Jack looked in that dark doorway. I wanted to bring that vision home with me.

CHAPTER THIRTEEN

Another benefit to heading home rather than spending the night was that I was in my own bed the next morning when Corinna texted me to tell me she was down the street and to ask if I wanted to meet for brunch.

This was typical Corinna. Planning in advance was not her strong suit. She often blamed it on her unpredictable audition schedule, but I did not buy that, since she was last minute (or "delightfully spontaneous" depending on who was describing it or how annoyed I was with her at the given moment) on nights, weekends, and holidays. It was just the way she operated. She was subject to her own whims and eccentricities. We all played along, used to it, with only the occasional grumblings.

Today, I was not grumbling. Today, I was positively thrilled to have a willing and ready audience with whom I could share my latest unexpected adventure.

"Still in bed," I texted back. "Give me ten minutes to throw on some clothes."

"No problem. The Alcove?"

"Sure. I'm bringing Miles because he needs a walk."

"Great. I'll get him a cappuccino."

I laughed as I raced to wash my face and make myself semi-presentable. At any given moment, it was guaranteed that Corinna would look cuter than me, prone as she was to little Mary Janes and ballet flats, coordinated with cute polka dots and fitted dresses. On a Sunday morning, odds were I was wearing sweat pants, which were exactly what I pulled on, coordinated (if you could call it that) with a pink hoodie and my army camouflage baseball cap. Thank god L.A. rarely believed in dress codes.

"Hey girl," Corinna called, waving at me from her table in the far right corner. "I'll hang on to Miles while you go in and order."

I occasionally suspected Corinna loved Miles more than me. I left him to her mercy, knowing there would be several Instagram photos of her kissing him online before I had finished placing my order. Miles feigned tolerance, but I suspected he secretly enjoyed the attention and girlish squealing.

By the time I got back to the table, with my order number in hand, Corinna had Miles on her lap and was bouncing him like a baby. Miles did, in fact, look content. I laughed at the two of them.

"Should I leave you guys alone?"

"Very funny, lady. Sit. Tell me what I missed last week."

"Well, first, how was *Southland*?"

Corinna just beamed in response. Like most L.A. actors, she was in perpetual fear that each job would be her last. So anytime she booked anything, it felt like a minor victory, a rebuttal to the universe for the doubts and rejections.

"It was great. Three full days of shooting. I'm the mother of a drug dealer. It was all very intense and emotional."

"The mother of a drug dealer? And how old was the drug dealer? Six?"

"Twelve, actually."

I sighed. "Well, that's depressing."

Corinna nodded in agreement, but she was beaming too much to be convincing.

"When does it air?"

"I don't remember. In a month? I'll email you the info when I get it from my manager."

"Great."

I spotted our waiter heading towards us with our food, so I cleared room on the table to make way for our two enormous salads. Corinna and I had both ordered the salmon salad. Typical. Miles, sadly, got moved to the floor so Corinna could eat.

"And what about you, lady? What trouble were you getting into when I was shooting? Is the girlfriend gone yet?"

I shook my head.

"What? Are you serious?" Corinna's fork froze in mid-air, halfway to her mouth, a huge piece of salmon threatening to fall back on the plate.

"I am, in fact, serious. Not only is the girlfriend still around, hovering over L.A. like an oppressive fog, but Rafael actually canceled plans with me last night because the two of them had a fight."

"Did you talk to Rafael about the girlfriend? Have you said anything yet?"

"No." Corinna gave me an accusatory stare. "But wait! I was *going* to. I was all ready to talk to him about it last night, but then he canceled."

I could tell she did not believe me.

"Did you ask him why they were fighting?"

"No. Should I have?"

"He just said he was canceling, and you said okay, and that was the whole conversation?"

Corinna was even chewing thoughtfully. I could practically see the wheels turning in her brain as she tried to make sense of the whole thing. Good luck with that, is what I wanted to tell her. I had been trying to make sense of it for even longer than her, and I had gotten nowhere.

"He said he was canceling because they had had a fight, and I said okay, and that was the whole conversation."

She nodded, continuing to contemplate the mess I had gotten myself into. I tossed Miles some salmon while I watched her think. She clearly was coming to no conclusions, or at least no satisfactory conclusions.

"So what happens next?" she asked.

I shrugged. "I have no idea, honestly. But something else happened."

"Oh yeah?" This made her perk up.

"I had sex."

Corinna dropped her fork on the table and stared at me. "With Rafael?"

I shook my head. "No. With Jack."

"With Jack? Who the hell is Jack?"

Right. I had not told her about Jack. "I didn't tell you about Jack because I didn't think it was a big deal. And it's new. And you were busy. Shooting and stuff."

She paused dramatically, ever the actress. "You had sex. With someone new. Who is not a big deal. While I was too busy to find out about it. Did I get that right?"

I smiled. "Yeah. I guess you're right."

"Adrian, are you okay?" She gave me the kind of look your mother gives you when you say you have lost your appetite or when you think you might have a fever. That sort of concerned look, scrutinizing your face for signs of illness or ailment.

I smiled even more widely. "I am, in fact, okay."

"Adrian. You don't just have sex with people. You date them, and you analyze them, and you try to figure them out and who they are and where it's going to go—" she waved another salmon-laden fork as if to reflect where my relationships were going to go "—and only then do you sex with them."

I shrugged again. "Last night was different."

"Were you drunk?" Still with that scrutinizing stare.

I had to think for a second. She took my silence as all the confirmation she needed.

"You *were*. You had drunk sex." She patted my shoulder proudly. "Good for you. We've all got to do that sometimes. I just didn't think you had it in you. Now tell me who he is."

So I told her about Jack, and his gorgeous looks, and his magic shows, and his beautiful house, and the crazy chemistry we had, and she hung onto every word.

"Adrian, this sounds great. Much better than Rafael. When are you going to see him again?"

"I don't know. He didn't say. He travels a lot. I don't know. I don't think he's a relationship guy, either. I think he's too attractive for a relationship."

"You mean, like Tyler?"

I laughed. "Yeah. Like Tyler. Fucking hot guys. What a waste of a gene pool."

"Well, you never know. Sometimes hot guys can get serious."

I raised my eyebrows at that. "Oh yeah? Give me one example."

Corinna looked down at her salad, and I watched her doing a mental tally of all the men she had dated. Much like I had already figured out, all the really hot guys had persistently remained unavailable. The good guys, the sweet guys, the ones built for dating, were always the quirky ones, the ones with character or "personality." The really hot ones had just sailed through life too easily. Why commit to a relationship when they could just get a new girl the next day?

She and I both knew better, and we usually steered clear of the actor/model types. Even if they seemed nice at first, they always evaporated into nothingness over time. Better to go for the hot guy's best friend, or his brother. The one who had not been able to rely on good looks and so had been forced to develop charm and integrity to compensate.

"You're right," she said, lifting her eyes back up. "But still."

"But still."

But neither of us were convinced.

***

I did not hear from Rafael that day. We had not had an entire day without texting since our friendship began. It felt strange, disorientating, and it made me sad. I compulsively checked my phone throughout the day, but there was never anything from him. No text, no email. Just silence.

My brain began entertaining all kinds of possibilities. Had he and his girlfriend reconciled, making their relationship stronger than ever? Had he and his girlfriend split up, leaving him reeling and devastated and guilty about whatever had (or had not) happened between us? I did not know what yesterday's fight with her had been about. What if it had been about me? Or what if he had heard about me and Jack? What if he was angry at me? Or disappointed? What if I would never hear from him again? With every passing hour, I was convinced I had lost him.

By the time I was ready to give up on the day and go to sleep, and there had been nothing, I was sure I would never hear from him again. I felt sick and miserable. I had not heard from Jack, either, but that paled in comparison. Not hearing from Rafael was the worst. I lay in bed, trying to sleep, routinely checking that my phone was *not* on silent.

I ended up giving up around one a.m. and taking half a Xanax. My stomach was churning. I needed to sleep so that I could function at work the next morning. I knew Alfredo had a conference call scheduled first thing and that I had to write copy for a new lipstick campaign. It felt impossible to imagine being easy and breezy and glamorous when I was miserable inside, but somehow I would have to pull it off.

It was not only that it felt strange not to hear from Rafael, but the fact that I was not hearing from him the day after he had canceled on our plans, the day after he had fought with his girlfriend, the day after I had slept with Jack, all conspired to make me come up with every twisted theory under the sun for why everything was ruined and lost.

I finally fell asleep a total mess, knocked out thanks to chemical intervention.

The next morning I woke up to two text messages.

One was from Jack: "I was out surfing all day yesterday, but thank you for a great night. We should hang out more often."

The second was from Rafael: "Miss you. Dinner tonight?"

Both texts made me feel bathed in love and desire. All the negativity of the day before evaporated magically as I clicked back and forth between the two texts, reading and rereading them. "Yay," I thought. "Yay, yay, yay." I smiled at no one and rolled over to hug Miles. I was thrilled. Suddenly, work seemed manageable again, even if it included Alfredo, a difficult client, and a new campaign.

The only problem was that I already had plans for later in the evening with my friend Tyler. And they were not typical plans. I had no idea how Rafael would feel about them. But I would not know until I asked.

I grabbed the phone and texted Rafael back.

"Good morning. I'd love to have dinner tonight. The thing is I'm supposed to meet my friend Tyler around nine at the strip club near my house. I don't need to stay long, maybe an hour maximum, but I am supposed to meet some girl he is dating who works there. Want to have dinner first and then come with?"

Worst-case scenario, he could always decline, and we would just have dinner. But maybe he would be into it? He was such a strange guy sometimes, so different from anyone else I had ever met, that I often had a hard time predicting what he would do. And obviously, when it came to his feelings for me, I could not read him at all. So I figured it was worth a shot.

My cavalier attitude took a beating, though, as he did not reply for a couple hours, during which I once again became a compulsive phone checker, my stomach a nervous mess. I was sitting at my desk, on my second cup of coffee, trying to come up with different ways of saying "endless lip color" when my phone finally beeped.

Turned out I had nothing to worry about.

"Sorry, left my phone in my apartment and was with

Peter. Yes, let's have dinner around 7:30 and then go meet Tyler. I'd like to meet your friend and the strip club could be fun."

So there was that. Okay. Done. I grinned, the stress lifting off my shoulders. I instantly thought of five different ways to say "endless." And then I remembered I still needed to text Jack.

CHAPTER FOURTEEN

The night was surreal. First, I picked up Rafael, and we went to get the Thai food we had not gotten the day before. It was great to see him. It felt like I had not seen him in forever, but it always felt like that. Whenever we were apart, it seemed like an eternity.

And whenever I spent time with him outside of the Castle, it reminded me what a different person he was when he was "off duty," and how special I felt to be experiencing *that* person, the private person, the non-public persona that a much smaller group of people got the chance to know. I loved how much more relaxed and open he was, how he would joke and laugh and be a total dork. At the Castle, he was always more formal and reserved, as if he was constantly being judged.

Most men look better in a suit, more distinguished and classy, but not Rafael. He looked good in a suit—it was not that he looked bad—but he looked *infinitely* more appealing out of one. In regular clothes, he looked cute, cuddly, more accessible and more relaxed, and this was just compounded by his out-of-the-Castle personality. Today he was wearing a cotton long-sleeved polo shirt with jeans. I could not help smiling as he got in the car. He looked a little rugged and very European. Whatever was happening with us, whatever annoying complications there were, it was good to see him.

We hugged each other awkwardly across the parking brake, before looking at each other for a moment. We were smiling like awkward teenagers. It was so obvious that we liked each other, that we enjoyed each other's company, that I could not help patting him on his thigh with my hand as I told him that it was good to see him. It was the only physical contact I felt I could get away with.

"It's good to see you, too," he replied, and we both stupidly smiled at each other some more.

And then I drove to get us Thai food.

My favorite Thai place was near my house, conveniently also only a few blocks from Jumbo's Clown Room, the strip club where we would be meeting Tyler. I liked the restaurant for a variety of reasons (like the breadth of their menu, the affordability and quality of their food), but I especially appreciated the fact that it was never crowded, thus allowing Rafael and I to slip into a quiet corner booth by the back window.

One of the things that appealed to me about booths was that, depending on how you sat, there was not always a table in the way. Legs could touch. Booths created an illusion of greater intimacy. You could slip back and forth, alternating between being closer together versus getting a better look at each other.

To be honest, I was torn between which option I wanted. I loved being close enough to press my knee against his— watching him look down at the menu and then look up at me through his long black lashes—but I also loved being able to stare at him. It was hard to believe that someone like him was real. I kept expecting him to disappear, like one of his many illusions, which is probably why I had had such a meltdown after not hearing him for one day.

But for now, for today, he was real, and he was beside me. When I slid over a few inches, I could feel the warmth of his leg against mine, I could see the pores on his face, I could pick out individual eyelashes. It was impossible not to stare.

And if our conversation had not been so engrossing, I probably would have just sat and stared. But the conversation, as it always was with him, was mesmerizing, and our fresh spring rolls delicious, so the whole meal ended up being full of sensory delights. I enjoyed everything about it and him.

The primary topic of our dinner discussion was a new show that Rafael and Peter were preparing. Their show at the

Peller had gone so well that the Magic Castle had invited them to come back and do a longer version in the Palace. This not only entailed a revamping of some of the routines from the Peller show but an addition of several new ones, about twenty minutes more material. It also entailed a new blast of publicity. Rafael showed me several images from a recent photo shoot to ask my opinion about which would be most effective for this new show.

I flipped through the images on his phone. They were all pretty great—and then I got to one that made me stop dead in my tracks. My heart fluttered in my chest as I looked up to stare at him.

"Rafael, are you serious? This one is amazing. I can't believe you didn't show this one to me first. This is great."

Words limited me. The image was "great," but more than that, it was *spectacular*. It was pin-up worthy. It made me want to go back to high school so that I could put it up in my locker and swoon over it between classes. Rafael in person was obviously sexy enough to drive me to distraction, but this image was outrageous. This was over-the-top. This was sexier than Clooney. This made me ravenous for him.

"Will you email this one to me?"

He nodded, looking at me with a bit of surprise. He clearly did not get it. He was totally unaware of his own sex appeal, and this unawareness made him even sexier. He really was the awkward kid who had hidden behind the magic tricks, who had used the cards and the sleight of hand as a way to facilitate interactions with the real world, but then who had unexpectedly grown up into a very attractive man. Sometimes I wondered if he ever even looked in the mirror.

Rafael reached forward to reclaim his phone, but I would not give it to him.

"Wait," I told him. "I need a minute."

Without any shame, I stared at the image. More accurately, I devoured it with my eyes, wishing I could devour him in the same way.

Rafael, for all his sexiness and man-of-mystery qualities, was still sweet, romantic, and kind with an accent that made me melt. But the theme for this photo shoot was to turn both Rafael and Peter into thugs, seemingly at each other's throats. Their knuckles were slightly bruised, their faces marred with makeup that gave the illusion they had both been punched and scraped. In this particular image, Rafael was leaning against the wall, James Dean style, in a slim gray European suit (the kind Mark used to wear but which I instantly saw looked much better on Rafael, perhaps because he was actually European), with a cigarette in his mouth. Rafael did not smoke—he did not even drink—but anyone who would deny that the cigarette was sexy as fuck in his slim red lips, between his clenched jaw, had no idea what they were talking about. Rafael was hot in this image; there was no other way to put it.

"You're embarrassing me," he said, trying to get the phone out of my hands.

"Nah. You shouldn't be embarrassed. You look great in this photo. You should absolutely use this one. And you should send it to me immediately."

He laughed. "I'll send it right now."

He took the phone out of my hand and messaged me the photo. I was so mesmerized, I could not wait to go home and stare at it some more. I was like a teenager with a new Justin Bieber magazine spread.

"The rugged look suits you."

Now he *really* looked embarrassed. "It's just acting. And makeup."

"I don't care. You're still working it. It looks good."

"Okay. Thank you. I will accept the compliment. Now let's talk about something else."

I smiled at him. Poor little awkward Spaniard. He really had no idea how sexy he was. But I was happy to talk about something else. I could stare at the photo as much as I wanted to later. Now I had him to look at.

The rest of the dinner flew by as we talked magic and

television and real life. Rafael told me about the band he had been in when he was in Spain. It felt like only a couple minutes had passed, and then Tyler was texting me that he was on his way to Jumbo's and would be there in about ten minutes.

"Oh, we should head out. Tyler will be at there soon."

"No problem. I'll take care of the bill."

Another thing about Rafael that puzzled me was the fact that he always paid when we were together. He did not think we were on dates, did he? I chalked it up to his being a gentleman, but it did contribute to my confusion about what, exactly, we were doing. That and the chemistry and the constant texting. I told myself that I would have to say something soon. Just not right now.

We decided to walk the few blocks to Jumbo's. The night was cool, and Rafael wrapped his arm around me. Again—mind-fuck! But I was not going to ask any questions. I just wrapped my arm around him and, like a happy couple on a date, we made our way down Hollywood Boulevard, intertwined, body against body.

Tyler had not yet arrived when we got to Jumbo's, so I picked a table in the corner, far from the stage but with a direct view. The place was so small that "far from the stage" was a relative concept. It just meant that you were not going to be guilted into tossing a steady stream of dollar bills at the dancers. There was a little bit of sanctuary in the distance.

But that sanctuary was minimal, a fact further compounded by the fact that there were no private rooms at Jumbo's, so there was a likely chance that a lap dance would happen a few inches away from where you had the misfortune to sit. And I say misfortune only because I found there to be nothing sexy about the men at Jumbo's, and I had no interest in seeing them get off a mere couple inches away. In my reckless youth, I had briefly worked as a stripper, and I was grateful that I had never had to give a lap dance.

Jumbo's Clown Room was a Hollywood institution for

reasons that confused me. First of all, there were no clowns. There was also no nudity. It was basically a small dive bar of which a third of the square footage was taken up by a stage with a pole. The girls were not your typical strip club girls, meaning that they were rarely blonde, rarely had fake boobs, and often had tattoos.

Tyler's girlfriend, who showed up with Tyler to work her shift, was, in fact, blonde and without tattoos, but her breasts, small as they were, were definitely not fake. Tyler reminded us, as we all made introductions, that she was a former ballerina from the Ukraine. Beyond that, we did not have time for more conversation before she had to run backstage to get ready.

Tyler came and sat beside me, with Rafael still sitting on my right. We were at the end of the row, so Rafael was actually positioned in the corner of the bench. When Tyler got there, Rafael slid over so he was where the back and side of the bench came together, resting his right arm on the back of the bench. His left arm, to my utter shock and surprise, he placed around me, letting it lay across my shoulders. I was floored. This was the most public display of affection he had ever demonstrated, although, of course, we were not at the Castle, so maybe the rules were different. Whatever was going on, it was beyond confusing.

I saw Tyler notice the body language, but he did not say anything. I could tell he was processing the arrangement and inputting the new evidence. I wondered if Corinna would be pissed that Tyler had met Rafael before she did.

The music was loud, making conversation difficult, but Tyler and Rafael managed to exchange some pleasantries, each asking the other about their jobs, Tyler sharing experiences about a trip to Spain he had taken while in college, Rafael asking about downtown Los Angeles, which was still unexplored terrain for him, while I leaned back, letting them shout over me, as I watched the girls dance almost naked across the stage.

At one point, there was a spectacular moment when all the girls filed onto the stage together.

"This is great," Tyler exclaimed, pointing at the stage as if we could somehow miss what was happening. "It's shift change."

The girls, as a combined effort, lathered up the mirrors around the stage with some kind of foam. It took me a minute to figure out that they were actually spelling something out. Rafael and I both laughed as it became clear what it was: "We love your tips."

Tyler beamed as if the whole show had been his production.

And then the girls wiped it all down, the mirrors gleaming, although by no stretch of the imagination were they spotless. I would not have wanted to touch any surface of that bar with my bare skin. But I did not have to. I just got to watch. And I got to feel Rafael against me as I did.

Maybe it was the darkness of the bar? Maybe it was the fact that we were in a strip club? Whatever it was, Rafael seemed to be comfortable with me leaning against him, and his arm stayed wrapped around my shoulder for the rest of the time we were there. We sat like that, watching the girls strip and twirl around the pole, performing feats of acrobatic mastery in their g-strings, while dollar bills littered the stage. When Tyler had to leave, after about an hour, to go meet some work buddies, I was disappointed to disentangle myself from Rafael.

We all filed out of the bar, Tyler heading east to his car, Rafael and I heading west to mine. Again, as we strolled down the street, he put his arm around me, just another couple heading back to their car after a night out. Except we were not a couple. We were not even on a date. As Rafael chatted about this and that—the car he wanted to buy, a friend from Vegas who was coming to visit—I tried to force myself to say something, *anything*, that would amount to confronting the issue. I kept rephrasing it in my head: "What about your girlfriend? Are you guys still together?" "What exactly is going on between us?" "How do you feel about me?" and the best, "What do you want from me?"

But everything sounded clumsy, awkward, and confrontational, putting him on the defensive in a way I could not bring myself to do. And so I said nothing.

I drove him home, feeling increasingly depressed but unwilling to verbalize any of my anxieties. I just nodded as he talked, while inside I churned. I wanted so desperately to touch him, to kiss him, to hold him, to know that he was mine. This situation—where I was so close and yet so far—was making me miserable.

I glanced over at him talking away. He was relaxed and animated. He was happy. He was beautiful. He was too beautiful. Those eyes, a blue green, like the ocean off the coast of Hawaii, were framed by long black lashes that contrasted with the warmth of his skin. He always looked as if he had just been in the sun with that glowing tawny skin. I wanted to stroke and caress it, to run my finger along his cheek, to trace his cheekbone. I wanted to slip my finger in his mouth, feel the wetness of his lips, the edge of his teeth. Tearing my gaze away, I felt sick.

I faked it when he said goodbye, giving him the platonic hug that was becoming our "thing." He kissed me on the cheek, giving me a slightly puzzled look. He was a smart guy. I was sure he could tell something was wrong, but he chose not to push it, not to ask. Instead, he let me go.

Feeling miserable and tormented, I turned my car around to head back down Franklin Avenue. It took five seconds for him to text me.

"I couldn't wait to get back to my apartment before texting you."

Aw, fuck, *really*? My patience was wearing thin. What was this nonsense? Platonic in person, romantic by text? I was becoming exasperated. This was predictable and a waste of time. I did not respond. I just kept driving, staring straight ahead.

He texted me again a minute later.

"Are you okay? You seemed different tonight."

I still did not answer. I did not know what to say. I knew if I said anything, I would be compelled to address the issue at hand, and I did not know if I was ready for that.

As I was parking my car, I got another text.

"You looked beautiful tonight. I loved spending time with you."

Enough. *Enough, enough, enough.* I broke. I could not take it anymore. As crazy as I was about him, this was too much. It hurt too much. I could not do it. Even if it meant losing him completely.

"I can't hang out with you anymore," I typed.

"What? Why?"

"It's too hard. I want to be with you." Cringing at the drama, at the sappy soap opera quality to which I had descended, I pressed send anyway.

There it was. My cards were on the table. No magic tricks, no illusions. The only thing that was going to disappear was me. I was not strong enough to stick around, to keep doing this. Corinna was right. This situation was all wrong.

I stared at my phone. I could see the blinking cursor that told me he was typing a message. I waited, watching it, wondering what he would say. I sat in my car in the parking garage, looking at my phone, waiting for his response. I did not have the motivation to get up and walk up to my apartment. I could not leave the safety and warmth of my car.

When it came, it was not at all what I had expected.

"What if I make it easier?"

Huh? "What does that mean?" I asked.

"By being single."

My world spun in circles, like a malfunctioning carousel. I felt dizzy. I stared at my phone, but it was blurry. I could not see straight. I took a breath and closed my eyes. I waited for the spinning to slow down. When I opened them, I looked cautiously at my phone. The text was still there, staring at me.

The thought of Rafael being single, being *available*, was almost too much for my brain to process. I had been so busy mentally preparing for my disappearing act that I had anticipated an entirely different performance.

"Really?"

"Yes," he texted back. "Really."

Things were still spinning. I laughed. I was almost hysterical. I now felt trapped in my car, so I grabbed my purse and let myself out. I needed to go home. I had to process all this. I needed to walk Miles. The enormity of it felt too large for my brain. He kept texting as I walked to my apartment.

"I have been thinking about it for a while. It's part of the reason she and I had that fight the other day. I know I need to do it. I know I don't want to be with her. I want to be with you."

These were the kind of words I had dreamed of hearing for so long that, now that they were here, I felt vaguely suspicious, out of place, as if someone had cast me in the wrong movie.

"I want to be with you, too," I typed cautiously.

My hesitation did not come from any reservation—I *knew* that I wanted to be with him more than anything. My hesitation came from how very much I wanted it, and therefore my fears that this could not be real.

"If marriage was in my vocabulary at this point in my life, I would probably ask you to marry me in a few weeks. You are a constant surprise, even in little things. If you are always surprising me, I would say you are the right person to marry me. I would not get bored."

I fumbled for my key, so utterly distracted by what he was telling me that I just stood outside my apartment, illuminated by the streetlamp, while Miles barked from the other side of the door. I read and reread. This was all coming out of nowhere. I did not know what to say, so I said nothing. I could not text back.

"I am almost in love with you."

Pulling in a deep breath, I forced myself to open the door, walk into my apartment, and sit on the bed. I had to concentrate. I brought myself back to reality just enough to be able to greet Miles, who was jumping around my knees, and to respond. Now I did not have to think about what to say.

"I am almost in love with you, too," I told him.

I had known that for a while. I had known, in fact, that I *was* in love with him, but if he was going to use the buffer of "almost," well, then, so would I. We both knew how we felt, and it seemed as though, finally, we were going do something about it.

But my state of bliss was interrupted by a temporary pang of guilt.

"Wait. I don't want you to break up with your girlfriend just for me. That's not right."

"I'm not breaking up with my girlfriend for you. I am breaking up with her for me and for her. It is not right for me to be with her when I am in love with someone else."

And just like that, the "almost" buffer was no longer needed.

I did not know how to process this. I had no frame of reference. I did not know the right course of action in this kind of situation.

"Can I do anything?" I asked. "Do you want some space while you deal with it?"

I cringed after I pressed send. I had not meant to refer to his girlfriend as an "it." I had meant the situation, I meant dealing with the *situation*, but oh god, it seemed like I had referred to his girlfriend as an "it." I was a mess. Now I was second-guessing everything. I had never been in this kind of predicament before. I had always stayed away from men with girlfriends. I was not a home wrecker. I was not even a heartbreaker. I was just a nice girl who had accidentally fallen in love with a magician. I felt horribly guilty.

"Yes. That's a good idea. Space would be good. Let me

have a little time to deal with her and to let things settle. I do not want to drag you into it."

That sounded smart and sensible, so I agreed, even though all I wanted to do, more than anything else, was to get back in my car and speed down Franklin, and go to his apartment (which I had yet to see), and fall into his arms. I wanted to kiss him in the doorway like they do in the movies, with endless passion, music swelling in the background. Then he would swoop me up and carry me inside. I wanted to feel his body, take off his clothes, lie in bed with him, binging on the kind of physical proximity that had been denied to me until now. I wanted it so much, and the fact that he was only a few minutes away made it all the more frustrating.

And yet, I knew he was right. And so, for the sake of any future together, a future I so desperately craved, I said yes. I agreed. I told him to take a week or a couple weeks or what he needed. I told him he could text me if he wanted, but that I would not initiate. I would give him as much space as he needed, and he could tell me when he was ready for more. I hated giving up so much power.

I hated having to be patient, but I felt like there was no choice. If we were going to do this, I wanted to do it right. I did not want to rush into something and have him resent me for it later. I knew he needed to feel in control, even though everything about this situation was really out of our control.

We said goodnight, via text message, but this time our messages came complete with "x's" and "o's."

"Good night. Xoxoxo," I wrote.

"Good night, sweet dreams. Xxxxxx," he replied.

And that was the last message I got from him for two weeks.

CHAPTER FIFTEEN

I knew I had no one to blame for the silence but myself, but I still hated it. It had been my idea to offer him space, it had been my move to force the issue, and even though the end result was something I wanted, not hearing from him made me miserable. It made me miserable because I had gotten used to hearing from him many times a day. I had gotten accustomed to knowing he would always be on the other end of a text if I needed him. I enjoyed seeing him and not being able to do that made me sad. Nothing I did—hiking, shopping with Corinna, Cardio Barre classes, another visit to Jumbo's with Tyler—could distract me.

I did not know how long it would take until I heard from him again (a week? a month? two months?), but the most gut-churning part was not knowing what would happen when I did. Would he really be free of the girlfriend? Would the trauma of trying to end a two-year relationship make him reconsider, make him treasure her all the more? Would the euphoria of freedom result in a bachelor-style frenzy of acquisition and plunder? Would he *ever* be mine? Or was I just waiting for inevitable disappointment?

Every day, when I woke up and looked at my phone, and there was no message from him, I felt deflated. Every night, when I looked at my phone before I went to bed, not to mention the hundred times I looked at my phone throughout the day and there was nothing, I felt depressed. Tiny wings of hope would lift me up when I did get a message, only to be crushed again when it was from someone else. It was never from him. From him there was only silence. Dead communication. He had disappeared. The ultimate magic trick.

The worst part was that I knew where to find him, but I could not go looking. I could not show up at the Castle, I could not go to his apartment. I had to honor his wishes. I had to respect his space if there was a chance that this was going to work. I had to trust that he would contact me when he was ready to talk, and I had to hope that I would want to hear what he had to say when he did.

One day passed. Then two. Then three. Then four. Then a week. I felt like crossing them out on my calendar, but that felt too depressing. Counting down is only effective if you have a deadline, a terminal date, a date you are working towards. In this case, I had no idea when I would hear from Rafael again. And with each passing day of silence, I started to suspect I never would.

Not hearing from him, and not knowing when I would, was killing me.

Luckily, there was Jack. Sweet Jack. With whom I thought I had had just had a one-night stand, but who seemed determined to prove me wrong. He was not pursuing me in the traditional sense—this was no knight in shining armor business, there were no roses on my doorstep—but in the casual way of the twenty-first century male. He would text me occasional photos of random things—like a particularly delicious meal he had cooked, an especially spectacular sunset at the beach, or a funny sign he had driven by. He would check in periodically and ask me how I was doing, and if anything interesting or striking happened in his life (like when he met Mark Wahlberg at a *Good Morning America* taping), he would share it with me.

I asked him once, after he sent me a photo of some beautiful clouds, if he sent these images to all the girls.

"C'est l'arte de seduction," he wrote back, and I laughed. I laughed because it was funny, but I also laughed because he did not answer my question. Typical evasive guy. I wondered how many different girls he was texting.

Ten days after the showdown with Rafael, Jack texted me

to ask if I wanted to come over to watch an episode of *Homeland*. Not only had I already seen the episode, but it was late, and I had to be at work early the next morning, so I said no. Rather than reading it as a personal rejection, Jack merely texted back to ask if I wanted to get dinner on Wednesday, instead. Part of me thought I should say no, that I was somehow staying true to Rafael by waiting for him, but the other part of me thought, why not? I had no idea when Rafael would return, or what he would say or want when he did, so I figured I should not stay home until then. And I *did* like Jack. So I said yes.

"Perfect," he texted back. "Do you like sushi?"

"Yes…"

"Good. I'll pick you up at 7:30. Dress nice. Send me your address."

I had to admit, I was kind of thrilled. I had never had much patience for indecisive men, and my absolute favorite kind of guy was one who took charge. I loved being told merely when to be ready and what to wear. I preferred this much more to the way Rafael always put me in charge of decisions and plan-making.

"Do you want me to tell you where we are going?"

"No, I like surprises," I replied—and I did. I was looking forward to this a lot more than I had anticipated. It would be a lovely distraction, and I had to admit that I was really looking forward to seeing Jack again.

Wednesday evening, I stared at my closet. Dress nice? How nice? What did that mean, exactly? In L.A., dressing nice could be as simple as leaving the flip-flops at home. I texted him to ask.

"An eight on the swank meter," was his reply.

Got it. Okay. I was enjoying this more and more. I liked his precision and sense of humor. I grabbed a black and blue striped Bebe dress—tight fitting, wide neck, perfect with my black stiletto boots and tights. I fastened a chain link belt around my waist, added some eyeliner and mascara, and was good to go. I looked in the mirror. With my motorcycle jacket, I felt complete. I was dressed up, but not overly formal—still kind of rock and roll. I could work a cocktail party without feeling under or overdressed. I was satisfied. I hoped he would like it, too.

He texted me when he was out front, and I grabbed my purse and hurried out to meet him. This was technically our first date, since the last time had been more of a group outing, even if it had ended with us alone together, so I felt a little nervous. I wondered how well the conversation would flow, if we would have anything even to talk about. Would we like each other? I was not sure exactly what to make of the situation —I kept being surprised by his continued interest— but I was looking forward to getting to know him better.

Jack was waiting for me outside of his Jeep.

"Hey, you look great," he said, reaching forward to give me a hug.

"Thanks," I said, leaning back, his arms wrapped around me, to look at him.

He smiled.

"It's good to see you."

We checked each other out in the light of the streetlamp.

He was attractive, very attractive. He was also taller than I remembered, even with my stiletto heels, and he was wearing a slim cut black suit, white shirt, and black tie that made him seem even sleeker and more attractive. I was impressed that this was my date. His intensely blue eyes stared into mine. I traced his right cheekbone with my finger. His cheekbones were David Bowie–worthy.

"It's good to see you, too," I replied.

Jack leaned in, brushing some hair off my face. His right arm was still curled around my waist, but his left hand snaked down, cupping my ass, as he pulled me in even tighter. He slipped his tongue into my mouth, and my muscles felt slack, my body completely suspended by his, as I melted into him. His kisses were sweet, kind, but full of desire. I momentarily forgot we were standing on the street, forgot to feel self-conscious, my tongue exploring his mouth, feeling the ridge of his teeth, the pressure of his lips, until a car drove by, and the lights startled both of us, bringing us back to reality.

He released me, and we both laughed awkwardly.

"Let me get the door for you," he said, coming around to the passenger side of the car.

I climbed up and inside the Jeep, settling in to my seat as he came back around to his side.

"Ready?" he asked.

"Yes."

"Should I tell you where we are going now?"

I shook my head. "Nope. Surprise me!"

"Alright." He smiled at me and turned the car on. "Let's go."

We drove down Sunset Boulevard toward downtown. My fear of us lacking in conversation topics was only slightly well-founded. This was not like an evening out with Rafael; the air did not crackle. But still, it was pleasant, the chemistry delicious, and the conversation decent.

Jack regaled me with anecdotes from the Lakers game he had recently attended and some private Hollywood parties at which he had performed. Apparently, Brad Pitt and George Clooney were both big fans, and he had once been hired by Katy Perry to perform at John Mayer's birthday. He had good stories. Magic was such an odd career choice. I had respect for anyone like Jack or Rafael who not only made a living at it but also made a *good* living at it.

We took Sunset Boulevard all the way into downtown, heading south on Spring Street, finally parking when we got to Sixth Street.

"We've got about," Jack glanced at his watch, "half an hour to kill before dinner. Want to grab a drink?"

"Sure."

We walked down Spring Street, a busy strip lined with coffee shops, bars, and restaurants. We picked a bar called The

Falls that neither of us had ever been to. It was a well-decorated place, warm with a mix of 1970s kitsch, elaborate chandeliers, and walls lined with fake logs of wood. We perched on two stools along the bar and surveyed the drinks menu. I chose one called "The Rustic," described as a mix of gin, grapefruit juice, agave, and tonic. Jack went for one called "The Hunter" —bourbon, orange juice, honey, and orange bitters. Both drinks arrived quickly, in iced glasses with slices of lemon.

It felt festive sitting here with him on a Wednesday night, drinking our fancy cocktails, me in my little dress, and him looking so sophisticated in his suit. He was already gorgeous, but as the alcohol hit my system, he became even more outrageously attractive. Whenever he smiled—those strong white teeth, those brilliantly blue eyes—I swooned just a little. Even his stories about the NBA were interesting because it was so nice to look at him. It did not matter what words were coming out of his mouth because I got to watch that mouth move. I got to watch those lips.

The best part was that I knew I could kiss those lips whenever I wanted. Which is what I did. I leaned over and kissed him his warm, soft mouth. He kissed me back, his arm around my shoulder, the two of us balanced precariously on our bar stools, both of us tasting like alcohol and citrus. While not an exhibitionist, I have always loved public displays of affection, when you fall into each other and the rest of the world ceases to exist even as it surrounds you, where the heat of physicality comes in teasing little quantities, interrupting the cold businesslike nature of the everyday.

Apparently Jack liked public displays of affection, too, or at least he did not mind them, because he kept kissing me. We would smooch, and then drink, and then smooch a bit more, and then he would tell me more about some NBA player or some party, and then I would interrupt him with another kiss. I was sure the bartender was happy to see us leave when our thirty minutes were up.

Jack led me out of the bar and to the right. I still had no idea where we were going, so I was a little surprised when he walked me to the coffee shop next door.

I turned to give him a quizzical glance.

"Don't worry, I'm not taking you out for coffee," he said, laughing. "This is the surprise part. Trust me."

We walked into the coffee shop, which, from the outside, appeared to be closed and shuttered. I was more than a little confused, but I was sure he had something good planned.

Jack led me through the front section of the coffee shop, past the coffee bar, and through to the kitchen where an elaborate table was set up with a white rose centerpiece and place settings for twelve. About ten people were milling about, drinks in hand, snacking on edamame.

"Where are we?"

Jack smiled. "It's a pop-up sushi restaurant. One night only. I know the chef. I've performed at some of his events. He takes over various kitchens and does exclusive, invite-only meals. You eat whatever he serves. But it's all sushi."

Pretty cool. I was impressed. I followed Jack into the kitchen toward a man wearing a bandana around his head.

"This is Jason. The chef."

"Hey, man, how's it going?" Jason beamed at Jack, giving him a big hug. "And who is this lovely lady?" he asked, turning to check me out.

"This is Adrian," Jack said.

I reached forward to shake his hand. "It's nice to meet you," I said. "Thank you for having us. And your flowers are beautiful. White roses are my favorite."

"It's my pleasure to have you—and I'm glad you like the flowers. My brother owns a floral shop, and white roses are his favorite, too." Turning to Jack, Jason pounded him on the back. "I love this guy. He's my favorite. I can't ever get enough of him. He's always so busy performing, I've got to book him at an event in order to get to see him...Or offer to feed him!"

Jack laughed. "Well, you've got us tonight. I hope you don't let us down!"

Jason shook his head. "Never. I've got great fish. Absolutely fresh. You're going to love it. But until it's ready, help yourself to drinks." He gestured toward a table full of bottles. "Wine, sake, beer, Korean vodka, whatever you want."

Jack and I moved toward the beverage table, leaving Jason to resume chopping fish and rolling seaweed.

"Have you ever had Soju?" Jack asked.

"No, what's that?"

"It's Korean vodka. People drink it straight. It's a little sweeter and has a higher alcohol content. Usually about 20% but sometimes 45%. That's partly why it is so popular. It's also popular because you can sell it with only a beer/wine license."

"Huh. I didn't know that. I've never heard of it."

"Do you want to try it?"

I shook my head. "No, I'm okay. I'll just do white wine." I was not feeling brave or reckless enough to try something new, much less something that might be 45% alcohol.

Jack poured glasses of white wine for both of us, and we went to take our seats around the large table.

The dinner was long but delicious. Each sushi course was delivered one at a time, since Jason was the only one preparing the food for the group of twelve people. There was something decadent about eating that way, small servings to be relished, and it gave me lots of time to drink my wine (slowly), feeling the alcohol move through my system, as Jack and I laughed and flirted and played footsie under the table. We intermittently took breaks from being fixated on each other to make small talk with our neighbors —Glen, on Jack's other side, was an investment banker, while Marie, on my other side, was the manager of a luxury apartment building.

Everyone else was too far away or too involved in their own conversations to chat with us, which was fine, since I mainly wanted to talk with Jack, anyway. Well, that was not exactly true. I mainly wanted to *make out* with Jack. The drunker I got, the more fun I had being inappropriate. He kept telling me to calm down, but he was only partly serious, as he kept filling my wine glass and groping me under the table.

It all made for a very memorable evening, everything intermingling with the pleasure of being with a very gorgeous man. By the time our meal wound to a close, finished off by vanilla mochi ice cream and huge red strawberries, I felt blissed out. Alcohol, sushi, and Jack were all wonderful aphrodisiacs, and the combination made for an exquisite cocktail.

Jack and I walked to his car, hand in hand, and it felt legit. It felt couple-y. It felt good and right. I was not thinking about anything. I was not questioning anything. I was just enjoying the moment and the way his hand felt in mind. I enjoyed looking at him, at his striking face. I loved the way his body felt, his muscular slimness under the well-fitting suit.

When Jack got to my house, he asked me if I wanted him to walk me to my door. There was no hesitation before my reply.

"Yes, and I'd love for you to come inside."

He parked, and we walked up the path to my apartment, groping each other like a couple of school kids. We practically tumbled into my apartment, buzzed on alcohol and sexual desire. I told him to get comfortable as I took Miles out for a quick bathroom break. When I got back, Jack was waiting for me, sitting on the edge of the bed. His shoes were off, his tie loosened, but otherwise, he was still fully dressed.

"You didn't take off your clothes…" I said, but it was more a question.

He shook his head, grinning. "No. I thought you could do that for me."

I smiled as I walked over to stand in front of him, my legs between his. I reached forward and loosened his tie even more before yanking it off and throwing it on the chair. Then I

173

slipped him out of his jacket and threw that on the chair, too. The buttons on his shirt I opened one at a time, slowly, torturously, my eyes never leaving his. By the time I got to his belt, I could tell how much he desired me, and it made me desire him even more. I ran my hand over the hard ridge in his pants, and he moaned. I pushed him down on the bed and pulled his pants down. They went on the chair, too. He was naked except for his boxers. I was still fully clothed. I had to do something about that.

I pulled my dress up over my head, then slipped my boots off, followed by my tights and then my bra. And then my underwear. I was fully naked. Except for the moment when I was pulling off my dress, our eye contact had not broken. We stared at each other. I took off his underwear and climbed on top of him, naked body on naked body. He ran his hands over my breasts, putting one, then the other, in his mouth, running his tongue across my nipples, lightly grazing them with his teeth. Now it was my turn to moan. He kissed me between my breasts, beneath them, above them, and I whimpered, pressing my hips against his, rubbing myself against his thigh.

I ran my fingers through his hair as he kissed and sucked and fondled my breasts, and I writhed against him, desperate for more, wetness leaking down my leg. He must have felt it, since he slipped one finger between my legs, inside me, gently pressing, before pulling it back out and bringing it to his mouth. He licked his finger.

"Delicious," he whispered, before sending his finger back into me. He rubbed in gentle circles around my clitoris, slipping his finger in and out, while I whimpered and clung to him.

When I could not stand it anymore, I took him and slid him inside me. I was so wet, there was almost no friction. He grabbed me and flipped me around, so he was on top and I was on the bottom. His hands still under my ass, and he pressed himself inside me. Pleasure raced through me, and I shivered. He moved faster and faster, one hand under me, the other hand tugging on my breasts, my nipples as hard and swollen as he was. I could feel my orgasm coming, the waves of delicious sensation, and my toes clenched, my entire body clenched, as he pulled me close to him, moaning. He moved faster as his own climax ripped through him, and his moans drowned out mine.

"Adrian, my god," he panted, as he collapsed on the bed beside me.

I smiled, looking at him, at the beads of sweat on his gorgeous face, and I traced the line of his jaw with my finger.

"You're beautiful," I said.

"So are you."

I could feel myself beaming as we stared at each other, half delirious, the post-orgasmic bliss combining with everything that we had consumed at dinner.

"Do you ever bring magic into the bedroom?" I asked.

"What do you mean?"

"I don't know...I mean, I've never slept with a magician before...I just wondered, do you ever perform in bed?"

He laughed. "You mean, like do magic in bed?"

"Yes. Exactly."

Jack had to think about that for a second. "One time, I was with this girl who really wanted me to dominate her. I think she wanted some version of my stage show. Anyway, I tied her up with magicians' rope in some knots from which she could not escape until I tugged on the rope...And once I let a lady tie me up with the understanding that I would escape and then take her by force. But I think that's about it." His words emerged slowly. I could tell that he had never really thought about this before.

"You've never wanted to do more?" I was insatiably curious.

"I guess not. I'm not really turned on by role-play; I like real life. I have to play an exaggerated version of myself all of the time on stage, so in the bedroom I like to be me, and I like the women to be them. Magic is fun, but it always feels like pageantry to me."

Jack looked at me and smiled. "Does that make sense?"

I nodded. It made a lot of sense. There was something about his openness that I found endearing, but he was also so open that I was unsure how to react to the things he said. Jack just *was*, and it unnerved me a little. I kept wanting to analyze him, but I could not get traction. He seemed so easy, so relaxed, but there was an intensity in his eyes that made me think nothing would get by him.

"I think both magic and sex take place in the brain...and both involve focus. Especially with you."

He ran his finger along my cheek as he said this, and I could feel my skin tingle as he touched it. I reached out to grab him and pull him closer. Our fingers explored each other's bodies, legs intertwined, sweaty and exhausted but relishing the feeling of skin against skin until we finally fell asleep in each other's arms.

CHAPTER SIXTEEN

Jack had to go to New York the next day for some magic shows, but he texted me while he was gone, and it felt tingly and new and teenagerish. He was cute. The text messages were not profound, but they were sweet, and it made me feel good to know that someone was thinking of me and paying attention to me. He sent me photos—of Soho, the Empire Hotel (referencing my love of *Gossip Girl*), Columbus Circle, the Guggenheim. Any landmark he thought would make me wistful and remind me of my New York days. He even sent photos of his audiences, when he could snap them from behind the curtain, and shots of himself standing beside marquees with his name on them. It was all very adorable.

This did not distract me, however, from the fact that Rafael was not contacting me. I continued to be tense and restless, checking my phone at frequent intervals, always feeling deflated when I confronted with a blank screen. And when I got a message, it was never from him. I resorted to taking Xanax (half a pill) nightly. It tormented me not to know what was going on at his end, what he was thinking or planning or wanting.

Until one day, in the early evening, out of the blue, just after I had gotten home from work, I got a text message.

"Hi, how are you?"

I stared at my phone. I did not know what to say. It was like spending years wishing for a pony, and then, unexpectedly, when one arrives on your doorstep, you are at a loss as to what to do with it.

I settled for: "I'm okay, how are you?"

His response took a few minutes, during which I nervously stared at my phone, tapping my fingers against the back of the case, waiting, almost as if for the delivery of my death sentence.

"Life has not been easy. I needed space and time to think of a lot of things. The situation is complicated. I hope you know what I mean and understand why I have not been in touch."

I did not know what he meant. I had no idea what he meant *at all*. The situation was "complicated," meaning they were still together? The situation was "complicated," meaning it was over but it had taken a while? And the most important question, where did I fit into all this?

"Yes, of course, I understand," I told him, lying, hoping the truth would reveal itself through whatever action he took next. I did not have the energy to ask my big questions. "You do what you need to do."

"Thank you, I appreciate that."

Pause. Silence. The blinking iMessage cursor told me that there was more to come. I waited. Nothing came. I got impatient. I wrote again.

"What would you like now? Do you need more time? Can I do anything?" I asked.

"I would like to see you."

Well. Now that was a surprise. And a pleasant one. I liked the idea of him wanting to see me.

"Okay. When?"

"Whenever you are free."

"I'm free now." Why waste time?

"So am I."

"Alright, I will pick you up in fifteen minutes."

"See you then."

I had no idea what to make of this turn of events, but I could only hope that seeing him in person would bring some clarity. At the very least, I hoped he would update me on what was going on, on what was so "complicated," and what, if anything, was going to happen between us. Because the situation, as it was, was driving me crazy.

All the churning anxiety, all the doubt, all the indignant internal monologues, however, vanished the second he got into the car. I had not realized how much I missed his physical presence until he was seated beside me. I knew how much I missed hearing from him—but a large part of that torment came from not knowing if I ever would hear from him again. As soon as he was in front of me, and I could give him a hug, all the questions evaporated. It felt so right. All I wanted was to be beside him, to hold him, to watch him talk, to look into his eyes, and I was willing to do whatever it took to make that a reality.

"Where do you want to go?" I asked.

He shrugged. "I don't care. You decide."

"Do you want food? Are you hungry?"

"No, I had a late lunch. I don't need to eat. But we can go get food if you're hungry." As usual, he was putting the decision on me. Sometimes his passivity drove me nuts.

I shook my head. "I'm not hungry. It's such a warm evening, do you want to sit outside somewhere?"

Los Angeles was being blessed, as it often was, by a prolonged summer, which meant nights that were warm with a hint of a cool breeze. Beautiful weather, perfect for being outdoors. I drove to Barnsdall Park, a small arts complex perched on a hill near my apartment, off of Hollywood Boulevard. Seemingly unassuming from street level, when you snaked your way up the long driveway, you were rewarded with breathtaking views of Hollywood and beyond.

I wanted to walk off some of my restless energy, so I parked at the bottom of the hill, and Rafael and I hiked our way up the driveway. Rafael was not in as good shape as I was, and, with a sweater on, he was also overdressed. By the time we got to the top, he had little beads of sweat on his forehead and was a bit out of breath. I wanted to stroke his face, but I kept my hands to myself.

We sat on the grass and watched the sun set. We were not technically touching, just sitting shoulder to shoulder, but

179

there may have been some leaning going on. We sat in silence, feeling each other's company and soaking in the view. With the breeze, it really was a gorgeous night. Neither of us said anything until the sun was at the horizon, the sky drenched in pinks and purples, turning deep blue at the points furthest from the sun. Only then did Rafael start to speak.

"So I told her."

"You told her what?"

"I told her the relationship had no future."

"Okay. And...?" I was too scared to think or react. I just wanted more information.

"Well, she argued with me. That is why it is complicated. I want her to understand where I am coming from. I want her to understand that this is the right move for both of us."

"Okay..." My voice trailed off. I did not know what else to say. The ball was so clearly in his court. I had no power over this situation. I did not even feel entitled to have input at this point. I did not know what he was expecting me to do.

He looked at me. He was clearly expecting *something*.

"I don't know what to say, Rafael."

"Maybe I am not being clear. I told her. I told her that I did not want to be in this relationship with her. She argued with me, but then she understood. I am trying to do this the right way. I am trying to handle this correctly. I want to respect both of you. But I told her. I want to be with you."

"So where are we now?" I was at a loss. I wanted a straight answer. I needed help sorting through this confusion.

"We are here, now, together. Isn't that what matters?"

I looked at him and sighed. His eyes searched mine, as if for an answer I did not have. Reaching out, he took hold of my right hand. He held it between both of his hands, his beautiful fingers wrapped around my wrist, tracing the skin of my arm.

"You're so gorgeous," he whispered.

He reached up with his right hand and stroked the side of my face. As if with some magical power, he wiped my brain clean. The worries and self-doubt evaporated. Butterflies whisked their way around my stomach, up into my lungs, and into my heart. My mouth felt dry. I stared at him. Rafael leaned closer, his gorgeous face inches from mine. I shivered slightly. It might have been because of the recently vanished sun, or it might have been from the crazy chemistry swirling around us, making the air sparkle.

"Are you cold?" he asked.

Before I could answer, he wrapped his arms around me, holding me. My mind was swirling, my body tingling. This was all too much to absorb. I touched his face with my left hand, caressing his cheek, stroking the line of his perfect nose and the edges of his mouth. His lips parted under my touch. I could feel the coolness of his breath.

"I could get lost in your eyes," I whispered.

"If you do, I will have to come and find you."

I smiled.

One of his hands slid around my neck and across my collarbone. My pulse quickened. I could hear my heart pounding in my ears.

And then he kissed me.

It was tender at first, with an edge of desperation, but then the desperation took over. He kissed with a hunger that shocked me. He shoved himself into me, the stubble on his face rubbing my skin, his tongue ravaging my mouth. I tumbled down on the grass. He was on top of me, his kisses deep and desirous. His passion surprised me. I had never seen this side of him before or even imagined it existed. He always seemed delicate, refined, a little shy—and now he was trying to consume me. His tongue deep in my mouth, his arms pulling me close, my lips already feeling swollen.

"Rafael," I said, pushing him away. "We're in the *park*."

He did not care. His eyes looked drunk, intoxicated, bleary with desire. As much as I wanted him, I was too self-conscious—and too sober—to be ravaged on the wet grass in a public park like this.

Running his fingers through my hair, he tugged just

enough to make it hurt but not enough to make me want to stop him.

"I want you. You know that I want you, right?" He was looking at me with an intensity I had never felt before.

"Yes. Yes, Rafael. I do." I smiled, stroking his face affectionately. "And I want you, too, but not here. Not like this."

We sat up, brushing the damp bits of grass off our shoulders. He looked at me and then kissed me again, tenderly this time. His mouth was warm, his tongue soft. I ran my tongue around the outside of his mouth, tracing his lips, and he grazed my tongue lightly with his teeth. With a little more decorum than before, we kissed until it got so cold that even our heat could not distract me from it.

I took his hand and, together, we walked back down the hill to my car. We did not say much. There was not much to say. The evening was still, and I felt at peace.

When we got to my car, I drove him back to his house. We held hands the whole way, unless I needed my right hand to drive, and then he placed his hand on my right thigh. This was how it would be, I thought. This was what it would be like to date Rafael.

We kissed again when we got to his street, a combination of sweetness and passion. It was hard to let him go, but I had to get up early the next morning for work, and I did not want to push him. I knew he was working through a messy situation, and I did not want to force him to do it any faster than felt right to him.

He lingered in the car for a few minutes. It was clear he did not want to leave, but he eventually did, after several more kisses and prolonged gazing. For the first time, I felt okay with the situation. As I drove away, I did not feel tortured or tormented. Things were moving in the right direction. Soon, we would be together. Officially and legitimately. I had the kisses and the rubbed raw face to prove it. Wincing, I looked in the mirror. I would have to remind Rafael to shave more often.

***

By the time I had slathered moisturizing cream onto my face and crawled into bed, I was a strange combination of exhausted and overcome with adrenaline over what had just transpired. I knew I had to sleep, I knew that we were nearing a deadline at work, I knew that I had to put this behind me. Getting worked up would not help anybody. I glanced at the time. Could I call Corinna? It was late. If I started talking to her, I would be up for another hour. And I had to get to sleep. I had taken so much Xanax to help me sleep when Rafael was not talking to me that I felt guilty taking another one tonight. I had no reason to be depressed or anxious. But I could not sleep.

I decided to try some melatonin. I had bought some a while back to help with jetlag, but it had given me crazy dreams, so I had shoved it in the back of my cupboard and forgotten about it. Maybe tonight would be a good opportunity to give it another shot. Maybe the crazy dreams had just been connected to the mental confusion of jetlag. I grabbed a pill and stuck it under my tongue, letting it dissolve. I got back in bed, staring at the ceiling, visions of Rafael dancing across the shadows.

I could finally feel welcome sleep rushing over me, and I rolled over, pulling my eye mask down over my face as I drifted away.

Rafael was holding my hand, pulling me through the long hallways of the Magic Castle, only they were longer and darker than in real life, and they were empty. The Magic Castle was deserted.

"Where are we going?" I asked.

He merely smiled at me, shushing me with his index

finger against my lips, and pulling me faster. We raced up stairs and downstairs, but mainly down, traversing what felt like a maze, curling our way into the labyrinth of the castle, until, with a spectacular exit, we suddenly emerged in the Peller theater, the same place where I had first seen Rafael perform.

But all the seats were gone. There was just the stage, lit-up, and the rest of the room was in darkness. I turned to Rafael for explanation. He smiled again, reaching forward with his hand, pressing his finger against my mouth to silence me again. Leaving me standing there, he pushed the curtain aside and, reaching back, he grabbed hold of a folded table. Pulling the table out with care, he unfolded it and centered it underneath the spotlight.

As it clicked into place, Rafael gave the wooden table a whack with the palm of his hand, and the surface of the table was suddenly covered with soft green. Satisfied, he turned and looked at me. He reached out with his hand as if motioning for me to come closer. I stepped forward, and he took my hand. As he ran his left hand down my body, my clothes simply fell to the ground.

Rafael gestured toward the table. A stepping stool I had not noticed was just beneath it. I climbed onto it and made my way onto the table. The table had seemed weak and flimsy, but it did not creak or bend as I lay down across it. Lying down, I looked up at Rafael as he looked down on me. He smiled and pulled a deck of cards out of his pocket. He carefully slipped them out of their box, putting the box back into his pocket. I stayed motionless, watching him above me.

He held his hands over my torso and began shuffling the cards. They flowed from one hand to the next. His hands slowly grew wider and wider apart, but the cards did not fall. They kept flowing back and forth, like water streaming first in one direction and then in the other. He brought one hand lower, and the cards flowed downward after it, and then, as he angled his hand, the cards flowed over my torso, landing in a perfect row across my skin, each card with its back facing up.

I craned my head to see what he would do next.

With his right hand, he gave the deck what seemed like a tug, and then the cards flipped over in succession, like a string of dominos, but instead of falling down, they just inverted, so now the backs of the cards were against my skin. It was beautiful. Then Rafael ran his hand along the cards, and as he touched each card, it flew into the air and turned into a dove. My mouth hung open, as I, speechless, watched as fifty-two doves flew up into the darkness and disappeared.

Rafael looked up at the disappearing doves before looking down at me. He smiled, running his finger across my skin, tracing the line of where the cards had just been. My limbs felt heavy. I could not move. I opened my mouth to speak, but nothing came out. All I could do was watch him. His hand moved down my torso, tracing the line of my hips, before slipping between my legs. He reached inside me and, with a serious expression, pulled out a card. He held it up so that I could see. It was the Joker. He shook his head with a look of exaggerated disapproval. He reached back inside and pulled out another card. It was another Joker. He looked even sadder.

Running his hand back up my body, he lingered briefly on my nipples and then my collarbone before making his way up to my face. He gently slipped his hand between my lips and opened up my mouth. Reaching inside, he pulled out another playing card. I could feel my eyes widen even though I still could not move my limbs. He held the card up. It was the queen of hearts. He smiled, pleased. He then opened up his mouth with his fingers, slowly, as if the hinges had rusted, and he reached inside. His entire hand fit in his mouth, and, when it came back out, he was holding the king of hearts. He smiled, holding up both cards, the queen with his left, the king with his right.

And then, with a dramatic flourish, he clapped his hands together, and both cards disappeared in a burst of fire. I closed my eyes for a second, blinded by the brightness of the flame. When I opened them, Rafael was gone. I was alone and naked in the Peller.

I tried to move, to get off the table, but I was frozen. I opened my mouth, but no sound came out. I tried to talk, to shout, but all I heard was a slow buzzing in the background. It grew louder and louder until finally I realized it was my alarm clock. My eyes heavy, my mind groggy, I rolled over and looked at the time. It was time to get ready for work.

CHAPTER SEVENTEEN

Alfredo barged into my office just as I was finishing my second cup of coffee. The first cup I had had on the drive to work in a desperate attempt to recover from the side effects of the melatonin. I hoped the second cup would have more of an effect. He wanted to know if I had heard from the client yet. This meant that he wanted me to contact Sally Herschmann because he was too proud to call her himself.

When I first started at the company, the official account executive was a disaster, so afraid of pissing people off that she pissed everyone off. In her desperate attempts to get Sally to like her, she would routinely underestimate the amount of time it would take to complete a project, which led to us consistently being late on *everything*, Sally hating us and threatening to take her business elsewhere, and the account executive eventually getting fired.

Even though I had been hired to write copy, and even though I was still technically as a freelancer, Sally liked me so much that I was put in the unique position of being account executive just for her and her hair-color and cosmetics company. The company said it was a temporary arrangement, on a per-project basis, but my contract kept getting extended.

I knew that they would not get rid of me because of how well I got along with Sally, even if they stalled on giving me a proper full-time contract. Sally liked that I never sugarcoated anything and that I told her exactly what was going on and how bad things were (if they were bad). The only times I lied to her were about delivery dates. Instead of promising work to her early, and disappointing her, I always tacked two days on to whatever the creative department told me, which meant we consistently delivered on time, if not early.

Did I mention that Sally liked me?

So whenever Alfredo needed anything from Sally, he always came to me first.

"No, nothing yet today or yesterday." I glanced over at my phone. No blinking message light. "No voicemail or email."

"Okay. Make sure she knows that she has to get us revisions by lunch today if she wants the project finished this week."

"I know that, and I'm pretty sure she does, too. But just in case, I'll remind her."

"Great, thank you," he said. As he turned to leave, he said over his shoulder, "You look tired today. Get more sleep."

I was shocked. Alfredo never said anything personal to me, *ever*. He definitely never mentioned my appearance, either good or bad. We never made small talk, never talked about our weekends or the weather, much less how I looked. This was highly unusual. I pulled out a mirror and scrutinized my reflection. Did I look that horrible? The black circles under my eyes were a little more pronounced than normal, but was that enough to make Alfredo comment? I sighed. Rafael was taking a toll on me. I would need more coffee and some under-eye concealer before dinner tonight.

Tonight felt like my first proper date with Rafael, our grand debut. I spent an hour getting ready, putting on makeup, even curling my hair into Farrah Fawcett–like waves. I wore a slim, low-cut sweater and a pair of jeans with boots. I was excited, like a teenager getting ready for prom, any fatigue quickly eradicated.

I could not wait to see him, and I actually ended up being about ten minutes early to pick him up, so I just sat in the car and checked Facebook as time inched forward at an excruciatingly slow pace. I could not wait to see his gorgeous smile, his beautiful eyes framed with those lashes. I could not wait to see him and be able to touch him, to hold his hand, to kiss him, to eradicate whatever weirdness had lingered from that dream like cobwebs across my day.

When he got in my car, he practically pounced on me. He did not even put on his seat belt. I did not see him lean over. Somehow he was on top of me, almost in my seat, devouring me, his kisses covering my face. His passion, again, left me breathless.

I pressed him away for a moment in order to get a little air into my lungs.

"Let me look at you," I said, and he sat back so that I could.

His face was flush, his eyes intense. His lips were luscious. I could not resist them. I grabbed him and pulled him over to me. I had to taste him. First just soft strokes of lips against lips, over and over, and then pressure building, his tongue pushing into mine, tongues tangling, consuming each other's mouths.

"Should I come inside?" I asked, barely able to get the words out between his kisses.

He shook his head, his mouth making its way across my face and down my neck, sending tendrils of saliva in its wake. He ran his tongue across my collarbone, and I moaned. I reached over with my right hand, feeling his thigh, and then between his legs. I could tell how much he desired me.

"Let's skip dinner. Show me your place instead," I suggested.

He just shook his head and kept kissing me. Why would he not let me come to his apartment? Surely he was not concerned about a messy bedroom or a bathroom without toilet paper or any of those other bachelor situations? I wanted him, and I wanted *all* of him. I did not care about the rest. What man did not want that?

"Why not?"

"I'll tell you later," was all he said, totally engrossed in kissing my shoulders and licking my ear.

"Rafael, stop. You're driving me crazy!" I pushed him away, looking at him. "You're torturing me. Let's go be alone together."

"You torture me, too. But you know it will happen. I know it will happen. So it just makes it that much sweeter how much we want it."

"But you don't want me now?"

"I'm not ready to show you my apartment."

Not only was he avoiding the original question, but now I had a whole other question to ask.

"Why not?" I smiled because there was a certain charm to his hesitation even if I was a little put off.

He looked down at his lap, averting his eyes from mine. The moment suddenly felt awkward. My stomach clenched slightly. This could be bad.

"Because she still has things there."

"Oh." That did not seem like such a big deal. My stomach started to unclench. "From when she was last here?"

"Yes."

"Why did she leave them? She didn't want to take them with her?"

"She left them because she is planning to move here." He glanced up at me and then looked away again.

"Oh." I was starting to understand. And I was starting to feel horrible. "When is she planning on moving here?"

"In a few months."

"I see." As much as I desperately did not want to know the answer, I had to ask the obvious question. "Is she still going to move here?"

He sighed. He would not look at me. "I don't know. That's part of why it's complicated."

"Will she move here even if you two aren't together? Or is she moving here to be with you?"

"I hope she moves here even if we aren't together. Moving here is the right decision for her. She already has her visa."

"So…" My voice trailed off. I knew I was interrogating him, and I hated that feeling, but he was also not giving me a straight answer. There was something here that was enormous and unwieldy, and I could not get a grip on it.

He finally lifted his head and made eye contact. I stared into his eyes, as if the answer was somewhere in there. It was not.

"Rafael."

"Yes."

"So if she is moving here anyway, even if you aren't together, then what's the complicated part?"

"Well..." He seemed to be at a loss for words, and I was desperately trying to understand whatever it was he was failing to communicate. "I don't know if she will move here if we are not together. She is not as strong and brave as you are. I am worried she will not come if she thinks she will be alone here."

"Wait. I'm sorry. I'm confused. You guys did break up, right?"

He cleared his throat. He rubbed his palms on his thighs as if to wipe off the sweat. His eyes were focused anywhere but at me. This did not look good. I was growingly increasingly nervous.

"I'm working on it."

"What does that mean?"

"It means I am working on it. It means I am trying to do this in the way that is right for everyone. I am trying to treat everyone with respect."

"So you didn't break up with her?"

He sighed. "I tried. I told her I didn't want to be in the relationship anymore. But she cried. She was really sad. She argued with me. We fought. We fought more today. I need to do this gently. In stages. I need to make sure she still moves here."

Something was not making sense.

"Why is it so important for you that she moves here? If you don't want to be with her...?"

"I know that being here is the right decision for her. It is the right move for her career. She is an actress. She needs to be in L.A. And I am trying to treat her the way I wish I had been treated in the past."

I was at a loss. I got where he was coming from, but I still did not understand. What I did understand was the bottom line: *they were still together.*

He looked up at me. "Do you want to get dinner?"

I shook my head. "I don't think so. I'm not hungry anymore."

Rafael looked sad. Seeing him look sad made me even sadder. I felt like I had lost something I did not even know I had, and I wanted it back. I reached forward and took his hand in mind. We sat in silence for a few minutes, both of us staring out the front windshield of my car.

"What do you want to do?" he asked me.

Fuck. The passivity again. "In general or right now?"

He laughed. "I meant in general, but right now could also apply."

I shrugged. "Right now, I think I want to go home. In general, I'm not sure. I have to think about it."

He nodded, looking at me with an expression of concern. A concern that was probably valid, since the situation felt pretty fucked up. I figured I might as well break it down, for his benefit as well as mine.

"I guess we have a couple options. One is, we try to be friends, although realistically, I'm not sure how well that would work. The second is we have a torrid affair, knowing that we are going to be together, and that it's just a matter of time. And I will try not to think about your girlfriend or feel guilty. And the third—"

He watched me, waiting for me to finish. It was not easy.

"The third is—that we don't see each other until you're finished."

Rafael nodded, as if digesting it all.

"How long do you think it will take?" I asked, even though I was not sure I wanted to know the answer.

"I don't know, honestly." He sounded so sad that it broke my heart. I squeezed his hand and waited for him to continue. "It could be a week, it could be a few days, it could be a couple weeks." He paused, looking down at his lap again. "I just don't know. I want to do this right."

"I get it. I get it. Not completely, I'll be honest, but I get that you want to do the right thing. It's just that—"

Again, I felt like I should keep my mouth shut, but I also felt like I had nothing to lose. "It seems a little like leading her on. I mean, if she thinks she is moving here to be with you, but you don't want to be with her, shouldn't you make that clear? And then she can decide on her own if she wants to come or not? It is her life, after all. And it's a pretty big decision."

He nodded, looking again like the weight of the world was on his shoulders. "This is all true. And it would be true if she were like you. But she's not like you. Imagine a sheltered child. She still lives with her parents. She's not like you."

"But if she's so young and naïve, should she really be moving to a city like L.A. by herself, where she won't know anyone? Maybe she should stay in Spain?"

He shook his head. "No, there are no career opportunities for her in Spain. She needs to come to L.A. The roles are here. The managers. The agents. This is the right place for her. And I'm sorry…" He gazed at me, and I felt like I was about to cry. I wanted to hold him and never let him go. "I'm sorry, but I need to help her."

I nodded. There was nothing to say.

"So which option would you like to choose?" he asked.

I sighed. I leaned over, resting my head on his shoulder. "I don't know, honestly."

I interlocked my arm in his and just inhaled his scent. There was something about him that was still so reassuring even if he was also causing me so much stress. I knew on a very real level that this would be a goodbye, however temporary. That once again, he would disappear from my life, and I wanted to savor every last moment.

"You are too damn sexy," he said.

I laughed, tilting my head to look up at him. "Where did that come from?"

"It's true. I was thinking it, so I said it."

I smiled, resting my head back on his shoulder, squeezing his hand in mine.

"We will make love, you know that, right?" he asked.

I nodded.

"And it's going to be super intimate and beautiful when it happens."

I nodded again.

"And it will happen soon. I promise you that. I want nothing more."

I squeezed his hand in affirmation. "I believe you," I told him. "Let's think about what we want to do next, which option we want to try."

"Okay. Maybe talk tomorrow then? Will we be able to decide by then, do you think?"

"Yes. I think so."

I gave him a long hug, holding him close, not wanting to let him out of my car or my sight. But eventually I did, and, as I watched him walk away, it felt like we had said goodbye.

***

I did not know if it was the smart choice, but it did not take long to decide which option I wanted. I intentionally did not consult with Tyler or Corinna. I assumed they would disagree with me, but I did not care. I did not want their judgment over a situation they could not understand.

At this point, I was starting to doubt whether Rafael and I would end up together—either because he would stay with his girlfriend or because by the time he and I were finally ready to date, we would realize we were not right for each other, anyway.

So I chose to live in the moment, to take advantage of the opportunity that I could have *right now*. Nothing lasts forever, anyway.

"Let's have an affair," I texted him.

"Are you sure?" he replied instantly.

"Yes. I can handle it. I will compartmentalize. Let's do it. I want to be with you. It will be fun. And…I've never had a torrid affair before."

"☺"

Did a smiley face mean yes? I waited to see if he would say anything further. He did not.

"Are you into it?" I asked.

"Yes."

Pause. Blinking cursor. More to come.

"I think so."

More pause. More blinking.

"I'm a little nervous," he said.

His nervousness made me more nervous. "Well, of course, me too. But don't over think it. Let's just enjoy it."

"Okay."

Rafael was not doing a very good job of convincing me that he was into it. Now I was second-guessing myself. I did not know if I should back off or push harder. I wished he would be more assertive.

"Since you don't want me to come to your apartment, how about I pick you up after work and bring you to my place?"

Pause. Blinking cursor. I was now regretting having said anything. Was this all a huge mistake?

"Okay."

Well, then, *okay*. That took long enough.

Of course, I spent the day engaged in an internal debate about just how huge a mistake I had made. He was still taken, I reminded myself. I should be patient. I should wait. I should not force anything. But he was too beautiful, too appealing, too distracting on every level—mentally, physically, emotionally—for me to stay away. I forced myself to concentrate on my work, on sending client emails and making appropriate phone calls. I refused to call Corinna.

Luckily, today was not one of those days when I had to generate original content. Today was more of a management day, putting together schedules, following-up, integrating feedback into work that had already been generated. But the worst was when I had to sit through a PowerPoint presentation by Alfredo, who was too in love with the sound of his own words to wrap up any meeting on schedule. I could not follow a single thing he said, my eyes staring at the bright orange tie Alfredo was wearing, listening absentmindedly to the CRM figures he was outlining and the ways he thought we could improve them.

It was impossible to stay focused, my mind constantly wandering to thoughts of Rafael, remembering what he had felt like and tasted like while anticipating what his naked body would feel like today. His face, those fingers, his brilliantly blue eyes were there every time I closed my eyes.

By the afternoon, I was tense, distracted, and very impatient. The day stretched on interminably. I could not stand it. I could not sit still at my desk. All I could do was Google Rafael, staring at photos I found online, watching his videos, desperately trying to satiate the craving that was consuming me, while checking the time every few minutes.

I finally broke down and called Corinna.

"Tell me about your weekend," I said. "Distract me."

"I just hung out with this guy I met on the *Southland* shoot."

"An actor?"

Corinna had a knack for finding men everywhere— and all kinds of men. Her last boyfriend had been a drummer in a rock band. Another recent guy had worked for some mutual funds agency. It did not matter what kind of men she found, they all adored her, at least at first. But none of the affairs lasted long, either because she got bored or they got distracted. Los Angeles seemed to breed a culture of easily distracted men, a topic of frequent complaint among my female friends.

"No, thank god. He's a gaffer. We mainly hung out at his place near the Grove. We had dinner at the new Nobu in Malibu. That was cool."

I did not even know there *was* a Nobu in Malibu now. That's how uncool I was.

"And?" I asked.

"And nothing. Tell me about you. What's happening with your international playboy?"

"We've decided to have an affair. Or, I guess I decided that we should have an affair."

"Wait—I thought you've *been* having an affair?"

"Can you technically be having an affair if there's no sex?" I actually had wondered that while this whole thing was going on.

"Yes, Adrian, you can. But obviously sex makes everything better. So will there be sex?"

"Hopefully."

"Soon?"

"Tonight, I think."

She squealed. The only thing better than Corinna having sex was Corinna hearing about other people having sex.

"So he's ended things with the girlfriend?"

"Well, no. Not yet. That's why it's an affair."

"Okay. Now I'm confused. So what exactly is going on? Has he told her about you?"

"Uh, I don't think so."

She sighed loudly. I could not figure out if her disapproval had to do with the fact that I was not demanding better treatment for myself or her certainty that Rafael was dicking me around.

"I thought he already broke up with her? I thought you two were official or something?"

"I did too, but…"

"But what? Did they get back together?"

"It's complicated."

Corinna laughed. "It's complicated? Breaking up with someone is complicated? No, honey, *staying* with someone is complicated. Breaking up is easy."

"He told me he loved me," I said, somehow hoping that would appease her. I had not originally planned to share this bit of information.

"Really?" I could feel her skepticism and disapproval dripping through the phone.

"Yes."

"He loves you, but he won't break up with his girlfriend?"

"Corinna! Stop! He's working on it."

"All right. *Fine.* I'll give you and him the benefit of the doubt. So he's working on it...and you two are having sex tonight, anyway? Despite the fact that he has all this 'work' to do?"

"Yes. We have decided to have a torrid affair."

"A torrid affair? I like the sound of that. I could get behind that. So you're doing the affair thing until there's no more girlfriend thing?"

"Yes." I ignored her sarcasm. "Exactly."

"So the girlfriend thing, at least, is finite? You believe him? It's gonna end soon?"

"Yes." I tried to sound convincing for her sake as well as mine.

"Okay, fine. Will you call me tomorrow and tell me what happened? Unless, of course, you can call me tonight?"

I laughed. "Yes, I will tell you everything."

"And don't think I don't know about your little strip club outing. Tyler told me everything."

I should have known he would. "Yes, it's true. That happened."

I knew she was shaking her head on the other end of the phone. "I can't believe Tyler got to meet him first. Once this affair kicks off, maybe I get to meet him, too?"

"Of course. Absolutely."

"Do you two only hang out at strip clubs?" She snorted.

"Very funny. I'll set up a dinner or a trip to the Castle or something. Don't worry. You'll get to meet him."

"Good." She seemed pacified by my promise. "Well, have fun tonight. And remember everything so you can tell me later."

"I will. Bye."

The conversation had killed a bit of time, but it had barely distracted me from anything. Shortly after a lunch break during which I could not eat, I gave up and walked down the hall to the bathroom. My cheeks flushed with self-conscious embarrassment, as if everyone could see into my head and read my inappropriate desires.

Walking as quickly as I could, I ducked into a stall, relieved no one had stopped me. My mind was a mess. It was everywhere but here. Well, that was not true. It was not *everywhere*. It was, in fact, in one very specific place, focused on one very specific guy with whom I was utterly consumed. This current situation, of having him but not having him, was making everything worse. My desire was insatiable. The door had been opened, Pandora's box exposed, and now I could not shut it again.

I locked the bathroom door and unfastened my pants. I slipped them and my underwear down to my ankles and sat on the toilet. I leaned my body against the wall and sat like that for a minute, enjoying the reassuring coolness of the tile, the calm quiet of the stall. I was alone with my thoughts for the first time all day. No one could see me, no one could judge me, no one could read my mind.

Breathing deeply, I tried to relax. Unable to help myself, I slowly ran my right hand over my breasts. I moaned quietly. There was no mercy. I was not in control of anything anymore.

Reaching my hand under my shirt, inside my bra, I

tugged gently on first my left and then my right nipple. I imagined Rafael was there, pulling on them, sucking on them, and I moaned again, a little louder this time, feeling my insides beginning to melt, wetness dripping down my bare thigh. I needed more.

I slipped my left hand under my bra so that I could bring my right hand between my legs. I hesitantly rubbed my clitoris. Could I do this? Would I really be able to make myself come at work? Or was this just an exercise in increased sexual frustration?

Desire surged through me, Rafael's face and body all I could think about. I remembered feeling his passion in the park and in the car. I pressed harder with my right hand and pulled harder with my left. The pleasure ran through my body as I pictured him between my legs, his fingers on and inside my body.

As my fingers circled faster and faster around my clitoris, I leaned even more against the bathroom wall, sagging against the tile, legs spread even wider across the toilet. I shivered as the pleasure started to rise through my body, making my toes tense up and my nipples stiffen. I could feel myself about to come, dangling on the precipice, hovering, waiting, in that in-between moment right before all is about to explode.

I pushed a little harder and tugged a little more, and then I went flying over the edge. My head was a Technicolor explosion of quivering pleasure and images of Rafael—his eyes, his hands, his mouth, those lips, the pressure of his swollen desire against the fabric of his pants.

I sat there for a minute, my hand between my legs, feeling the receding waves of sensation, my other hand resting inside my bra. I was out of breath.

But I also felt good. So good that I temporarily stopped thinking about the fact that Rafael still had a girlfriend and only thought about how amazing it would be to finally fuck him.

CHAPTER EIGHTEEN

Even though I had told Rafael I would pick him up on my way home from work, I lied. Instead, I went home to change clothes. It was not a matter of "slipping into something more comfortable," but more a matter of slipping into something more *uncomfortable* instead.

All afternoon, despite my interlude in the bathroom, I had not been able to stop thinking about getting Rafael to myself, utterly, completely, and carnally. Now that it was finally happening, I wanted to make it amazing. I wanted to celebrate the event. I wanted to give it the attention and effort it deserved.

So I went home and took off all my clothes—and then I put them back on. But, this time, I added another layer underneath. I put on a pale pink and black satin garter slip. The top half was like a bustier, holding my breasts up and pushing them together, making them look larger and more full than they actually were, while the bottom part included a garter belt, with little clips that I attached to thigh high black tights. I pulled my black dress back over the ensemble, tugging it down until no seams were showing. There was no way of knowing what was underneath until I took it all off.

Satisfied with my strategizing, I grabbed my pale pink trench coat (only I knew what it matched), and headed out to pick up Rafael.

I texted him when I was a few minutes away, and he was waiting for me when I got to his building.

"Hey," I said, as he slid into the car.

"Hey," he said, smiling at me.

I felt nervous, jittery, and excited. Like Christmas morning.

"Did you have a good day?" I asked.

He nodded. "Yes. Our new show is going up at the Castle next week so Peter and I are doing all the last minute preparations."

"Oh my god, next week! I forgot it was so soon. I thought it was later in the month."

"Nope." He shook his head. "It starts Monday!"

"Monday. Wow. Do you want me to come on Monday?"

"No, don't. The show won't be good on Monday. You can come any day after that."

"Do you want me there?" I asked, suddenly feeling insecure. "Does it make a difference to you?"

"Are you kidding? I would love you there. I would love you to be at every one of my performances, but I don't want to bother you that much."

I laughed. "Okay, I can't do every one, but maybe I can come a couple times next week. You have three shows a night, right? All week?"

"Yes. That's right."

"Cool. Okay. I will come. Maybe on Tuesday for the first one? Let me look at my schedule, and I will figure out how many I can come to."

"Great."

He smiled at me. I smiled back and reached over to take his hand. I drove the rest of the way to my house that way, holding his hand, adrenaline and nerves making my skin tingle. Or it could just have been the feeling of his flesh against mine.

Now that things were about to happen, I was starting to feel shy and self-conscious. I tried to push those thoughts down and away. I tried to focus on how good it felt to hold his hand and how much better it would feel to hold his body.

But I still felt awkward and clumsy as I led the way into my apartment. I could tell he was a little awkward, too. My grand plans of disrobing in a spectacular fashion fizzled out as he sat on the couch, and I sat on the armchair facing him. This was not how I had imagined it happening.

It did not help matters that Miles was not a fan. Every once in a while, Miles took an inexplicable aversion to certain people. He hated the UPS delivery guy and the upstairs neighbor on the right. He hated skateboarders and bicyclists. He was fiercely protective of me, so rapid movement or menacing strangers were also on his short list.

But for the most part, he was affectionate with my friends. With me, of course, he was never anything but love and kisses and snuggles, so it was always startling when he took a dislike to certain people, especially if they were people I knew and cared for.

But Miles barked and gave the occasional menacing growl at Rafael's direction. I kept one grip on his collar and made him sit beside me, waiting for him to chill out. Eventually, the whole drama proved distracting and annoying, so I got a frozen raw bone out of the freezer and gave it to him. Preoccupied and satisfied, Miles dragged the bone into the dog bed and started gnawing happily.

That dealt with, I pulled my chair closer to the couch so that our knees could touch, resting my hand on his leg. He did not reciprocate. I tried some small talk, asking him if he wanted water or tea, but he said no. I rubbed my hand lightly on his knee, hoping to elicit some kind of response. None was forthcoming. He was not even looking at me. He was looking downward, at some indeterminate point. I wanted to hike up my skirt so that he could see the line of flesh above my stockings— anything to get his attention. I was starting to feel desperate.

"Rafael…" I said, my voice trailing off uncertainly. If I could only get him to look at me, I would kiss him.

He did not say anything. He looked up at me and then away again.

"What's going on, Rafael?" I moved my chair even closer so that I was practically sitting right next to him. "What's the matter?"

There was a long pause. I could tell he was about to say something, so I waited. My stomach churned. This could not be good. He took a deep breath and exhaled slowly. I was starting to feel like I was going to throw up. My bustier was cutting into my skin, my thigh highs sagging at the knees. I felt intensely uncomfortable. I wanted to be anywhere but here. I was suddenly consumed by an overwhelming desire to be alone with Miles.

"I thought I could do this, but I don't think I can." He looked at me, sadly, clearly conflicted and embarrassed. "I wanted to. I really did. But I can't. I'm sorry."

I nodded slowly. I got it, I really did. I understood where he was coming from. But that did not mean that I did not still feel like shit, though.

He looked at me, watching for my reaction. I gave the tiniest hint of a smile. I was trying desperately to be supportive and understanding, but, really, I just wanted to cry. I wanted to get in bed and pull the blankets over my head. I could not say anything because I had nothing left to say.

I looked back at him, at his gorgeous lashes and the soft strong line of his nose. I studied his jaw line, the blue of his eyes, the black curls of his hair, the small gathering of dust on his glasses. I looked at him, and I exhaled, slowly, trying to release the frustration. Trying to let it all go. This felt like the end.

"Shall I take you home?" I asked.

He nodded.

Dejected, like two children deprived of their birthday party, we walked to my car in silence. I drove him home, the only sound in the car coming from the stereo. It was my Metric cd, again, ironically, and I remembered the joy I had felt listening to that song the day of the play, when Rafael had sent me that text that started it all.

"You look even more beautiful in the daylight," he had said, and I could picture the way the clouds had looked in the sky as I had read the text. I remembered watching the clouds and realizing that I was falling in love with Rafael.

And now, it felt like the end of the story, the music more of a slap in the face, reminding me of failed opportunities, dashed hopes, and what could have been. I told myself, glancing over at him in the passenger seat, that this might not be the end. Maybe this was just a brief interlude. Maybe it was a matter of a little more time. But a small voice in my head was not hopeful. That voice told me this was it. I had lost my chance, a chance I never really had in the first place. A chance reserved for a girl in Spain whose ownership over Rafael remained triumphant. In that world, my love for him and his love for me was irrelevant. It was her turn, and it might never be mine.

We gave each other a hug goodbye, but it was the kind of hug people give each other when they have already disconnected, when the mental separation has superseded the physical one. It was a perfunctory goodbye, a symbolic gesture, echoing politeness and social norms more than any sort of real emotion. The distress I was feeling was being kept at bay by maximum self-control.

I was too busy keeping myself together to worry about how Rafael felt, or how hard any of this was for him. The only thing I could think of, which trumped any sort of sympathy I might have had for him, was that he was in control here. I was fundamentally powerless. He was, despite his quiet charm and awkwardness, desired by two women, and it was up to him to decide whom he wanted. The position may have been hard for him, he may have been conflicted about the best course of action, but the point still remained—he had the power, and I did not.

That feeling of complete powerlessness, of knowing that I needed to wait for a day that might never come, made me miserable. When I got home, alone at last, I did exactly what I had wanted to do earlier. The only thing I could imagine doing. I got in bed and pulled the covers over my head and went to sleep, Miles curled against the backs of my knees.

CHAPTER NINETEEN

I felt just as miserable the next day when I woke up. I knew that this did not have to be the end, but it felt like it. I hated knowing that this girl in Spain, this girl I had never met and probably never would, had her claws so deep into the guy I loved that I might never get him away.

I also hated feeling like the other woman. I had never been a mistress before, and I definitely had not set out to be one. But yet, here I was. The other woman. The one with no stakes, no claims, no hold over anything. It was a horrible place to be.

I rolled over in bed, and Miles licked my face. I held him for a few minutes. It was Saturday morning. I had an entirely unplanned day ahead of me, and that was a terrifying prospect. I was way too unhappy to be left to my own devices. I grabbed my phone and texted Ryan. It had been ages since I had seen him. In fact, now that I thought about it, the last time had been that night at the Castle. Wow, what a lifetime ago.

"What are you up to?" I asked.

"I was just about to head to the Silver Lake Reservoir for my morning constitutional," he texted back. That was the semi-ironic way he always referred to his daily stroll around the lake.

That sounded divine. "Perfect! Can Miles and I join you?"

"Absolutely. And lunch after?"

"Yes. See you in half an hour?"

"Sounds good. By the dog park?"

I confirmed and instantly felt better. That was the same dog park where I had adopted Miles several years ago. The Silver Lake Reservoir was actually two huge basins of water.

They were encircled by a fence, unfortunately, preventing passersby from getting too close to the water, but at least it was a beautiful view. The Reservoir really did provide water to 600,000 homes in Los Angeles, but most people I knew thought of it as a scenic place to stroll or jog. It also featured the infamous dog park, a basketball court, and a nursery school. But Ryan and I generally just used the walking path that encircled the Reservoir for our strolls.

This morning would be no different. We usually met once every couple weeks for a catch-up session that multi-tasked as a workout and a dog walk, so the fact that we had not seen each other in ages was unusual. Seeing him today would be perfect. I threw on my workout clothes, grabbed a handful of pumpkin seeds to tide me over until lunch, and headed out to meet Ryan.

When I got there, he was sitting on a bench by the dog park. He looked relaxed and happy. This made me even happier to see him. Ryan was from the Midwest, and even though he had been in Los Angeles for a couple years, he still had the Midwestern congeniality and sweet nature which made him one of my favorite people, and worth hanging on to even if we had met through Mark.

I slumped on the bench next to him and gave him a hug.

"You look great," I told him.

He smiled. "And you look like something is bothering you."

I laughed. "Yes. This is true. And I'll tell you all about it as we walk. Shall we?"

He nodded, and we both hit the path, Miles leading the way.

I did not feel like getting into my stupid tortured love affair quite yet, so I coaxed Ryan into going first. I wanted to get the full update on his life before I rehashed any of my drama.

Ryan had his own drama to talk about, and it was a wonderful diversion from mine. The producer of the television show he was working on had started hitting on Ryan at work. Bringing him coffee in the morning, taking him to lunch, showing more than a casual interest in Ryan's weekend and nighttime plans, and generally paying an excessive amount of attention to him while at the office. The situation had not crossed any specific lines but still verged on the inappropriate. There were hugs that lasted a little too long, arms around shoulders in situations where that was unnecessary, and pats on the back that seemed to verge on fondling.

Ryan and I discussed what he could do about it, and whether anything even needed to be done. The situation was complicated for a variety of reasons. One, the producer was Ryan's boss. Two, the producer was married (to a woman) and therefore technically unavailable. Three, the producer was exceptionally hot, so it was not as though the attention was entirely undesirable. The question was how Ryan should handle it, if he should take any action to make it stop, or if he should just enjoy it.

It was so much fun to talk about that I selfishly did not want Ryan to make it stop. I enjoyed discussing and processing it. While workplace sexual harassment is a serious problem, this did not feel like a problem. At least not yet. For the time being, it seemed like a way to make the days more entertaining for both Ryan and myself, and it could possibly result in a passionate love affair. And a passionate love affair could be a very good thing. Especially for Ryan, who rarely dated for reasons I did not entirely understand.

"What about *your* passionate love affair?" Ryan asked me.

I snorted. "Which one?"

"Is there more than one?" he asked me, grinning, arching an eyebrow.

I could feel myself blushing. "Yes and no. In a way, I've got nothing. In another way, I've got two. But it's two that are really zero. So I guess it's still nothing."

"Adrian...I have no idea what that means. You better

start talking. We've wasted enough time talking about my workplace nonsense. Dish."

I told him about Jack first, since that story was shorter and neater and easier to get through.

"Where is he now? When was the last time you saw him?"

"Jack is in New York now doing some magic shows. The last time I saw him was..." I had to think. "A week ago?"

He laughed. "It's all a blur, huh?"

"I'm a little embarrassed, but, yeah." It suddenly occurred to me that I sounded more than a little slutty.

"And is it a blur because of the other guy?"

"Yes."

"And why isn't Jack your main guy? He seems kind of great."

I had to think about that for a minute. I had not really considered Jack seriously before, as blinded by Rafael as I was. "Honestly, I don't think he wants a relationship. I think he's one of those too attractive guys who doesn't want to commit. He likes keeping his options open."

"And how do you know that?"

I laughed. "I don't know. I think I'm just suspicious of anyone *that* attractive! Plus he travels all the time, so it's hard to build any kind of momentum when someone is gone so much."

"And the other guy is Rafael?"

"Yes."

"Okay. So what's happening with *that*?" he asked. "I haven't met Jack, but Rafael is hot, too."

"He is, it's true. Obviously, I think he's gorgeous. But it's hot in a different way."

"You mean, in the quirky, angular, artsy way?"

I laughed. "Yeah. And, unfortunately, *nothing* is happening with that."

"Oh. And that's the problem?"

I nodded, feeling tearful and wistful again.

"And *why* is nothing happening with that?"

I explained exactly what was going on with the girlfriend and the "complicated situation" and the breakup that just would not quit.

"And what is so complicated about it?"

"Well, that's what I don't totally understand," I told him. "I guess he's trying to be the good guy here, and I get that, but I feel like he's getting her here under false pretenses."

"And that doesn't seem like a good guy move."

I shook my head. "No, it doesn't. That's what doesn't make sense."

"In fact, it feels like a pussy move."

I laughed. "Yeah. You're right."

"Are you sure he's a good guy?"

"I think so."

"A breakup is one conversation, really."

"I know. That's what Corinna keeps saying. Every breakup I've ever had has come down to one conversation. If we had been living together, the awkwardness might linger for a while until one of us moved out, but I have no idea how anyone could stretch a breakup over so many weeks. Especially when the other person is living in another country, so you don't even have to deal with them being in your face."

"That's true. And after your relationship with Mark, you have plenty of breakup experiences. You'd know all about it."

Ryan punched me affectionately in the arm. I punched him back.

"Very funny. Stay focused."

Ryan obligingly wiped the grin off his face. "Do you think maybe he isn't really going to break up with her?" he asked.

That was secretly my biggest fear, one so secret I had not even acknowledged it to myself. But looking at all the facts, it was impossible to ignore it. I sighed, feeling incredibly worn out.

"Can we sit for a minute?" I asked.

"Sure." Ryan looked at me, concerned. "Are you okay?"

"Yeah." I sat on the bench and sighed. "I just feel like an idiot."

"You're not an idiot. You're a romantic. You fell in love. You didn't mean to."

"Yeah, I guess. I still feel like I should have known better. I should have been more careful. Or something. I should give up on him, right? I need to move on. He's just a waste of time. I can't believe he sucked me in."

Ryan shook his head. "Don't waste time and energy thinking like that. What you have to think about now is what you're going to do to make yourself feel better."

I laughed. "You mean, 'Operation Get-Over-Rafael'?"

He grinned. "Yes, exactly. O.G.O.R.. We can call it 'ogre' for short."

"I like the sound of that." I looked at him gratefully and squeezed his hand. "I can do that. I *will* do that. Thank you. For listening and for everything else."

"Of course! No problem. And now get your ass off this bench. We've got another mile left ahead of us, and we've got to figure out what 'ogre' will entail."

Tugging my hand, he pulled me off the bench. Miles bounded ahead, grateful the break had been short. Miles loved this loop as much (if not more) than both Ryan and I did. I followed, already feeling a little better now that I had a plan of action. As Ryan and I finished up our walk, we figured out exactly what that plan of action would entail.

Basically, to put it bluntly, it entailed being a hussy.

Jack was going to be back in a week or so. I was going to text him to keep the flame alive. I liked him, even if I was doubtful about any long-term potential. In the meantime, I would also get my ass out of the house, in as many tight dresses as possible, to various parties and events. I would reactivate my online personal ad, as well.

I was not looking for long-term right now. I was looking for distraction. I was looking to flush my system. I was looking to Get Over Rafael. And if, along the way, he did manage to ditch the girlfriend (finally), well, then I would cross that bridge when I got to it.

But until then, I would not be holding my breath. As Ryan reminded me, I was far too fabulous to sit around and wait for some guy who might not even show up.

CHAPTER TWENTY

Despite my enthusiasm, I was still surprised at how quickly Operation Get Over Rafael kicked into gear. The next day, I got invited by my friend Robert to evening cocktails by the pool at his friend Mitchell's house to celebrate the warm weather. Bathing suits were encouraged. Drinks and small snacks would be provided.

Robert had been one of my first friends in Los Angeles. I had met him in one of those ways you only meet people in the movies. I was at the Hammer Museum, at a photography exhibit, and he happened to be standing next to me, the two of us scrutinizing the same photograph.

"It's so clearly London," I said, sort of to him but also just to state an obvious point.

He laughed. "You mean the grey skies and grim architecture? Yes, clearly London."

We ended up roaming through the rest of the exhibit together, discussing matters as diverse as New York (we both hated Williamsburg and its grim architecture), television (we both had a proclivity for shows like *Six Feet Under* and *The Wire*), and art. After concluding the exhibit, we grabbed some lunch at the health food restaurant around the corner and became fast friends immediately after that.

Robert was one of those bohemian types, with a bushy beard, sparkly eyes, and an opinion on everything from organic coffee to international politics. He made most of his money as an author of children's literature, which seemed somehow appropriate in its randomness, but he also freelanced as a curatorial consult for art auction houses and was an occasional contributor to *Artforum*.

I did not know Mitchell well. All I knew was that he was

one of Robert's closest friends and a successful producer—as in an *actual* producer whose movies people had heard of, as opposed to the thousands (if not millions) of "producers" in Los Angeles. I had only met him once before, at the member's only Soho House in West Hollywood. A highly exclusive restaurant and bar, Soho House catered to creative types, but what that really meant was creative types who could afford the annual membership of $1800 (unless you wanted access to Soho Houses in other locations, and then it was $2400) and who managed to have their application approved. If you were someone like Cameron Diaz, Brad Pitt, or Harvey Weinstein, there was obviously no problem. If you were someone ordinary, it was a little more difficult. However, once you were a member, you were allowed to invite guests, which was how I ended up at the Soho House one Friday night, courtesy of Robert, who was there courtesy of Mitchell.

I had a lovely time drinking expensive cocktails while admiring the breathtaking view and the poshness of it all. It was also enough of an opportunity for me to ascertain that Mitchell was very good-looking, dashing, and incredibly sophisticated. All of which, I assumed, put him out of my league, so I did not pursue anything that night and made do talking with Robert.

But now things had changed. I was in the midst of "O.G.O.R.," and so everything was different. Not only was Mitchell fair game, but it was a pretty safe bet that there would be other dashing and sophisticated men at the pool party that night, and my ability to wear my bikini and/or a cocktail dress with excessively high heels put the odds even more in my favor. I was determined to snatch someone up, and that determination was boosting my confidence and motivation. I had a mission to complete, after all.

When I got to Mitchell's house, which required some careful navigation of the streets north of Sunset Boulevard in Beverly Hills—winding, glorious streets with enormous houses and fancy cars —I had to double-check that I was at the right place because there was a huge gate across the driveway and no foreseeable way to get in. There was a small door with a keypad to the left of the driveway, but Robert had not given me a code or instructions, so at first I thought maybe I was at the wrong place. But I checked my text message, and yes, this was the address Robert had given me.

I walked up to the door and noticed that, imperceptible from the street, it was open a crack. Okay, so far so good. I pushed it open gingerly and peered through. Holy shit. I knew Mitchell had money, but I had no idea it was *this* kind of money. It was officially the largest house I had ever seen, enormous, expensive, and incredibly tastefully mid-century modern. I was in awe. I also felt ridiculously out of place. All my confidence evaporated. I felt like a scruffy teenager from the wrong side of the tracks. I swallowed and contemplated turning around.

But then I took a deep breath. Robert was expecting me. Ryan would be disappointed with me if I gave up. I *wanted* and *needed* this invite. And no one could tell how much (or how little) my clothes cost. I had worn a bikini, per instructions, and then a slim white dress on top, which doubled as beach cover-up attire and, with the heels I was wearing, could also pass cocktail dress code. Feeling squirmy inside, I reminded myself that I simply had to act *as if*, and no one would know the difference. I had just as much of a right to be here as anyone else. And maybe I would get a date with a rich guy out of it. That would be a perk. I did not usually come across rich guys in my normal social circles.

I climbed up the path leading to the house. The grounds were perfectly landscaped, the luscious green lawn interspersed with palm trees and the occasionally "rustic" large rock. It felt very Beverly Hills but with echoes of the au natural. The house was only two stories, but it was significantly larger horizontally than vertically, sprawling across the landscaped grounds. The massive front door seemed to be set within an even more massive window, glass above and on both sides of the thick wood paneling.

I raised my hand as if to knock, but then I noticed a small postcard taped to the window to the left of the front door. It was a picture of a man floating in a pool, holding a cocktail. "Come on in" was scrawled by hand above the man. I smiled. Cute. The door was, indeed, unlocked, and so I did come on in.

The inside of the house had an open floor plan, living room spilling into dining room, and the far wall, the wall I was facing, was all glass, open to the pool. It was gorgeous. I stood and stared for a minute, taking it all in: the spectacular chandelier above the dining room table, the floor to ceiling bookshelf, the Rothko above the fireplace, the white leather couch against the wall of glass, the winding staircase leading up to more private regions, and then, to my right, the spacious and ultramodern kitchen. I sighed. So this was how the other half lived.

The inside of the house was deserted. Everyone, as I could see through the glass wall, was by the pool, reclining on chairs, holding drinks, talking in small groups, with a few swimming in the pool. Robert was manning the barbeque.

There we go, I thought. I would go talk to him. That would be a good place to start.

Dropping my bag discreetly behind one of the deck chairs, I headed over to say hello to Robert.

"Hey, how's it going?"

"Adrian! You made it! You found the place okay?" Dropping the grilling utensils to the side, he gave me a big hug and a scratchy beard kiss.

"I did."

"You did or your phone did?"

I laughed. "Well, my phone did. I just followed directions."

He grinned at me. "Well, I'm glad you're here. Would you like a drink? Some food?"

"Robert, this house is *amazing*."

He nodded. "Yup. It is. Mitchell's got bucks and a lot of good taste."

"Clearly! I think it's the nicest house I've ever seen."

Robert shrugged. "You still haven't seen mine."

"Ha. Right. That's true. I should do that sometime."

Robert and I always met out—at art openings, movies, restaurants, bars—so we had yet to go to each other's apartments. I felt as though I might have offended his ego a little bit with my exuberance over Mitchell's place. It must be tough for a guy to have a best friend with significantly more money. I changed the subject by asking about the food and letting Robert serve me some chicken and vegetable kabobs. They might have been a little messy to eat, but I could always get in the pool after and rinse off.

Plate of food in hand, I went to sit by the pool. Dangling my legs in the water, I ate slowly, listening to the conversations taking place around me. I was enjoying the listening so much that I did not even notice when Mitchell appeared beside me until he sat down, slipping his feet into the water.

"Hey," I said, startled. "How are you?"

Mitchell smiled at me. "I'm good. How are you? Thanks for coming."

I had never been this close to him before, and I was a little distracted by how long his eyelashes were. For a second, I caught myself comparing them to Rafael's. Whose were longer? Then I realized what I was doing, reminded myself of O.G.O.R., and brought my attention back to Mitchell.

"I'm sorry, what did you say?"

"I asked if you would like a drink," he repeated, looking a little amused at my spaciness.

"Sure. Yes. That would be great."

"Perfect."

He got up gracefully, his long legs straightening and elongating, reminding me a bit of a praying mantis. It was not just that he was tall and lean, but that he seemed to be floating on air. There was an ease to his body, to the way his joints seemed to operate. It was like watching a dancer.

Finishing up my food, I wiped my mouth and slid my plate onto a nearby table. I hoped there were no smears on my face or hands, but I felt clean. Before he could get back, I slipped off my dress and adjusted my bikini. When he returned with my glass of sparkling wine, I was effortlessly, oh-so-casually, reclined, cleavage perfectly adjusted, bikini bottoms low across my hips. I was in character. He would not sneak up on me this time.

"Here you are," he said, leaning down to pass me my wine.

"Thank you." I smiled, looking up at him through what I hoped were fluttering eyelashes. "Why don't you sit with me for a few minutes? Take a little break from hosting?"

He smiled. I could not tell if it was a smile of pure pleasure or patronizing pleasure, the way parents are enchanted by the amusing antics of their children. There was something so smooth about him that I could not help feeling clumsy and oafish. But I had to keep acting as if. *As if.* Because, really, what choice did I have? I had promised Ryan a full report, and I could not let him down.

Regardless of the cause of his smile, Mitchell sat beside me, dangling his legs in the water. He was wearing khaki shorts and a pristinely white t-shirt.

"Hi," I said, suddenly nervous.

"Hi," he said.

We sat and smiled at each other a little bit, and then I diffused the moment by asking him about his current projects. He told me about his latest movie, some upcoming trips he had planned with his parents, which then transitioned into him telling me about his parents and his childhood. The main things I got from what he said was that he was currently producing a movie while in pre-production on a few more, that he was close with his parents, and that, as an only child, he had spent a lot of time alone growing up.

I knew it was too good to be true. You can only monopolize the host of a party for so long before people notice. Just as I was starting to feel comfortable with Mitchell, some older women arrived, and he got up to greet them. I decided to get in the water and swim rather than sit by the pool unattended. Slipping all the way in, the water felt delicious, and I floated for a while, letting the various conversations flow around me. At some point, Robert got in with me, bringing me a cocktail with slices of fruit. He had one glass for me and another glass for himself. We leaned against the wall of the pool and sipped.

The sun was setting, and it was now noticeably warmer in the water than outside of it. I was reluctant to get out of the pool. Robert felt the same way, and we just stayed, leaning against the wall, our drinks periodically refilled by the waiter Mitchell had hired for the evening. It was remarkably pleasant. Times like this made me love Los Angeles. The setting sun sent its final rays over the house, turning the sky a dusty pink. Before long, it would be dark, the only illumination the strings of lights hung over the pool and the candles set up along the railing of the deck. There was an intimacy to the evening that had not been palpable during the day, the darkness bringing everyone closer to together.

As it grew late, people began to leave. I knew I should probably go soon, but part of me did not want to brave the cold I would feel as soon as I left the water. Part of me also did not want to leave until I had had the chance to talk to Mitchell again. Unfortunately, ever since our conversation, he had been swept up by first one group of people and then another. Despite my grand plans to finagle at least one date out of the evening, most of the people at the party were either older women or men with dates. It was not as fruitful a gathering as I had anticipated. Ryan would not be pleased.

Mitchell, I knew, was single. But, unfortunately for O.G.O.R., he seemed to be one of the few men there who was. I consoled myself with the fact that I was having a lovely evening, and there were far worse ways to watch the sun go down.

It grew increasingly cold and dark. There were only a few people left by this point. Mitchell came over to sit beside Robert and me, holding two large and fluffy towels.

"Not that you have to get out any time soon, I'm enjoying you enjoy the pool, but whenever you want them, these are for you." He rested them on a nearby chair.

We stayed in the water for a little while, Mitchell sitting above us, but soon it became cold even in the pool, and Robert and I hauled ourselves out, grabbing the towels. Robert sat on the chair where the towels had been. I looked around briefly to figure out where I should sit. As if he had planned this all along, Mitchell spread his legs so that they draped over the sides of his chair, leaving a large expanse of free space between his thighs.

"Why don't you sit here?" he offered, gesturing to the space.

A bit surprised but certainly pleased, I did exactly that, sitting on the edge of the chair so that my back was to him. I was uncomfortable making myself too at home with his body, so I left space between us. He quickly remedied that, however, by moving closer to the end of the chair himself, his legs on either side of mine. Wrapping his arms around me, he held me like that, the two of us on the verge of cuddling. Robert seemed completely unphased. Perhaps he had predicted this all along?

As if we had done it a hundred times before, the three of us sat like that, me leaning back against Mitchell, his arms around me, Robert facing us. When people left, Mitchell did not get up, merely bidding them goodbye from his perch by the pool. Soon, unfortunately, it grew so late that it was time for me to leave, too.

I extricated myself from Mitchell's arms, went to the bathroom to take off my wet bathing suit and change back into my dress, and then I went to say goodbye to him and Robert.

"I'll walk you out," Mitchell said.

Robert merely waved from his armchair. He knew better than to interfere with this goodbye. Smart man.

Mitchell and I walked to his massive front door together in silence. Now that we were no longer intertwined, the moment felt awkward, as if we had just slept together and now had to figure out if we actually liked each other.

But I knew that I liked him. It might not be earth-shattering love, but he was cute and charming, and I was definitely ready to invest some time in him.

At the very least, today had given me several hours in which I did not think (more than a few times) about checking my phone to see if I had heard from Rafael. That could only be viewed as progress.

Opening the door, I leaned forward to give Mitchell a goodbye hug. Glancing quickly over his shoulder, as if to make sure no one was watching, he whisked me outside to his front stoop, pressing me up against the outside wall of his house. We looked at each for a minute, his face inches from mine, and then he leaned over and slipped his tongue in my mouth. It was a little unexpected, perhaps a bit rushed and not exactly what I had in mind, but it was not bad. It was, after all, what I had been hoping would happen eventually, if not tonight.

I wrapped my arms around him and kissed him back. There was a certain sloppiness to his kisses which seemed in marked contrast to the fastidiousness with which he did everything else. But it was sweet, and passionately aggressive, and sort of conspiratorial in the nook, so I felt satisfied as I walked to my car. There may have been few single men at this party, but I had snagged the best one of them all. I had gotten what I came for—and more. Operation Get Over Rafael was off to a good start.

I called Ryan as soon as I got in the car.

"Tell me everything," was the first thing he said.

"I got the big one," I told him, laughing, winding my way

down Beverly Glen toward Sunset Boulevard.

"You got the big one? What does that mean?"

"It means the host of the party kissed me."

"Wait, what? You already got kissed?"

"Yes. Totally. Serious make-out action in the dark as I was leaving."

"How did you pull that off?" he asked.

"Honestly, I have no idea. But somehow I did."

"Well, good for you. Are you going to see him again?"

"I hope so. You never know with these things."

"Are you going to call him?"

"No. Absolutely not. The ball's in his court. I don't even have his number. Although…I guess I could get it from Robert."

"Nope. Don't call him. A guy like that needs a little challenge. Let *him* get your number from Robert if he wants it."

"Yes. I agree. Okay! I'll let you know what happens."

"Definitely do."

O.G.O.R. was moving right along. When I got home, I already had a couple responses to my newly activated personal ad. There was one that caught my eye in particular. It was from a good-looking guy whose very posture seemed overtly physical and no-nonsense. I could make out the outlines of his biceps through the fabric of his dark blue button-down shirt. He was leaning against a white brick wall, wearing a Yankees baseball cap and thin black glasses. There was something about the directness of his gaze that made it hard for me to look away. With his broad shoulders, he looked strong and confident. I was tired of men who were afraid of me or afraid of making decisions, who were coy, easily intimidated, and passive. I liked this guy. He seemed like he could take charge and take me. Like he would not break under pressure.

His message, too, was cute.

Um, this is awkward but my pooches saw your dog in your profile picture and are trying to get us together.

Strong *and* sweet. I wanted to curl up against that torso, to rest my head on that shoulder, to be held by those arms and those hands. I clicked over to his profile to read more about him.

NY_Ricky's profile said he was 42, white, non-religious, a Cancer from New York, with a chiseled body type (yes, I could see that in the photos), and his profession was director I was instantly intrigued. I read more. The whole profile was full of the whole I'm-a-great-dancer-great-cook-avid-traveler-*Downton-Abbey*-watching-artist-type-who-thinks-kids-are-cute-and-I'll-talk-to-you-all-night shit, and I fell for it. I decided to write him back.

Aw, that's so cute of them. So matchmakery. And it's also thoughtful of them, because I always find that first email—the "initiate contact" email—to be the hardest to write, so they gave you an excuse. Tell them thank you from me. And tell me more about directing—what? who?

I clicked send and went to take a shower. When I got into bed, I saw that I had a text message from a number I did not recognize. I opened it up.

"Hi, this is Mitchell. I got your number from Robert. I hope that's okay. I had a lovely time with you tonight—especially walking you out... I'm leaving for London at the end of the week, but maybe we can hang out before I go? Maybe have our own pool party? Let me know if you are around."

"That sounds divine," I replied. "For you, I am around."

I smiled. Things were heating up. What an unexpected but delightful evening. I did want to see him again, and maybe "NY_Ricky" would write me back, too.

But as I drifted to sleep, I could still feel the emptiness behind my sternum, a literal pain in my heart from the absence of Rafael. I missed him most at these times, when the lack of a goodnight text felt most pronounced. I also missed the good morning texts, and the during-the-day texts, and the conversation that felt more alive than any plebeian interchange

I might have with ordinary folk, the sexual tension so acute I could not stand being in the same room as him without touching him. I also missed the trips to the Castle, surrounded by magic on stage and beside me, the complete allure of the impossible and the extraordinary, the exquisitely fascinating place that was Rafael's mind and world. I clearly needed O.G.O.R. to take effect as soon as possible.

I dragged Miles up from the foot of the bed and convinced him to curl up beside me. We fell asleep that way, me holding him at my chest, as if his warmth might help fill that space, might temporarily distract from the void around me, the void reflected in the all too frequent silence of my phone.

CHAPTER TWENTY-ONE

The next day was Monday, so I had to go to work, but that did not mean that O.G.O.R. had stalled. Around ten a.m., I received a text from Mitchell.

"Dinner by the pool Thursday?" he asked.

"Yes, please."

I grinned, my spirits lifting already. They lifted more an hour later, when I heard from NY_Ricky.

That's as sweet and gentle an answer as I'd expect looking at your beautiful pix. (being serious) I'm rick by the way. I'm an actor, dancer, director. And at the moment, a gypsy I guess. I'm working on a new tv show for ABC. I do Broadway in NY and film/tv in LA. And other things. But there's already too much to tell you in a message. Would you be open to a drink some evening soon? I'm in Sherman Oaks at the moment but moving all over the city.

Wow. Just like that, two guys. I had plans with Mitchell for Thursday, but my weekend was free, as was Wednesday. I messaged Rick back with some options. And then I texted Ryan with all the developments.

"Two guys? Lady, you work fast!"

"We'll see if either of them pan out to anything…"

"It doesn't matter if they do or don't. All that matters is that you are fabulous and that you are MOVING ON. You've got to channel Carrie and get all S.A.T.C. on their ass."

I laughed. "You're ridiculous. Nothing about this is Carrie Bradshaw!"

"Yes, it is! You just don't realize how exciting your life is from the outside. You've got the men (even if you've got the heartbreak, too), you've got the parties, and you've even got the Beverly Hills hookup. Enjoy it! Love the drama. At

227

least it's not boring."

He had a point there. Nothing about this was boring. And it was keeping me distracted.

Before lunchtime, Rick had written me back, saying that Wednesday would be perfect. We confirmed to meet for drinks at eight p.m. at Harvard and Stone, a bar near my house on Hollywood Boulevard. Renovated about a year and a half ago, I had avoided it when it first reopened, leaving it to the swarms of hipsters who adored the bar's industrial aesthetic, with its exposed brick walls, massive steel door, and bare light bulbs. But now that the hipsters had moved on to the next chic and rugged hangout, I actually liked the bar, especially mid-week, when there was guaranteed to be at least one free couch in the vicinity of the fireplace.

The night I met Rick, there were indeed numerous empty couches by the fireplace. I had gotten there before him, so I ordered myself a Prosecco at the bar and settled into the couch closest to the fireplace. In typical L.A. fashion, although the day had been warm, the weather had cooled off as soon as the sun had set. By eight p.m. I needed a light jacket, and I definitely appreciated the fireplace, both for its visual aesthetic and for the warmth and soft light it provided.

Rick arrived a few minutes after I had sat down. We recognized each other immediately, even though he was not wearing the Yankees cap from the picture.

"I'm so sorry I'm late. Have you been waiting long?"

I shook my head. "Nope, just got here."

"I wanted to buy you a drink," he protested, pointing to the glass already in my hand.

"You can buy the next one," I promised.

A weird habit of mine was that, on these kinds of dates, with perfect strangers I might never see again, I preferred buying my own drinks. It made me feel as though I did not owe them anything.

A little defeated, he went to the bar to order his own drink. While he was doing it, I checked him out. He was shorter than I had expected. I could not remember how tall his profile said he was, if it even did, but I definitely had thought he would have a more imposing physical stature. He also had a weird profile—the back of his head seemed strangely flat. Most conspicuous, however, were the wrinkles around his eyes and mouth. He did not seem to be forty-two, but I felt awkward bringing it up. Not that it really mattered, since I believed age to be a state of mind, but I also took issue with people who lied on their profiles.

No matter, I told myself, as he walked back to the couch with his drink. I would put all that aside for now and get to know him, flat head notwithstanding.

Getting to know him was more pleasant than I expected. We did all the obligatory questions—siblings, childhood, places lived, career trajectories, etc. His life was interesting, but as I did the math, calculating when he must have graduated college in order to have spent his ten years acting, followed by his years as a chef, and then his last two decades as a director, it did not seem possible that he was forty-two.

"When did you graduate college?" I asked him. I may not have been particularly good at math, but I knew something did not add up.

He must have been able to tell because he paused and looked down at his empty glass, as if the answer was lurking amongst the ice cubes.

"I graduated in 1976."

I was *born* in 1976, and I was currently thirty-six. So there was no way he was six years older than me. As I looked at him, adding up numbers in my head, he confessed.

"I'm not forty-two."

"Oh." At least I was not an idiot. "How old are you?"

He hesitated. "I'm fifty-eight."

That was not what I had signed up for.

"You're *fifty-eight*?"

He could not tell from my reaction if I had exclaimed because I was angry (at being lied to) or if I was shocked (because he did not look fifty-eight), but I had exclaimed because I was both. I had never been on a date with someone that much older than me, and I was not sure how I felt about it. Fifty-eight left him closer to my mother's age than mine, and that made me feel a little strange. Fifty-eight definitely left him too old for me, regardless of how much younger he looked. I wanted someone of marrying age, someone who wanted to have a family, and my vision of that did not include Dad taking the kids to first grade when he was seventy.

I did not want to be rude by getting up and rushing out, so I decided to have that second drink he insisted on buying me, and then I would make a graceful exit. He was pleasant to talk to, even if he was not as sexy in person as in the photos. He was slimmer and slighter than expected. Those broad shoulders I had drooled over were not so broad now that they were in front of me.

But c'est la vie. This was the risk of online dating. There were no guarantees and plenty of surprises. At least the small talk was bearable, and all the more bearable with the help of my second drink.

By the time I was ready to leave, I felt fond of him, even if decidedly not interested in anything further. Somehow, however, he had picked up on an entirely different set of signals.

When I stood up to go, he stood up, as well, and gave me a hug.

"Would you like me to walk you home?" he whispered in my ear.

Something about that felt creepy to me, as legit and gentlemanly as the spirit behind the offer might have been.

I shook my head. "No, that's totally fine, I'm only a few blocks from here. I can walk."

"Are you sure?" he asked, seeming lecherous as he leaned over to me. I could smell his drink on his breath.

"Yes. Quite sure. I'll be okay."

I stepped back, out of range of him and his breath, but he

only stepped closer.

"I'd love to see you again."

I nodded in what I hoped was a friendly but noncommittal fashion.

"Maybe tomorrow night? Or is that too soon?"

"I have plans tomorrow night. Sorry."

I grabbed my bag and made as if to leave. Unfortunately, he just followed me out of the bar and onto the sidewalk.

"How about Friday night?"

"I think I have plans Friday night, too. Why don't you call me?"

He grinned. "Yes, of course. Absolutely."

There was a pause that felt to me like the evening had concluded, so I turned to walk away down the street, but he grabbed my wrist. What did he want now?

I twisted around to look back at him.

"Can I kiss you?"

"No." I shook my head. "I really need to go home. It's late."

He nodded, as if accepting my excuse as valid, but he did not release my wrist.

"I can't wait to see you again."

He smiled, and I swear he licked his lips. Totally creepy. I tugged my wrist free and strode down the street. I had not even gotten to the corner before he texted me.

"You are gorgeous. Radiant. Tonight was great."

I did not answer.

That did not stop him from sending another message.

"I can't wait to see you again. And to kiss you."

I rolled my eyes. Again, I did not answer. I just walked faster. He texted again.

"I hope to see you Friday, let me know."

And a minute later, as I was unlocking the door to my apartment:

"xoxox R"

Ugh. Really?

Well, that had been a bust. At least tomorrow there would be Mitchell. And hopefully after Mitchell there would be others—anything to get over Rafael. Anything to distract me from the sense of loss and rejection.

When I got into bed, I noticed that there was a new message on my phone. I had not heard a beep; it must have come through when I was washing my face or something. My first reaction was, ugh, more from creepy Rick dude. But no, it was from Jack.

"Just thinking about you...how was your evening?"

Aw, that was cute. I was not sure what to say. Should I be honest? Should I lie? I still was having a hard time figuring out what Jack wanted. He really did not seem like the monogamous type, so maybe he would want to hear stories about my dating disasters. Or was that tacky to share?

I settled for cryptic and just texted him back that my evening had been okay—and how was his?

"Not bad...Had the night off. Did some reading and thought about you. Why only okay?"

What the hell, I would be honest. I was a horrible liar, anyway. "I had a crappy date."

"Of course you had a crappy date," he replied.

"Why of course?"

"Because you weren't with me. ☺"

"Ha. Very funny."

"It's true. Your only good dates should be with me."

I was not entirely sure how to respond to that. I could not tell if he was being serious or playing around.

"Tell me. Have you been on any good dates recently that were not with me?"

I had to think about that for a minute. Technically, my meetings with Rafael were not dates, so I could not include him in the mix. And before Rafael, there had been Mark, which felt like a different category. Mark felt like a bad habit.

"You're right," I confessed. "My best dates lately have been with you." It was true.

"Good. ☺ Let's keep it that way."

Now I felt guilty about my upcoming date with Mitchell, but until Jack felt like boyfriend material, until he actually asked me for monogamy, or even implied that he wanted it or was offering it, I figured I should keep all my options open. Hell, I did not even know when I was seeing Jack again. If he wanted me, he was going to have to be a little more proactive. If he wanted me, he was actually going to have to be in town.

CHAPTER TWENTY-TWO

What does one wear to a private pool and dinner party at the home of a man who has everything? I wanted to wear one of my little cocktail dresses, since that felt datey and appropriate, but it felt strange to put a bathing suit on underneath. Mixed messages. Were we really going to swim? If I showed up in pool attire, and he had a romantic dinner prepared, I would feel awkward. I stared at my closet for a while in consternation. I could not figure out a decently sexy dress that would also work around a bikini. What to do?

At the risk of deciding wrong (what if he *had* wanted pool attire?), I settled on the sexy and just threw a bikini into my bag. I could always change when I was there. And, in case I needed it later, I put a second dress into my bag, as well, that I could slip on over a bathing suit. Although, I figured, if we did swim, I would probably towel off, and then any dress could go back on. But whatever. I was prepared either way.

Putting on some waterproof mascara and eyeliner, I studied myself in the mirror. I looked presentable, if a little tired. Work had been long today—Alfredo had kept coming into my office with changes to the latest project proposal, wanting to add elements that would push us beyond the client's requested deadline—and last night still lingered in the residue of bad dates. I hoped Mitchell would put both out of my mind. I could get used to having a rich Beverly Hills boyfriend, as foreign a concept as that was to an East Side girl like me. It was easier for me to find men with scruffy facial hair and hoodies than those with IRAs and lengthy IMDB profiles, but maybe opposites would attract. Lord knows, those hipster dudes never appealed to me.

The ride westward on Sunset Boulevard felt like a

symbolic exodus from hipster to money. Sunset Boulevard went all the way from downtown Los Angeles to the ocean, through dirty and vibrant Echo Park, past Williamsburg-esque Silver Lake, with its urban chic and trendy shops, into Hollywood, both dirty *and* chic—depending on the time of the day and the proximity to certain nightclubs—and always full of tourists teeming around the intersection of Hollywood Boulevard and Highland Avenue, before going through a generic patch of strip malls and storefronts.

Then, suddenly, you were at the Sunset Strip, home of Los Angeles rock and roll standbys, like the Viper Room, Whiskey a Go Go, Rainbow Bar and Grill, and the Troubadour. Now that alternative music culture had moved to Echo Park and Silver Lake, I was not sure how many L.A. natives went to these venues, or what kind of people these natives were, since I did not do more than drive through the Sunset Strip. It always felt like a tourist trap to me, a Disneyfied take on the punk scene I had lived with in New York's East Village when I was in my twenties. The massive billboards, flashy stores, tourist crowds, and steep parking charges also kept me away.

Above the Sunset Strip, however, was where the rich people lived. Prime real estate for movie stars and producers, that was where the big bucks started, and, as soon as I passed the Sunset Strip, the world changed drastically. Suddenly, Sunset Boulevard was a dark, tree-lined street, the chaos and lights of the Strip now a distant memory. I was headed into Beverly Hills. Mitchell lived just a bit further west and north, up in the windy roads that characterized much of Los Angeles's wealthy neighborhoods. It was almost as though, if you could find your way without getting lost, you belonged.

Once I passed the Sunset Strip, I knew I was only a few minutes away from his fancy house, and that was when I started getting nervous. This was my first time alone with him, and I felt flustered before I had even arrived. I drove down the dark and winding Sunset Boulevard, with no storefronts of any kind to light the way, just trees and grass, the brief brightness of the Beverly Hills Hotel a warning that I was about to make my turn up Benedict Canyon. Then it was a matter of snaking my way up more dark streets, where street signs (if you were lucky to see them) were often nestled in trees. Obviously, Beverly Hills was not for the uninitiated or those with bad nighttime vision.

After I parked outside Mitchell's massive gate, my stomach started doing flips. I, again, felt like a little girl who had somehow wandered to the good side of the tracks, and who, at a moment's notice, could be discovered and shipped back to where she belonged.

It did not help matters that the door through which I had entered on Sunday was now securely closed, and I still did not know the keypad code. I called Mitchell and told him I was out front, at his gate. He told me what code to press, but, of course, since I was trespassing in an area far above my pay grade, I could not figure out how to get the door to open. He had to walk down to the gate to open the door manually. I felt mortified. This was not getting off to a good start.

"Hey, how are you?" he asked, beads of perspiration on his brow. He seemed nervous.

"I'm okay, how are you?"

He nodded, as if in confirmation, and started walking back toward the house, ahead of me.

Awkward.

When we got to the front door, I started to walk through it, but he grabbed my arm.

"Let's recreate Sunday," he said, sheepishly.

Okay, that was cute. I grinned. I tossed my bag with bathing suit and extra dress into the foyer, and then I let him press me against the wall for a repeat kiss. His face was damp with sweat, which was a little unpleasant, but the kiss was okay. Not sensational but okay. There was some potential there—at least, that was what I was trying to convince myself.

After the kiss, he took my hand and led me into the

kitchen, and I remembered just how amazing his house was. Now that it was empty of other guests, it felt larger and even more extravagant. There was a huge vase full of tulips perfectly centered on the enormous dining table, beneath the spectacular chandelier that would not have fit into my apartment. There were paintings on all the walls that probably cost more than I had ever made in my life. The couch, along the wall of glass facing the pool, could fit seven adults comfortably. Everything in the kitchen looked state-of-the-art, spotlessly clean with marble counters and four stools around the center island.

"Would you like a drink?" he asked.

Yes! Alcohol would be great right now. "Please. What are you having?"

"I just opened a bottle of white wine. Would you like some? I can also make you a cocktail."

"White wine would be perfect. Thank you." I was not ready to get cocktail drunk until I knew what was going on.

"Here you go," he said, handing me a glass of wine.

Even the glass was beautiful, delicate crystal with a thin gold band that I traced with my finger. I felt hesitant. This man was rich. Like, lots and lots of money rich. Why was I here?

"It's real gold," he said, a little embarrassed.

"Really?"

"Yeah. Twenty-four karat. Gift from my mother."

I liked that he seemed a little embarrassed. It was cute. Maybe this would be okay after all. I took a sip of the wine.

"How is it?" he asked, nervous and overly concerned.

"It's great. Delicious." I tried to sound reassuring.

"Perfect!" He beamed. "Would you like anything to snack on? Dinner is almost ready, I'm just grilling some fish outside."

I shook my head. "I'm good. I'll wait for the fish."

He smiled and then his mouth gaped. "Oh, the fish—one second!"

Grabbing some tongs from the counter, he rushed outside in a panic.

I perched on one of the stools, drinking my wine. I was not sure if I should follow him outside or wait in the kitchen, so I opted for the path of least resistance. I was terribly afraid of doing the wrong thing. I felt uncouth and clumsy, like my limbs were too long for my body, as if I desperately needed to get sent off to charm school. I gulped the wine down as if it would help—or at least dull the pain of my awkwardness—but it did not.

When he came back into the kitchen, with a plate of perfectly grilled salmon and some sides of corn, I felt just as tongue-tied as before. So I did what anyone would do on a first date when conversation stalls—I asked him about himself. I had already covered his childhood, family, and work at the party, so I could not repeat those questions. Instead, I brought up the ultimate default, I got him talking about his house. He obviously loved it, and he was happy to go on and on about the various renovations he had done since buying it.

Despite my attempts at conversation, there were still patches of silence, during which I pretended to be thoroughly distracted by my food. The clang of our silverware against the expensive plates was, at times, the only sound in the room. Oh well, I was trying.

We finished the salmon, corn, and salad he had prepared—all exquisitely tasty—and polished off two glasses of wine each, and then he brought out dessert, an incredibly rich chocolate cake, half of which was missing.

He laughed as he presented it to me. "It's left over from a birthday party. I hope you'll have some. I need to finish it!"

"It looks delicious," I told him. The last thing I needed before putting on my bathing suit was a huge slice of chocolate cake, but I had never been good at turning down decadence.

He cut a significant slice and served it to me on a small china plate. The slice barely fit on the plate, and when I dug my fork in, the cake fell over, bits of chocolate frosting landing on the counter.

"Oh my god, I'm so sorry!"

"Don't worry about it," he said. "Just use your fingers. Lick it up." He laughed self-consciously, trying to be sexy and failing.

I grinned, scooping up the frosting with my index finger and slowly, teasingly, I ran the frosting over my bottom lip before slipping my finger into my mouth. The frosting was rich and cool against my tongue. He stared at me, riveted, as I brought my lips together, sucking my finger clean. I slipped my finger in and out of my mouth, staring at him until I burst out laughing. I, too, could not always be sexy, and when I tried too hard, I just felt ridiculous.

He laughed with me, but it was a self-conscious laugh, his eyes still fixated on my mouth.

"You've got—you've got—there's just—"

"Do I have food on my face?"

"Yes, uh, just let me."

He leaned forward and carefully, cautiously, ran his index finger by the right corner of my mouth. There was, in fact, a renegade piece of frosting lurking there. He caught it and then slid his finger into my mouth. Following along with this game, I slipped my tongue around the tip of his finger, and he moaned. I grabbed his hand and slid his finger deeper into my mouth. Two could play this game.

His eyes were intense, mesmerized by my actions. They widened and then closed briefly as I pressed his finger all the way into my mouth, building up the pressure of my lips around the base of his finger. Clenching the counter with his other hand, he moaned again. I ran circles around his finger with my tongue before I slowly pulled him out of my mouth.

I smiled at him, but his eyes were dark and serious. "That was almost as delicious as the cake," I told him, and he laughed nervously, his expression lightening.

"Do you want some more?" he asked me.

"More you or more cake?"

He grinned. "Whatever you want."

"I'd like to swim now, actually."

I had caught him off guard. "Oh, really? Okay. We can do that. Do you want to change?"

Emboldened by the recent events, I shook my head. Keeping my eyes fixated on his, I unzipped my dress and let it fall to the ground. Not shifting my gaze, I unhooked my bra and let it drop to the floor, as well. I then slipped my underwear down over my hips, and it fell to my ankles. Still without taking my eyes away from his face, I kneeled down just enough to unhook first one heel and then another.

I stood, fully naked, in front of him. I let him look for a second and then, with a smile, I ran through his kitchen, out the big glass door, and jumped into the pool.

The water was warm and felt incredible on my bare skin. Swimming naked had always been one of my favorite activities, and it was a source of constant frustration to me how rarely I got to do it. Tonight I would make the most of it. Like a mermaid, I slipped through the water, swimming from one end of the narrow pool to the other. By the time I doubled back to the first side, he was in there, waiting for me. He was also naked.

I swam up to him and wrapped my legs around his waist. With my hands around his neck and shoulders, I hovered, gravity-less, my face inches from his. We stared at each other like that for a moment, his arms holding me close, pressing into my back. And then we kissed. Maybe it was because we were drunk, maybe it was because we were naked, maybe it was because we were alone, maybe it was because it was a repeat performance, but this kiss was better than the one on Sunday. He was still a little overly aggressive with his tongue, the movements more rapid than ideal, but I could get into it. And get into it I did.

The wetness of his mouth blended with the wetness enveloping us, the warmth of the water cupping us, like we were floating in some kind of embryonic delirium, and I was glad that I did not have to stand, that I did not have to maintain balance, that I could lose myself in his mouth, in his lips, in his tongue. He felt strong as he held me in the water, his broad shoulders like my life raft, my body thoroughly intertwined around his. I could feel my lust building inside me, and I could feel his desire against my naked body.

I knew I was being a horrible tease, but I was not ready to have sex with him. There was not the immediate chemistry or connection I had felt with Jack or Raphael. Mitchell still felt foreign to me, someone whose surface I had only just begun to explore, and most of who he was remained a mystery. That same quality that made me feel like an awkward little girl around him made me feel way too insecure to share myself with him in that way. It felt rushed. I was not ready. It was too soon.

Pulling back from him, I unwrapped myself and darted under the water to slip through his embrace. I swam underwater to the opposite end of the pool before re-emerging.

"You're so far away," he complained.

I smiled. "I'll come back."

I was not trying to avoid him, but I was trying to slow things down. I knew how much I wanted to have sex with someone, to feel the temporary intimacy and warmth, if only to make me feel better about Rafael, but I did not want it to be with Mitchell, like this, tonight. I would be using him, and I would just feel cheap.

At the same time, though, the night was young. I could still have some fun.

I swam over to him and then past him. He reached out to grab me, but I swam too fast, just out of reach. He laughed and swam after me. We encircled each other like that, him playfully pursuing, me using my swimming skills to evade him—until I got bored, and then I let him grab me.

One arm around my waist, he pulled me to him and kissed me hungrily. I kissed him back—and then I swam away again.

"Hey! Come back," he protested.

Swimming back, I kissed him, and then darted away again. He swam after me, grabbing hold of my leg, tugging me over. This time, he pressed me against the edge of the pool so that I could not escape and pushed his tongue back into my mouth. Letting him kiss me, my back leaning into the marble of the pool, I snaked my hand down the side of his body and placed it around him. I squeezed, and his breath caught, his body weakening. He grabbed hold of the edge of the pool with his hands to keep himself from slipping away.

I moved my hand up and down, slowly at first, then building up speed, my fingers tightening around him. I could feel his hips tilting toward me, his body weak and taut at the same time. I kept up the pressure and the pace, and he moaned again, his breath quick and shallow in my ear. I wanted him to come, I wanted to render him totally in my power, and I moved fast and firm, my lips grazing the side of his throat before settling on his ear. I tugged lightly with my teeth.

"My god," he groaned, and I took that as all the encouragement I needed.

I flicked my tongue around the edge of his ear before taking hold again, a little firmer this time with the teeth. I tugged harder with my hand. He was practically panting, his fingers almost white with their grip on the rim of the pool. I ran my tongue over the side of his neck, and that tipped him over the edge. He cried out, and I could tell he had finished because of the primal quality of his cry and because all the energy in his body had gone slack. Whatever he had discharged floated away, an expression of ultimate relaxation spreading across his face.

He smiled at me. "Thank you."

I smiled back. "You're welcome."

He gave me a kiss, releasing his grip on the tile to wrap his arms around me again. We floated like that for a moment, two buoys in the middle of a lake, before he slipped one of his hands between my legs. I was grateful for the pool's water because he could not tell that I was not wet, or, at least, that my wetness was only from the pool. As hot as it had been to watch him come, my body was not aching for him. I felt curiously ambivalent about the notion of letting him make me come.

In fact, as his hand started to explore my insides, I realized that I was not ambivalent at all. I did not want to share this experience with him. I was not ready for that kind of vulnerability. I knew myself well enough, and I knew that, no matter what he did, how ardently he poked and pressed, I would not come. If I was not comfortable with someone, it was virtually impossible. My insides were hardened—and not in the good way. It was time to go home.

I reached down for his hand and pulled it up to my mouth. I kissed each one of his fingers before letting his hand fall back to the water. I kissed him once more on the lips, as well, and then I whispered in his ear that I should go.

"No," he said, shaking his head, and grabbing me close.

I let him hold me like that for a few seconds before repeating, a bit more firmly, that I really did need to go. It was, after all, a school night. I had a meeting with Alfredo at nine a.m. that promised to be exhausting. I pushed against his chest, and this time he let me go without protest.

I swam to the end of the pool and climbed up the stairs. Grabbing a towel from the stack he had on a chair, I dried myself off. He kept floating in the pool, staring at me with obvious desire. I knew he wanted more, but I was not in the mood to do any favors. Plus, I had taken care of him, so he had no grounds for complaint.

Suitably dry, I walked into the kitchen and put my clothes back on. As I was buckling the strap of my left heel, he came into the kitchen, a towel wrapped around his waist. He was still damp, droplets of water across his chest and shoulders, so I refrained from hugging him goodbye.

I just leaned over and kissed him on the mouth. He kissed

me back, our bodies separate, and it seemed like an appropriate goodbye. We were close but still estranged. The evening had been nice, I had enjoyed myself, but had I enjoyed his company as much as swimming naked? I was not sure. However, I resolved not to overanalyze. I would just enjoy. I liked Mitchell, he was smart and well-read and an excellent cook, and I would be happy to see him again, either alone or with Robert, but where things would go between us— that was still a mystery.

Driving down Sunset Boulevard, retracing my steps back to Hollywood, I left the windows open and the music loud. I needed to drown out my thoughts, to let the bass fill my car and my mind.

By the time I got home, despite the volume of the music and the events of the last week, I knew I had to admit something to myself. It was not other men who would help me get over Rafael. It was only time itself.

CHAPTER TWENTY-THREE

I decided to put O.G.O.R. on hold and let time work its magic. I went to Cardio Barre. I caught up on movies. I hiked with Miles. I did the Silver Lake Reservoir constitutional with Ryan. I had a girls night out with Corinna. Everything that could make time go faster, that could turn my mind off, that could distract me from Rafael, I did it. And to those who say time heals all wounds, I was forced to agree. With every passing day, it got a little easier. I thought about him less and less.

That is not to say I did not have pangs of sadness, but those moments grew further and further apart, until they only happened late at night, when everything grew silent and dark, and there was nothing distracting me from my thoughts. In those moments, after I got into bed and turned off the lights, I would let myself think about him as I fell asleep. It was a small reward for not thinking about him during the day. With time, though, the sadness took on less and less of an edge, until it was just an emptiness, that feeling you have when you have gotten rid of a piece of furniture. Something new might have replaced it, but the lines and form and colors of the original piece still lurk in that place it once inhabited, a ghostly shadow of its former self.

Eventually even that faded, and soon I only thought of him a couple nights a week, and then only briefly, in that state of semi-consciousness, when you are neither asleep nor awake. That felt appropriate, somehow, since that space was the realm of magic and magicians, the place for that which defied logic and rational thought, the mystical and the surreal. I let Rafael maintain residence there since I had no control over that area, anyway.

But during the days, when I was awake and coherent, I did not think of him. Rick had messaged me a couple times after our date, but I did not respond, and eventually he drifted away. Mitchell was in London, so I did not expect to hear from him. Jack had come back to L.A. briefly and taken me out for drinks before he had to head off to perform on some cruise.

He met me at my apartment, with a single white rose (he remembered my offhand comment from our sushi date which impressed me) and a small paper bag.

"What's this?" I asked.

"It's dinner. Or a snack. Or whatever." He grinned. "They should still be fresh, made this morning. Although you might want to toast them."

I peered into the bag. There were several bagels inside: pumpernickel, sesame, and cinnamon raisin.

"Bagels?" I asked, incredulous, standing aside to let him into my apartment as Miles rushed forward to sniff the bag. "Like, from New York?"

He nodded, grinning even broadly. "And who is this?" Jack asked, kneeling down to say hello to Miles.

"Jack, meet Miles. Miles, meet Jack," I said, but introductions were hardly necessary. Miles was covering Jack's face with kisses.

Jack pulled out a plastic bag from behind his back and handed it to me so that he could greet Miles properly. "Cream cheese, butter, and Swiss cheese. I didn't know what you liked on your bagels, so I figured I'd cover all the basics. They are fresh from this morning. Upper East Side deli..."

My jaw dropped. "Are you serious?"

"The cream cheese and stuff isn't from New York. That's from Ralphs down the street. Is your dog always this friendly?"

I laughed. "Actually, no. Sometimes he is quite shy, and sometimes he hates people. He's rarely this friendly this quickly." The two of them seemed to be fast friends, Miles nuzzling Jack and Jack scratching Miles behind the ears. "Should I be jealous?"

Jack winked at me. "You never know, I might steal your dog. He's pretty cute."

I grinned. "Hey, as long as you guys get along. And Jack, seriously, this is amazing. How'd you know I loved bagels?"

This time it was his turn to laugh. "Who doesn't love bagels?"

I nodded. "You're right. Especially from New York."

Bagels in Los Angeles were notoriously disappointing when compared to those from New York, and I usually made it a point to eat a few bagels every time I went back for a visit. But it had never occurred to me to fly some bagels back home. This was definitely a stroke of genius on Jack's part.

"And the rose? How'd you remember that?"

He shrugged. "I don't know. You said white roses were your favorite, so I figured that was information worth remembering."

I shook my head, blown away, and led him into the kitchen, Miles trotting at his feet. After some light toasting, the bagels felt straight out of the oven, and we ate all of them, the cinnamon raisin with cream cheese, the pumpernickel with the Swiss cheese, and the sesame with the butter. It was carb heaven.

After sufficient binging, we walked, hand in hand, to Harvard and Stone, the same place I had gone with Rick, to get our carbs in liquid form. Since it was a weeknight, the bar was quiet, and I got my favorite spot on the couch by the fireplace. It was nice to see him, and we kissed and talked for a couple hours, as he told me stories about his New York travels, and I shared my experiences from the years I had lived there.

He said all the right things, he made me laugh, he laughed at my jokes, he held my hand, he checked to see if I wanted more to drink every time my glass got low, and he asked how I got into copywriting.

"It happened by accident," I told him. "I was an English major in college—not because I liked writing, but because that's the major you choose when you don't know what you want to do, and you're bad at math and science. Anyway, I got stuck with this advisor, this grouchy guy with a cowboy hat who terrified everyone. For some reason, he liked me. His brother ran a small ad agency in New York, and a couple years after I moved to New York, he emailed me and said his brother had an opening, so I sent my resume over. It was perfect timing because I had just quit my job because my boss was an asshole, so I was unemployed and broke. I took the job because I was desperate, but I ended up loving it, so it all worked out perfectly. I've been doing it since."

"And why the move to L.A. then?"

"New York got expensive. And I had been there for six years. That's a long time to live anywhere. I figured I should try the west coast out before I got too old. I had never been to L.A. before, so I thought—why not give it a shot?"

Jack smiled as if that was the most amazing story he had ever heard. "Do you read a lot?" he asked.

"I read. I always feel like I don't read as much as I should. I used to keep a diary, too, but I stopped a few years ago. I guess I am surrounded by words all the time, so sometimes I need to run away from them. Do you read a lot?"

He nodded. "All the time. It's one of the 'perks' of traveling. I read on planes, in airports, in hotel rooms. I'm always traveling alone, so books are my friends."

That surprised me, for some reason, and my reaction must have showed.

"What? You don't think I read?"

I shrugged. "I don't know. I don't know you well. I don't know what you do—or read."

"I'd like to get to know you better," he said, leaning over to kiss me. I loved feeling his lips against my skin. I kept being surprised by how gentle he was.

I asked if he loved touring.

"I love performing, but the touring is hard. You spend so much time in your head and with people you don't know. Everyone smiles at you, but they never really listen. It gets hard after a while. It always feels good to come home." He paused and ran his finger down my arm. "I've been doing it a long time."

"Would you ever stop?"

He shook his head. "I could never stop doing magic. Not only because I don't know how to do anything else, but also because it's who I am. I've been doing it since I was six. So I'll keep doing it until I can't do it anymore. And if you are serious about performing, you have to tour unless you get lucky and find a stable gig."

"Since you were six? What made you start when you were six?"

He opened his mouth as if to talk and then looked down, hesitant. "This may sound crazy, but I was a nervous little kid. I was scared of spiders and the dark. I didn't like to go to bed at night unless the lights were on. I was kind of a mess."

I listened, riveted.

"And then my dad came back from one of his business trips with a magic kit for me. That was my first magic kit. He didn't know anything about magic, he just picked it up at some store in New York that was near his hotel. But I didn't care where it came from or why. I just fell in love with magic. When I did magic, I felt powerful. I felt like I knew secrets. And those secrets gave me power over my audience, but, most importantly, they gave me power over my fears. They made me feel like I was the wizard behind the curtain, you know? I started sleeping with the lights off. And the more I did magic, the less I was afraid."

He looked at me, self-conscious. "Is this too much? Am I telling you too much? I've never told anyone this before."

I shook my head and took his hand, holding it between mine. "No. This is great. I love hearing it. I love hearing about you."

He smiled. "Most magicians learn magic to crack secrets. To solve puzzles. For me, I learned magic because I wanted so desperately to believe that there was more out there. That life wasn't this dark and scary place. That it was a place full of joy and wonder and...well, magic. It's a paradox, huh? The magician who wants to believe."

"It makes sense," I told him. And it did. "That's what I love about magic. The childlike wonder. The amazement. The thrill of the impossible happening before your eyes. You want to believe it's real. And I love that you can perform the impossible."

After looking at me intensely for a moment, Jack leaned over to give me a long kiss.

And then I saw Mark.

"Holy shit."

"What?" Jack asked, looking at me with concern.

I instantly regretted my reaction. This could get awkward. "Nothing. Nothing." I looked away, as if turning my head would make Mark disappear. Or, at the very least, not see me.

Jack did not buy it. "What is it? Are you okay?" He scanned the room, knowing that I had seen something upsetting but having no idea what it was.

Mark was at the bar with some girl ordering drinks. I tried to stare covertly. I would not have made a good spy. My neck was starting to hurt, and if Mark looked over, he would have seen me in a second. The darkness of Harvard and Stone was working to my advantage, but only for the time being. Once they got their drinks, my cover would probably be blown.

"It's my ex," I said, gesturing with my head toward the bar.

Jack turned to look. "The douchebag with the actress?"

I laughed. "How can you tell?"

He laughed. "You can't?"

"Well, I know he's a douchebag, but it may have taken me several years to figure that out."

"Really?" Jack seemed incredulous. "You spent several years with that guy?"

Now I felt embarrassed. "He looks that bad?"

"Ah, well, you know. Guys like that are a dime a dozen in Hollywood. I think they all work at William Morris." He shrugged. "If that's your thing, you're certainly living in the right place."

"He's not an agent," I said, laughing.

"Oh yeah? He certainly looks like one. I thought those suits came custom with the job. That and the overpriced haircuts."

I laughed even more. Jack smiled at me. "You're made of much better stock," he said, tracing the line of my jaw before leaning in to give me a kiss. "And compared to that girl? She'd never make it past pilot season."

"What does that mean?" I asked, unable to get the smile off my face. I knew we were being catty, but I loved it.

"You know, she looks good in theory, so you shoot her in a pilot, and then you realize you couldn't possibly stand her for a whole season."

"Best analogy ever. You know this from experience?"

He grinned. "Let's just say I've had enough experience to know what to avoid."

"I've never dated an actress," I replied. "Or an actor. But I seem to have a weakness for magicians."

"You know something, Adrian?"

"What's that?" His tone got serious, and I felt nervous for a second.

"Sometimes it's just a matter of asking for what you want."

I leaned over and kissed him. He grabbed me and held me. I let myself feel his body against mine, the cinnamon-like smell of his cologne, the reassuring broadness of his collarbones, the strength of his shoulders. Even though Mark was only half a room away, even though he was there with some new hot piece of ass, I did not care. I was being held by

Jack, who, to quote him, was also made of much better stock.

We did not have a lot of time, since I had to work the next day and he had a six a.m. flight, so we wrapped up our conversation and left the bar hand in hand. I did not care if Mark saw. I did not even bother to look around the room to see where he was sitting. I did not care anymore.

When we ended the date with a couple of steamy kisses goodbye against Jack's Jeep Cherokee, I felt like they were more than just kisses. For the first time, there was a connection there, something of substance. And then Jack was off, full of promises to send me postcards and bring me more edible gifts upon his return.

With him gone and all silent on the Rafael front, I filled my time accordingly with work, Cardio Barre, Miles, and my friends. I corresponded occasionally with men via my personal ad, but, for the most part, I just stayed busy.

And then I got an email from Rafael.

Life has not been easy. I needed space and time to think of a lot of things. Hope you understand why I have been silent. I am not in the best place in my life. If you are my friend, you will understand. I am figuring life out. For now, I just need time for me and trying to understand where I am at. I need to make decisions and I want to have time and space to do them. Hope you understand. I am leaving for Spain next week for my mother's birthday. I am doing a solo show at the Castle all this week, and I would love for you to come. I miss our conversations. I know you may not believe this, but it is true. I understand why you may not want to come to the show, but if you can make it, it would mean a lot to me, and I would love to know your thoughts about it.
-Rafael

The first thing I noticed was how many times he used the word "understand." Obviously, he wanted me to *understand* him and his actions. The second thing I noticed was that he was going to Spain, which meant he would probably be seeing his girlfriend. I did not know what that signified, but I noticed it. The third thing that stood out was that he wanted to see me. He may not have asked to see me alone, but he was still asking to see me.

I did not know what that meant, either.

I did not reply at first. I reviewed the message in my head for the rest of the day. I read it and re-read it. I texted Ryan to ask him what he thought.

"Do you think I should go?" I asked him.

"Absolutely not," he said. "But will you? Yes."

I laughed. This was probably true. I had never been particularly good at saying no to Rafael. But still, self-preservation was at stake here. Would I be able to handle seeing him? Would all my hard O.G.O.R. efforts go up in smoke? It seemed as though I was over him. When I gingerly opened myself up and pressed on my heart, it felt like I was healed. When I tried to visualize what it would be like to see him, I continued to feel intact. Maybe I would be okay?

I had to think about this. I asked Corinna what she thought I should do. She said I should go but that I should bring a date.

I noticed that Rafael conspicuously did *not* mention the girlfriend in his email. If they had actually (finally) split up, surely he would have mentioned that. That would have been a news flash, after all. So the fact that he did not bring her up at all could only mean one thing: they were still together. But then again, he did mention that he was going to Spain. Maybe that was implicit code to tell me that he was going to break up with her when he was there? Maybe he was waiting to do it in person?

But if that were the case, he would have told me that important nugget of information. He had to know that I was thinking about this, he had to know that I was waiting for any kind of development on this issue, and yet he did not bring it up. If he had taken any sort of action, surely he would have rushed to report it? So the lack of information could only mean one thing—no news was bad news.

I was in a downward spiral of over-analysis, and all the answers were depressing.

I sighed. I should have known better. How often does someone marry the mistress? The wife may be tormented and disrespected, but, at the end of the day, she gets the flowers and keeps the husband. I was a mistake. A glitch in the matrix. And maybe the excessive pleas for understanding were just a thinly veiled apology.

If I had been a stronger woman, if I had been powered by convictions and high moral ground, I would have clicked delete on that message and erased him from my phone, putting him out of my mind and myself out of my misery.

But let's be realistic. I was not that kind of woman or I would not have ended up here in the first place.

To my surprise, when I really thought about it, my heart did feel healed, and my mind clear. Maybe I was actually over him?

Even if it was a foolish idea, I really wanted to see Rafael's magic show. I remembered, all too well, how spectacular his performance was with Peter, and I could only imagine how incredible he would be on his own. The desire to see his show trumped all other misgivings. I would go. Ryan was right. I could not say no. But I would take Corinna's advice. I would bring a date. It would protect me, serving as a buffer, and maybe it would make Rafael jealous at the same time.

Jack was still on his cruise, Mitchell was still in London, the personal ad was currently a bust, so I had to find someone else. I had met this guy Jesse at a party a few months before. Well, to be accurate, I had re-met him. I had originally met him a couple years earlier, when he lived next door to Tyler. Tyler had regular pool parties at his loft during the summer months, and so I would see Jesse often at those events, but our conversations were always brief and in passing. And then I would not see him at all until the following summer.

This last time, however, was different. This time, he talked to me at length, hovering beside me the whole time I was eating, offering me drinks and extra food, laughing at my jokes, asking questions about my life and my job and my dog. And then, when I left, he asked for my number.

We had not gotten together since, but he had texted me a couple times and made it clear that he wanted to do so eventually. The timing never seemed to work, and I did not consider him a serious prospect, so I had not invested much effort. However, I suspected he would be a great one-time date. I figured he would be a shoo-in to accompany me to the Castle to see Rafael's show, and I was right. I was not sure if he was more excited to see me or to go to the Castle, but regardless, he confirmed with enthusiasm, and I wrote back to Rafael.

Dear Rafael,

I'm sorry to hear that life is not easy for you. I am not trying to make anything harder for you. I'm not asking you for anything, and I am definitely not trying to pressure you. If I can do anything to help, let me know. The only thing that I care about is that there is a place for me in your life. Congratulations on the solo show at the Castle. I would love to come and see it, thank you for inviting me. Can I come with a plus one on Wednesday night?

Adrian

The email was strategically composed. I began it by being reassuring and supportive, because all these sentiments were true. I did not want him to break up with his girlfriend just for me. That would not be good for either of us and would not yield any sort of rewarding long-term situation.

If he was not going to break up with her, then I wanted to be sure I kept him as a friend. As long as I had him in my life, in some way, I would make do with that. The idea of losing him entirely was too horrible for me to contemplate, and so I wanted to make sure he knew that I still wanted a friendship if I could get nothing else.

At the same time, I wanted him to know that I would *not* be coming to his show alone. I did not specify that I would be coming with a date because I wanted him to wonder what my plus one meant, which I knew he would. I wanted him to see me with Jesse and to wonder what was going on between us, if it was serious or casual, if it mattered, if it was a threat.

This might have been cruel and manipulative of me, but so be it. He deserved it. Maybe I was a little vindictive, but it was definitely not as cruel as what Rafael had put me through. The more I thought about it, the more I thought Corinna's suggestion had been genius.

Rafael wrote back immediately.

"Perfect. See you Wednesday. You and your plus one will be on my list at the door, and I will reserve seats for you for the early show, if that works for you. I'm glad you can come."

Perfect, indeed. I marked Wednesday down on my calendar even though there was no way in hell I would forget that it was happening.

Jesse had never been to the Castle before, and he was beyond excited to be going. I was glad that I was not going alone, although I still was not sure if there was any potential in Jesse. He seemed to be a sweet guy in the few interactions I had had with him, but he was a bit overweight, with a thick beard, and I knew he smoked pot on a fairly regular basis. All three of those things were detractors from his appeal.

His brother, whom I had also met at the occasional pool party, was a sleeker, sportier version of Jesse who was often in the company of models, and I had always wondered if the extra weight was Jesse's subconscious way of setting himself apart from his stylish older brother. At the same time, if Jesse lost some weight, shaved the facial hair, and cooled it with the pot, he could probably pull a similar caliber of woman, but hey—maybe that was not what he was looking for. Obviously, at the moment, the woman he wanted was me.

And on Wednesday, I would be his. Beyond Wednesday, who could say?

Jesse picked me up exactly on time. To my surprise, he was all gentlemanly about it, getting out of the car to open the door for me, giving me a quick kiss on the cheek before I sat down, his beard not as rough on my cheek as I expected.

"You look lovely," he said.

"Why, thank you. So do you."

He did not *really* look lovely. The suit was a tiny bit too small, but he did look presentable, if not actually nice. The suit slimmed him in a way that a bathing suit, obviously, did not. And he was wearing a deep red silk tie that looked striking against a black shirt and a black suit. Points for outfit coordination.

And also points for behavior. When we got to the Castle, he came around and opened the door for me before handing his keys to the valet. I was touched. For a stoner dude, he knew how to act on a date. He also held the door to the Castle open for me, letting me lead the way in.

Again, I had the privilege of saying "We are guests of Rafael Delgado" to the girls at the front desk and again the honor of being whisked in with a nod and a wave. I let Jesse have the "Open Sesame" duty since it was his first time there, and he was appropriately geeked out about it. He was even more impressed when, as I led him up the winding path to the Parlour Theater, where Rafael would be performing that week, people knew who I was. Bartenders, waiters, house managers all nodded hello at me.

"Are you, like, totally VIP here or what?" he whispered after the house manager outside the Palace greeted me.

I laughed. "Hardly. I just know someone who is."

Jesse looked skeptical, and I could tell he was impressed when we got to the Parlour, and Manny, the house manager, showed us inside to the two reserved seats in the third row.

"Okay, so who do you know, and how do you get such fancy treatment?" he asked, incredulous, as soon as we had sat down.

I shrugged self-consciously. "I just know the guy we're about to see tonight. Rafael Delgado."

"And who is he?"

"He's one of the best card magicians in the world," I replied, more than a little boastful. I could not help it.

Sometimes I got so wrapped up in how I saw Rafael that I forgot how the rest of the world knew him. Because Rafael never did card tricks when we were together, because the last time I had seen him do magic was that night at the Castle with Mark and Ryan, I sometimes forgot that he had the ability to make things disappear and reappear, that illusions and tricks were what he did professionally, that he always had a deck of cards with him. But yes, he was not just the most magnetic and compelling person I had ever met. I had to admit that he was *also* one of the world's foremost practitioners of prestidigitation.

Prestidigitation:

1. Performance of or skill in performing magic or conjuring tricks with the hands; sleight of hand.

2. A show of skill or deceitful cleverness.

Deceitful cleverness. Yes. I should have thought of that before falling for him. Before trusting him. Before believing his promises. Maybe it had been easier for him to fool me precisely because of how close he was to me. Maybe, I suddenly realized, this had all been a terrible mistake, and my heart sank. He had told me once that he would take me to Spain, that he would show me his hometown, that he would introduce me to his family and his best friend from high school. Had it all been deceit?

Of course, that trip had never happened and would probably never happen. And now, of all the unexpected twists, I was here at the Castle again to see him perform, only this time there was another man beside me. In some way, I was back at square one. I was in the audience, Rafael was on the stage, and we were separated by a million metaphorical miles. Deja fucking vu.

"Would you like a drink?"

Jesse's question jolted me out of my downward spiral. I glanced over at him, and he pointed to the waitress who was standing in front of the stage asking for drink orders.

Oh, right. Since I never drank with Rafael, I forgot that the waitresses did that. "I'll have a white wine," I said to Jesse.

Ever the gentleman, he motioned to the waitress who ran up the aisle to us.

"She'll have a white wine, and I'll have a beer. A dark beer. Guinness or whatever you have."

"Perfect. No problem. Be right back!"

The waitress grabbed one more set of drink orders from some Asian girls before slipping past the line of entering people to run to the bar, and I turned to focus my attention on Jesse. I needed to remind myself that I was here with *him*.

I also needed to distract myself from the butterflies floating through my insides at the prospect of seeing Rafael. Operation Get Over Rafael had obviously not succeeded. Maybe it had been a mistake coming here tonight. Maybe it *was* too soon. Maybe I was not as healed and clear-headed as I had thought. But regardless, I was here, and I needed to get through it.

The waitress showed up with our drinks just as the lights were dimming and the house manager had begun his introductory speech. Jesse slipped her his credit card as I held our drinks. After he had signed the receipt, I passed him his drink. We did a whispered "cheers" and clinked our glasses as Rafael stepped through the curtain at the back of the stage.

Fuck. He was more gorgeous than I had remembered. This had been a terrible idea. I took a gulp of wine and prayed for strength.

Rafael did have amazing charisma. I watched Jesse watch

Rafael. He was predictably riveted. It was like getting a diffused version of the real thing, like watching a solar eclipse through a pinhole camera. It was too much to watch Rafael directly, so I watched Jesse watch him. I had to acclimate myself to his presence, to the sound of his voice, before I could see those eyes and that grin.

Even though I knew I was wasting precious performance time with one of the world's great magicians, the first part of the show was mostly a blur. I studied the veins on my hands, the wrinkles around my knuckles, the folds of my dress, the buckle on my purse, the expression on Jesse's face, as if I had paid admission to see those things rather than the guy in front of me.

And then, knowing that I needed to rejoin the moment, that I owed it to Jesse to be present, I forced myself to look up and watched the rest of the show.

Rafael had a deck of cards in his hand. He handed it to a man in the front row to shuffle.

"Sir, I would like you to be happy. Will you shuffle the cards until you are happy?"

The man willingly obliged, shuffling the cards effectively but in a way that made me appreciate how Rafael made the cards flow like water. With this guy, each card remained conspicuously separate, an individual beast in a pile of unwieldy beasts. Thump thump. It was a miracle no cards fell on the floor.

When the man was satisfied, he made as though to pass the cards back to Rafael. Rafael shook his head.

"This must be random. You cannot think I controlled this. You cannot think that I had anything to do with this."

He paused meaningfully, ever dramatic. I thought it was funny how over the top he was on stage, what a drastic role reversal this was from the relaxed and passive guy who rode in my car. On stage, his accent grew thicker, his gestures more emphatic, his persona more exaggerated.

"Now I want you to pass the cards over your head

without looking to see who is behind you. Just reach behind with your cards and let someone from the row behind you take them."

The man did as he was told, and a slim brunette took the deck of cards. She looked to Rafael, awaiting further instruction.

"Now I would like *you* to shuffle the cards until are satisfied."

This woman was better than the first guy. She shuffled the cards as though she played board games on a weekly basis.

"I see you have done this before," Rafael said, smiling.

She laughed. "I play poker."

The entire room burst out in laughter at the image of this petite woman playing poker. But the evidence was there. While she did not shuffle cards as though it was a work of art, she did shuffle them as though she knew what she was doing.

When she was satisfied, Rafael had her pass the cards behind her again. This time, the cards were mine for the taking, but I motioned for Jesse to grab them. Not only did I not want to shuffle cards in front of everyone, but I did not want an excuse for Rafael and I to interact. I wanted to stay as detached as I possibly could. Plus, I knew Jesse would adore the opportunity.

Jesse had a bit of a performative streak in him, and he shuffled the cards dramatically and flamboyantly, like a Vegas card dealer. Everyone laughed appreciatively, and Rafael nodded, impressed.

"Do you also play poker?" he asked.

Jesse laughed. "No. War."

Another round of laughter by the increasingly rowdy and restless audience. There had been so much buildup; they wanted to know where the trick was going. I had faith that Rafael had something astonishing in store. I watched patiently, first as Jesse finished shuffling the cards and then as he passed them back to Rafael.

"So now three of you have shuffled the cards to your

satisfaction, and I have not touched them. Am I correct?"

The man in the front row, the woman in the second row, and Jesse all nodded.

"So are all of you satisfied that the cards have been properly shuffled? After all, we have had a poker expert and a—" he nodded first at the woman and then at Jesse "—War expert."

A couple people snickered, but most were too enraptured to laugh. They knew something amazing was about to happen, and they were riveted. Rafael had us in his grip—me for perhaps slightly different reasons—but still, we could not take our eyes off him.

"So the cards should now be in a completely chaotic order, am I correct?"

The room nodded in unison.

"With no pattern or organization?"

More nodding.

Rafael exhaled dramatically. And then he begin putting the cards down on the table in front of him, one at a time. The first was the ace. The second was the two of hearts. Then the three, and the four, and the five of hearts. No one was breathing. We were watching the spell unfold. Then the six, and the seven, and the eight. He looked up. He looked at the man in the front row.

"Did you do this?" Rafael asked.

The man shook his head like a kid confronted with an empty cookie jar—only in this case, we all knew the man had not stolen any cookies. Rafael looked at the woman in the second row. She shook her head rapidly, too. Rafael turned his questioning gaze to Jesse. Jesse also shook his head. I knew that Rafael was just building more tension. The device was transparent and obvious, but holy fuck was it working. The room was dead silent. We waited to see what would happen next.

Rafael spread the rest of the deck on the table. Nine, ten, joker, and king of hearts. In perfect order, minus the queen.

Rafael sighed with pleasure, organizing the cards on the table, straightening their edges, perfecting their order in a neat little row, all to make it even more spectacular when he had his "shocked" discovery that the queen was missing.

"Did you take it?" he asked, confronting the poor guy in the front row, who just shook his head, without any clue what was going on. I started to suspect what Rafael had planned.

"Did *you* take it?" he asked, pouncing on the woman in the second row. She also shook her head, helpless and confused.

"Or you…?" He turned his attention to Jesse.

"Sorry, man. No clue where it went," Jesse said. He was enjoying this.

Rafael scanned the crowd before walking up the aisle to stand beside Jesse. "I have to say, I'm not sure if I believe you. You did have the deck of cards last."

Jesse held up his hands as if to show that they were empty. Rafael gave him a scrutinizing stare.

"Hm…" he said, as he seemed to ponder an idea. "If I were to steal a card, where would I put it?"

It was clearly a rhetorical question, and no one said anything. We were all desperately waiting to see what Rafael would do next.

"If I were to steal a card, the first thing I would do is give it to a beautiful woman for safekeeping."

Now Rafael turned his attention to me. I shook my head. I had no card.

"She *says* she has no card, but what does life tell us about beautiful women?"

"Don't trust them!" shouted some drunk guy in the back of the theater, and his friends cheered in support. People's patience was starting to fray. They were giving up on Rafael ever finding that missing queen of hearts.

A slow smile spread across Rafael's face. He nodded.

"Now you guys admit that the lovely lady in the second row was chosen by chance to shuffle the cards. I did not select her." Everyone nodded. "And then, in turn, this lovely gentleman was also chosen by chance." Everyone nodded again. "So there is no logical, rational way that I could have planned any of this, correct?" We all nodded a third time. The room, again, was dead silent. "May I, ma'am?"

Rafael reached forward toward my bag that was resting on my knees. This twist I had not foreseen. Speechless and confused, I handed him my bag. I had no idea why he wanted it. He held the bag up high and, in clear view of the entire theater, he slowly unhinged the clasp.

"Will you reach inside?" he asked.

I did—and to my shock, I grabbed the missing card. I pulled out the missing queen of hearts.

The room erupted into thunderous applause.

Rafael grinned, taking the card and handing me back my purse. He winked at me before turning around and heading to the stage, the card above his head, the room still clapping, the entire audience in awe.

Jesse turned to me and whispered in my ear, "Holy shit, you *are* VIP."

I could not help but smile.

For his next trick, Rafael invited an Asian woman from the front row to sit with him on stage. The two of them sat on either side of the small table. Rafael shuffled the cards, and then he had her select one. She wrote her name on it with a pen he pulled out of his pocket. He then had her slip the card back into the deck. He shuffled the cards again before pulling another card from the middle of the deck.

"Is this your card?" he asked, holding the three of clubs up to the audience.

She shook her head, looking extremely apologetic. "It's not."

He seemed shocked. "It's not?"

She shook her head again.

He shuffled the cards once more and retrieved yet another card. He held this one up to the audience. It was the five of clubs.

She shook her head a third time. She looked mortified that this was also not her card. Rafael looked embarrassed by his error. He ran his fingers through his hair.

"I don't know what's going on. This has never happened before. What *was* your card?"

"You were close," she said, shrugging, apologetic. "It was the four of clubs."

"So close," he said, shaking his head with disgust. "So close, and yet I missed it…Well, let's find it."

Rafael spread the cards on the table, face up, and began pawing through them, looking for the four of clubs. It was not in the deck. The card itself was missing. Rafael shook his head, utterly confused. He looked through all the cards on the table. No four of clubs. He pulled the lining out of the pockets in his pants. Nothing there. He turned the pockets in his suit inside out. Nothing there, either.

"Somehow I have lost another card." He looked up at me. "Could this one also be in your purse?"

I opened it and checked. No, no card. I shook my head. He seemed crestfallen.

Just as the audience was starting to wonder if Rafael had totally lost his game, there was a knock at the door. Rafael, startled, looked up.

"Is anyone here expecting someone?"

The audience collectively shook their heads. No one had any clue what was going on.

"Excuse me, then. Let me just get rid of them. Maybe they're selling encyclopedias."

Everyone snickered as Rafael walked over to the door and opened it. Peter was standing outside.

"Oh, Peter. What are you doing here? I'm sort of in the middle of a show."

Rafael gestured behind him to the lot of us. Everyone craned their heads to see who this Peter guy was. Peter looked terribly uncomfortable to have been put in this position.

"I'm so sorry to bother you, but I think you took my wallet by accident. I went to pay for a drink, and I have *your* wallet." Peter hunched his shoulders as if he was cringing. I felt bad for him. I think everyone did.

"Really? You have my wallet? I didn't even notice." Rafael pulled a black leather wallet out of the back pocket of his pants. Peter was holding an identical black wallet in his hands. Rafael opened up the wallet he was holding and exclaimed, "You're right! This is your wallet! The driver's license has your name and photo on it! How ridiculous."

Sheepishly, Peter reached forward and gave Rafael the correct wallet, reclaiming his own. "I'm really sorry. I think I took it when I was in your apartment earlier today."

"That's no problem at all! Have a good night!" Rafael waved merrily at Peter as he closed the door. He turned around to face us again. "So sorry about that mix up, you guys. Where were we?" He looked over at the woman who was still sitting on the stage. "Oh, right! Your card! I lost it. I'm *so* sorry about that. I feel horrible. Let me make it up to you. I'll buy you a drink. Would that be okay?"

The woman shrugged and nodded. No one had any idea what the correct protocol was for this kind of situation. We just went with it.

Rafael opened up the wallet he had just gotten back from Peter. He took out a twenty dollar bill to hand to the woman and, as he did so, a card fell out of the wallet.

"Would you mind getting that?" he asked the woman. He was busy organizing the cards on the table, putting them together into an organized pile.

She leaned down and picked up the card. As she picked it up, she exclaimed.

"What's that?" he asked, absentmindedly.

"It's my card!" she shrieked with joy.

"It's *your* card? You mean, the four of clubs that I lost?" Rafael leaned over to take a look.

She nodded rapidly, a grin splitting her face in two.

"Will you show the audience?"

She held it up so that we could all see. Not only was it the four of clubs, it was, in fact, the four of clubs with her signature. Everyone gasped with amazement. How had he done that? How was that even possible? The card clearly came out of a wallet that had not even been in the room during the trick. A wallet that Rafael had barely even touched. We had all seen the card fall out of the wallet—it had not even come into contact with Rafael's hands. It was definitely the original card because her signature was *on it*. Incredible. Logic defying.

To enthusiastic applause, Rafael bowed and smiled at the woman. "Thank you, everyone, and good night." With a final bow, he exited the stage, disappearing behind the red curtain.

I was speechless. Jesse turned to me, incredulous.

"Holy shit. You said he was amazing, but that was—that was mind-blowing."

I grinned at Jesse's enthusiasm. It *had* been an amazing performance. I still thought I might prefer Rafael and Peter as a duo, because their mutual energies were so different and yet complementary, but if I had to see either alone, it would obviously be Rafael. He was on another level entirely. That level of sophistication, performance, and intellect—no one could match him. This realization settled upon me as Jesse and I exited the Parlour. I was now suddenly very depressed.

There was no one out there like Rafael. There was no one I could date, no activities I could pursue, nothing I could do to distract me from that knowledge. There would be no replacement, no alternative. I just had to learn to accept things as they were and figure out a way to move forward. I doubted that would be with Jesse or Mitchell or Jack, but all I could do was keep going as best as I could and hope that, eventually, I would figure out how to get over Rafael. Maybe one day I would wake up, and none of it would matter anymore. Rafael would just be a novelty item from my past. That funny Spanish magician I fell in love with one summer. A guy I had never slept with and yet with whom I had had raging, mind-consuming chemistry.

Just as all this was cycling through my head, as Jesse heading back from the bar after getting us more drinks, Rafael appeared.

"Hey! You made it! So good to see you!" He swooped down, as if out of nowhere, giddy and euphoric from the adrenaline rush of his show. He gave me a kiss on his cheek and turned to say hello to Jesse.

I introduced the two of them, going through the social motions, but I was not really there. I was on autopilot. Jesse started in on the praise rave that everyone seemed to shower onto Rafael post-show as I stood there awkwardly, drink in hand, feeling like the world's biggest reject. Pull it together, Adrian. *Pull it together*. But I could not. I could not stand so close to him and know that I was not going to have him and feel okay. My despair morphed into anger.

Gorgeous as he was, sweet as he was, smart as he was, he was also a fucking jerk. He had mind-fucked me. He had sucked me in and spit me out. I had not signed up for this. I had done nothing wrong. He had made me fall in love with him, with his charming European shtick and his flirting and his empty endless promises.

Loyalty, huh? He had told me once that loyalty was tremendously important to him. That ideas could come and go but that friends and loyalty were what mattered—but clearly he had not meant loyalty to me. He had obviously meant loyalty to the girlfriend. The one he said he did not want to marry, the one he said he never wanted to live with again, the one he did not want children or a future with. Yeah, *that* girlfriend. The one he refused to break up with.

Meanwhile, here I was, one of the most amazing people he had ever met (or so he said), one of the few people who understood him (or so he had told me), someone he could actually imagine marrying (or so I had been led to believe), and yet I was not worth dating. I was not even, apparently, worth fucking, unless it was the mental kind.

"I have to go to the bathroom," I said abruptly, interrupting whatever conversation Rafael and Jesse were having. The two of them looked at me, startled and confused. Deer in the headlights. Fuck them. I slammed my empty glass down on the bar and rushed off to the nearest bathroom. I was about to lose it, and I was not going to let that happen in public.

The bathroom was small, one of those two-stall affairs with a lock on the external door as well as on the doors of the individual stalls. I raced inside and locked the external door, leaning up against it. Thank god it was empty. I took a few deep breaths, trying to get myself to relax. I needed to pull myself together. I was here on a date with Jesse, for fuck's sake. I needed to stop being such a baby about the whole thing. *Get it together, Adrian*! What the fuck?

I stared at myself in the mirror. My eyes looked enormous. I looked pathetic, weepy, and weak. But I was pissed, too. I may have been a victim, but it was because I had been lied to and manipulated. By a fucking magician. Lies and illusions were his stock in trade. What had I expected? Honesty and transparency? I mean, *really*? I was an idiot.

I took a deep breath and leaned over the bathroom sink to inspect my makeup. Even if I was falling apart on the inside, I had to look like I had my shit together. I would not give Rafael the credit of seeing me cry. I would not fuck up my date with Jesse. My eyeliner was only marginally damaged. I grabbed a paper towel and folded it in half, carefully wiping it along the edges of my eye, scooping up errant eyeliner. Perfect. I took another deep breath. It was going to be okay.

I got some lipstick out of my bag and applied a layer of Dior Addict "Kiss." It was a pleasant, cheerful pink, and it made me feel better already. I took one last deep breath, mustered up some reserve, and opened up the door. Rafael was standing outside.

"What are you doing here? Don't you have another show to prepare for?" I was caught off guard and felt thoroughly annoyed. Was he stalking me now?

He looked at his watch. "I have half an hour until the next show. And I don't need to prepare, it's ready to go."

I stared at him, an accusing look in my eyes.

"You're angry at me," he said. It was a statement, not a question, but I nodded anyway.

"Yeah, I'm angry."

"Can I talk to you?"

I shook my head. "I have to go find Jesse. I can't leave him alone at the bar."

"He's not alone. I introduced him to Peter. They're talking a mile a minute. He won't even notice that you're not back."

"Just because you don't notice me doesn't mean that other guys don't notice me."

"What?" Rafael looked genuinely confused. "What do you mean, I don't notice you?"

"Forget it," I said, attempting to push Rafael out of the way so that I could leave the bathroom. He would not move.

"No. We need to talk about this," he insisted.

"We don't have anything to talk about. I'm done."

"You're done? Done with what?"

I gestured widely. "With you. With *this*. With whatever the fuck is going on and has been going on. I'm done with it. It's *over*. I can't do it anymore."

Rafael looked stricken. His face went pale. He glanced around as if to make sure no one was watching and then he pushed me back into the bathroom. He quickly stepped in after me and closed the door behind him. Then he locked it.

"What the fuck are you doing?" I asked him. "Let me out. I don't want to talk to you."

He shook his head, staring at me intensely. "No. I need to talk to you."

"Fine. Talk to me." I crossed my arms across my chest defensively.

He was silent, just staring.

"Talk. Go," I said, but he just stared at me. I sighed dramatically. "Rafael. Really? Are you going to talk? Because if you don't have anything to say, I have to go."

And then, with a move so fast I did not even see it coming, Rafael kissed me. He kissed me in the second floor bathroom of the Magic Castle, outside the Palace Theater, while my date talked cards and poker at the bar. He spun me around and pressed me up against the bathroom door, and he kissed me. He kissed me in a way that he had never kissed me before, falling into me, his arms around my waist, my back pushed into the door, his shoulders, chest, and body warmer and stronger than I had remembered, fitting into me, around me.

Everything and everyone melted away, and this bathroom became my world. His lips against mine, his mouth open, my tongue against his teeth, each of us against the other, as close to each other as we could possibly be, like two bodies merging, a kiss of such hunger and desire that I could not breathe. I could not even remember how to breathe. All that mattered was getting him as close to me as I possibly could, clutching his body as he clutched mine even while every ounce of intellect shouted at me to stop, stop, stop.

And then someone knocked on the door, and Rafael pulled back, as if out of bad dream. He shook his head.

"I have to go," he said, and without another word, he left. He unlocked the door as I stood there, incapable of words or action, and he pushed me aside. As he rushed out, an elderly woman with silver hair in a huge bouffant came into the bathroom. She looked at me with curiosity and concern.

"Are you okay, dear?"

I could not even imagine the look on my face. I was in shock. I was sure my makeup was all over my face. I just nodded, dumbly, and, thank god, she went into the stall to do her business and did not try to talk to me.

All I could think was that I had to go. I had to leave. I had to get out of there. I could not be in the Magic Castle a single second more. I needed to go home. I was angry, sad, rejected, and frustrated in a dizzying mix.

I rushed to the bar and tapped Jesse on the shoulder. He pulled away from Peter for a second to look at me. It must have been obvious that something was very wrong because, as soon as he looked at me, I could see the concern on his face.

"Adrian? Are you okay?"

I shook my head. "No. I don't feel well. Maybe I drank too much. I need to go home. Can you take me?"

Jesse sprang into action. "Of course, of course. Let's go." He shook Peter's hand. "Goodbye, man, thanks for the conversation."

And then he turned to me. He meant business. Wrapping an arm around me, he whisked me down the hall, past the restaurant, down the stairs, and through the lobby. He was such an imposing figure that people just got out of his way. He was like Moses parting the Red Sea. All I did was lean into him and let him do his thing, and he did it well.

When we got to the crowded valet area, he sat me down on one of the benches outside of the Magic Castle before running over to the valet. I saw them conferring intently and some money change hands before Jesse came back over to sit beside me.

"I told him you were sick. He's letting us jump the line. They're getting my car next."

I was overwhelmed with gratitude. "Are you serious? You didn't have to do that."

He shook his head. "Nonsense. Of course I did." He patted my thigh sympathetically. "We've got to get you home. Like *yesterday*."

Even in my current state, I could not help smiling, and Jesse looked pleased with his own levity and its success. He held me until our car was ready, which, true to his promise, was the next car. I was impressed. Everyone else who was waiting was not so impressed, but who cared about them?

I let Jesse help me into the car and close the door behind

me. I was so glad to be in his car, out of the Castle, and almost home, that I just felt grateful.

"Thank you," I said, when he got into the car.

"For what?" He glanced over at me while shifting the car into drive.

"For being great tonight. And in general. For being so understanding about all this tonight."

"You don't feel well. It happens." He patted my leg again.

I leaned back in the car, processing that latest bit of information. For some reason, so aware was I of the drama and attraction between me and Rafael that I forgot other people did not know about it. Jesse had no idea what went down tonight. He had no clue. He genuinely thought I was sick. The fact that he was not very bright was yet another reason I did not think of him as a potential boyfriend.

But his oblivion also reminded me that this whole mess, this whole torturous mind-fuck of a situation that felt so huge and enormous and enveloping to me, was only in my head. To the rest of the world, it did not matter. The rest of the world did not care if Rafael and I were ever together. I tried to find solace and perspective in that discovery, but, tonight, there would be neither. Maybe tomorrow. Maybe next week. But not tonight. Tonight I was confused, and angry, and sad. And there was nothing I, or anyone else, could do about that. Even the postcards I got from Jack, from Vancouver to Anchorage and San Francisco, while they made it to my fridge, did not help me feel less alone.

CHAPTER TWENTY-FOUR

I committed to not texting Rafael. I would not initiate contact, I told myself. He clearly made the same promise, because I did not hear from him, either. All I knew was that he had gone to Spain for his mother's birthday. Even my pathetic attempts to stalk his Twitter feed yielded nothing. My late night weakness, when I woke up sleepless at three a.m., of scrolling through the updates on his public Facebook page also yielded nothing. I knew nothing. I had no idea what he was thinking or doing or feeling. All I had was silence—and my resolve not to contact him.

Corinna and I even started a pact where she told me that, if I even *thought* about texting Rafael that I had to text her first. And Tyler threatened to come over and dunk my phone in the toilet if he heard that I had initiated contact. Ryan was more forgiving, which was why he became the main person I vented to when I felt weak. I think Corinna and Tyler had simply run out patience, with me and with Rafael.

And then, one day, there was a text message from him.

"Look to see if you got an email from me but do not open it."

What? I had been reading in bed, Miles curled up beside me, but I could not resist. As much as I knew I should just ignore him, as much as I knew better than to respond, I flipped my laptop open and saw the email.

"Yes, I see it," I texted back.

"Good. You did not open it?"

I shook my head even though he obviously could not see me. "No. I did not. Aren't you in Spain?"

"Yes. But I can still send you email. Now think of a card."

"Ok...and then do I tell you what it is?"

"If you like."

"Three of clubs."

"Okay. Now check your email."

I flipped back to my email and clicked to open the letter from him. At first, all I saw were the words "Scroll down..." Then each line just featured a period, so it looked like this:

Scroll down...

.

.

.

.

.

.

I had to scroll all the way down the page and then some. And then there, at the very bottom of the email, was an image—of the three of clubs. Whoa. That was crazy.

"How did you do that?"

"A magician never reveals his secrets ;)"

Fuck. Who knew magic could be so sexy? Who knew it could be so alluring? I hated and loved him at that instant. And I knew, as long as we had any contact, that I would be under his spell.

"Rafael, you need to stop this."

"Stop what?"

"Stop messing with me. Stop contacting me. I can't do it. It's too hard for me. I know I keep saying that, but it's true. You can contact me when you are ready to be with me. Otherwise, wait for me to contact you. I will contact you when I am ready to be friends, when I am over you."

There was silence on his end. Just a blinking cursor. I waited.

"So your feelings for me will change?"

Was he kidding? "Of course my feelings for you will

change. I cannot continue with my feelings like this. It is killing me. I need to take my feelings for you and put them in a box and put that box very far away until we can be together—if that ever happens."

"Is it possible that you will lose the box? That you won't be able to find it again?"

"Well, yes. That is exactly what might happen."

"That makes me sad."

I was starting to get really angry. "It makes me sad, too. This whole situation makes me sad, too. But it also makes no sense. If you want to be with me, I don't know why you can't be with me."

"I told you, it's complicated."

"Yes, yes, I know it's complicated. I'm tired of hearing it's complicated. You're making it complicated. Love shouldn't be complicated. You either want to be with someone or you don't."

"Even when you are angry at me, it's so pleasant to listen to you, I get so focused that I believe my face becomes pathetic."

I melted. How could I not? However fucked up things were, however angry I was, I still adored him. Way to diffuse the situation, Rafael.

"Look, I do want you to do what is best for you. I don't want to force you into anything. I want you to have respect for your relationship and exit however and whenever you want—and maybe not at all, if that's what you decide. I know you need time to process and think and grieve and heal or whatever you need to do to work your way through it. And I don't want to rush you through any of that. That's not fair," I told him.

"Thanks. I appreciate it."

"But while you are doing whatever you need to do, we need to scale things back with us. You need space, and I need space."

I was trying to be zen about the whole thing, but I also

had to instill a bit more self-preservation.

"We can do that, but, what I have to do, I will do because is what needs to be done. I don't want space from you, and I don't believe that you want space from me, but I understand that this is difficult for you. It is difficult for me, too. I hate to lie to my feelings."

The cursor kept blinking, so I knew he had more to say, so I waited to see if he would explain more about how he felt or about what was going on.

"I really like you. Even if it's crazy and ridiculous, I feel right with you."

"I feel the same way, so I understand," I wrote back. "It's so funny, if you had asked me two months ago to design the ideal guy for me, it would not have been you. Not to be mean, but this whole situation is so unexpected, and now I can't get enough of you."

"☺ I would never pick you either, don't worry. I never thought I would like a person that has a dog, has tattoos, and takes dance classes."

"And I can't believe I go and fall for the first magician I meet. Who does that?"

Rafael sent me another smiley face. Somehow our argument had totally dissolved, and we were being mushy again.

"It happens if that first magician is me…and the girl is you."

"The whole thing is a little scary, right?" I asked.

"Yes, it is."

"I can't think straight about it, so it's hard for me to figure out what's going on." And it only seemed to be getting harder.

"I think we are in love."

My heart may have stopped beating for a few seconds.

"Rafael, what are you doing?"

"I am telling you how I feel. I am sorry if it is too much."

"The way you feel isn't too much. It's the fact that you are telling me this while you are in another country—with your girlfriend. You can't do this. You have to fix the situation."

"I do not understand it, either. I am not trying to make your life more difficult. I am trying to understand what is happening. And I cannot. But I also know enough to understand that the things that defy logic are the best ones."

"That's what you do for a living, so you would know."

"Yes. I know. You are so amazing that it's scary."

"Why scary?"

"Because your bar is already too high... if you push it, I may have a heart attack. You are so sexy that it is unbelievable."

"I am glad you think so."

What else could I say? My brain could not process the mixed signals fast enough. Every time I tried to have a straight conversation with him, he spun me around in circles. All I could do was agree.

"You need to sleep," he said, suddenly concerned for my wellbeing.

I had not even realized how late it was. It was almost one in the morning. I knew I had to go to bed, but I also knew that I had to say goodbye. This had to be it. Rafael and I had to stop talking until it was either time for us to move forward or I was really and truly over him. Because now I just felt lost and confused and like I was falling apart. The more contact we had, the more confused I was.

"Rafael, I meant what I said. About how it should be easy when it's the right time. This can't be some tortured love affair that we are doing because we want the challenge and the drama."

"I know. I am not interested in the challenge. I do not want drama. And I am doing what I need to do in order to move forward. I know what I want."

"I get it. I get you."

"I know you do. That's why you are into me, and I am into you."

"Yes…it's like our brains are dating even if we aren't."

"Yes, and our bodies are waiting."

I laughed. "It's an unusual situation."

"Unusual is what interesting people do first and others copy later," Rafael said.

That felt like the right note on which to end our conversation. That and the fact that I could no longer keep my eyes open.

"I am going to go to bed. I am still crazy about you, and I will miss you while we are not in contact," I told him.

"I will miss you, too. Good night."

And then, twenty seconds later, he sent his last message: "I love you."

I was too tired to process how I felt, but I doubted that I would have had much more clarity if I had been wide-awake. I did not know if I should be feeling sad, resigned, happy, or excited about the future. I did not understand what was going on. All I knew was that I loved him and that right now I could not be with him. Part of me clung to the hope that one day I would be able to be with him, but another part of me, the rational and reasonable part of me, knew that I had to eradicate that hope.

I needed to put my love and desire in a box and lock it up far, far away. Perversely, I needed to get over him if there was a chance that we would be together. Because pining for him like this, wearing my heart in a big open mess on my chest was making me miserable, and I was starting to resent him for tormenting me in this way.

But I did not know how to get over him. Nothing I was doing was working. I told myself to be patient with that big gaping heart, to expect nothing, and maybe, just maybe, I would be rewarded with something unexpected.

CHAPTER TWENTY-FIVE

This time both Rafael and I stuck to the plan. There was no contact for several weeks. No texting, no email. Nothing. I kept up my facade of moving on. I saw Jesse again, but it merely confirmed my doubts about him. The fact that his apartment reeked of patchouli did not help either. I met with a couple people off the personal ad site, I even had a sloppy hook-up with one after a few too many drinks, but I found no one of substance. I had no experiences of significance. I just stayed busy. I tried to meet up with Jack again, but he was busy and unavailable, always filming for this show or consulting for that show or out of town for an event. We texted occasionally, and the interest was there, but the timing was always wrong.

And so it went until one day, when I least expected it, I got a text message from Rafael.

"Back to L.A. Let me know when you can meet up."

And that was it. No further elaboration. No clue as to what he had in mind. Nothing.

I called Ryan and asked his advice. I felt like he was entitled to give better advice after having met Rafael. That and Corinna was off in love-land with her actor guy, so she could not be counted on to remember how heartbreak felt. I could not expect sympathy.

"What do you think I should do?"

"Are you serious?"

"You think I should meet with him?"

"Are you even considering *not* meeting with him? Really? You would go the rest of your life not knowing what he had to say to you? Just get it over with. See him. See what he has to say, if he has anything to say at all. And if he's still with that girl, then you know, and then you walk away. But you really walk away."

I nodded. He was right. "Should I ask him what he wants to talk about it?"

"No. Don't be a girl about it. Don't get into it over text. Just go. Meet with him. Let him talk to you in person. If he doesn't bring it up, you can either bring it up yourself or never see him again, because in *that* case, he's a total pussy."

"I think we've already established that he's a total pussy."

"Well. Yes. Real men with dicks take action. They don't fuck around. But maybe he's just slow. Some guys are slow. Give him one more chance, but *only* one more chance. Maybe he needed to deal with it—I'm sorry, deal with *her*—in person."

"You're right again. Okay. Fine. I'll give him one more chance. I'll see what he has to say."

"Good. And then text me after and tell me everything."

I laughed. "It's a deal. I'll let you know what the plan is."

I texted Rafael and told him I could meet him whenever. He proposed meeting the next night at the Castle. I liked that plan. I figured, now that I was testing out my new strength, that it was probably better to avoid being alone with Rafael, especially if the news was going to be bad, so it would be good to be in a relaxed and peopled atmosphere. And there would be activities to do—we would not just be staring at each other the whole night. Well, we probably *would* be staring, but at least it would not be awkwardly, over a silent meal.

I did not know what to wear. I did not know what to expect. I did not know what I should be preparing for. I stood and stared at my closet, drawing an unexpected blank. I had so many little cocktails dresses, but none had the gravitas I felt I needed for this evening. I needed something explosive and serious. I needed the big leagues.

For this, I would text Corinna. Not only was she the most fashionable person I knew, but she knew my closet as well as her own.

"What's the best dress I have?"

It only took her a moment. "The black Thomas Wylde one."

She was right. That dress was perfect. It was black (serious) with an asymmetrical cut up the leg (explosive) and a diagonal cut across the top, exposing one arm and shoulder (big leagues). I paired it with bare legs, stiletto boots, and a small black jacket. It was dramatic and incredibly sexy, while also very striking. It was both unusual and flattering. It made a statement. And tonight, when I was not sure how much I would be able to say, I needed my clothes to speak for me.

I knew I probably would not be drinking with Rafael, so I did something I never did. I had a drink at home before I left to "steady my nerves." Only one drink, because I was about to drive, but a drink nonetheless. I made myself a weak gin and tonic, and as I drank it down, I told myself that, whatever happened tonight, I would get through it. This was just one day out of my life.

For what it was worth, Jack would be back in Los Angeles tomorrow. He had even told me that he had been hired to consult on a television show, so he would be able to travel less and would be around more. I did not know what that would lead to. Despite my affection for Jack, it was hard to read the extent of his affection for me. His constant traveling made it hard for us to create any real momentum. But starting tomorrow, he would be in town for the long term. That meant something even if I was not sure exactly what.

I reminded myself that Rafael was just one of many people I had met in my life. I had had some crazy experiences in New York, I had made out with producers in Beverly Hills pools, and I had even once kissed John Cusack backstage after a rock concert. Who was Rafael but just one more on an ever-growing list?

He had told me once that we would be friends forever, regardless of whom he was dating or whom I was dating. I doubted that, but I still managed to take solace in his promise. But regardless, it was stupid to worry about all this now. Because now I was late. He would be waiting for me. Grabbing my keys, I took one last look at my face, fixed a makeup smudge, and raced out the door.

When I got to the Castle, he was already at the bar. During the drive over, I kept trying to predict what it would be like to see him. Would it be some dramatic reunion? Would we fall into each other's arms or would it be weird, awkward, and stiff? Would we be like casual friends, falling into a nice platonic groove?

I did not know what I wanted or hoped for, but I knew that, when I got there, and he was friendly, but in a distant and aloof way, I was disappointed. He seemed pleased to see me, but it was in the way that distant cousins are when they sit beside each other at a family event. We sat at the lobby bar, and he said nothing about my dress. The conversation felt stilted. Our usual flow was conspicuously absent. I had to scramble for things to talk about.

Normally, we could not stop talking. Tonight, I asked questions, and he answered them. Sometimes he asked me questions, and then I answered them. But these were not questions that mattered. These were questions about his trip, his family, his friends, and being back in Spain. He told me about his cousin, who was graduating college, and his mother, who was overjoyed to have her son at her birthday. He told me about a big dinner he had had with his friends, about a local band they had all gone to see, about a play his sister had been in. I did not care about any of these stories. I wanted him to tell me why I was there, why he wanted to see me, and he did not.

He asked me about Ryan, about my job, about Miles. He told me about his new workout routine and asked about mine. He was intrigued by my obsession with Cardio Barre. I felt increasingly frustrated and disappointed. This was not why I had come. I did not have time for this. But I lacked the impetus for a sudden exit. I had only just arrived. It would be strange if I left, even though my brain scrambled to come up with any excuse for a quick escape.

And as I failed to think of an excuse, I suffered through the bullshit. I sat while he talked to the people passing by who knew him. I restlessly checked my watch. I went with him to see a show in the Close-Up Gallery, the smallest theater at the Castle. It was some older British magician who was friends with Rafael so he wanted to be supportive, but I was not terribly impressed. The magician did a lot of the usual tricks: quarters coming out of thin air, scarves coming out of pockets and hats, plus the typical card tricks. Maybe I would have enjoyed it more if I had been in a better mood, but, at this rate, I just wanted to go home.

And that was what I finally told Rafael when the show let out. When he asked me at which bar I wanted to sit, I just said, "I'm tired, Rafael. I need to go home."

His face fell slightly, but he nodded as if he understood.

"Come, I'll walk out with you."

"You don't have to."

This was our usual routine. He would offer to wait with me by the valet, I would tell him it was unnecessary, but he would do it anyway, and I would enjoy the extra moments with him. Tonight, however, I really did not care. In fact, I preferred for him not to come. I wanted to get away from him. I was drained by all the superficial conversation.

But he insisted.

As we stood out by the valet station, he told me another Spain story, about some old friend from high school he had not seen in years whom he happened to run into at the restaurant where they had had his mother's birthday. I was not even listening, so distracted was I by my disappointment and frustration. The words coming out of his mouth felt like an endless stream of white noise that I did not even try to follow *Blah blah blah.*

When my car finally arrived, I wanted to cry with relief.

Escape was imminent. But then Rafael did something that he had never done before. He did not just say goodbye. He insisted on finishing his story. I had not even noticed it was still going on.

"We can't wait here," I said, annoyed. "People are getting their cars. I have to move out of the way."

"That's fine," he replied, easily, totally unfazed. Was he really so oblivious to my annoyance? "I'm almost done with the story. I'll ride with you in the car down to the street, and then I will walk back up to the Castle."

That seemed absurd to me—who really cared about his old friend and the stupid story?—but I was not going to argue. I was too defeated.

"Okay. Fine."

We both got into my car, and I drove down the steep hill to Franklin Boulevard. Of course, he was going into so much irrelevant detail that he was not even close to done by the time I got to Franklin, so I pulled over into a spot at the very far end of the parking lot and waited for him to finish.

I had not been paying attention to the story at all, so the only way I knew he was finally done was when he finally stopped talking. There was silence. I looked at him expectantly. Now it would surely be time for him to leave. He made no such move. I opened my mouth to tell him good night, but he leaned over and put his finger on my mouth.

"Shh," he said.

What the fuck?

His finger was on my mouth, so I waited, lips closed, to see what he was going to do next. The silence dragged on, the two of us just looking at each other in the darkness of my car.

And then he started to talk.

"It's over. It's really over. I'm sorry I did not tell you earlier. I was afraid. I was afraid you would not believe me because I have told you so many times that I was ending it. But this time I really did it. I did it. Not for you, but for me. And so that there could be an us. And I know that I took a long time to do it. Way too long, I'm sure, for many people, and I know that you may not have waited for me. And that's also why I was afraid to say anything. Because I'm scared not only that you won't believe me, but that now you won't want me. That you took that box with your feelings, and you really did put it away, and now they're gone, and I lost my chance to have the one person I really want. I'm sorry I couldn't act faster, and I'm sorry I couldn't tell you all this sooner. I kept trying. I wanted to. But I couldn't bring it out of myself. I was too afraid that you would not want me."

He looked down, away from me, finally taking his finger off my mouth. The emotions came so hard and fast that it was like a punch in the gut.

I realized that I could not do this. I did not want this. I had wanted him for so long that the sudden and unexpected absence of that desire felt like losing a limb. There was a hole where my love used to be, but I could not simply refill that hole on command.

He had told me over and over how complicated the situation was, but what I suddenly realized was that it had not been complicated at all. He may have bent over backwards to treat his girlfriend with respect, but, in the process, he had treated me like shit.

I thought about something I had read in one of the magic books Rafael had recommended. In an essay on the structure of magic, Roberto Giobbi wrote about the kind of people who choose magic as a profession, men who use magic as their vehicle for communicating ideas and emotions. For a magician like Jack, magic was about the show and the spectacle. It was a *performance*.

But for a magician like Rafael, magic was about illusion and psychological manipulation, artifice and misdirection. After all, sleight-of-hand magic does not really take place in the hands of the magician but in the heads of those who are watching. It was about constructing alternate realities, and it was from an alternate reality that I finally felt like I was escaping.

I looked over at him. He was so breathtakingly good-looking. But that was not enough.

"I'm sorry," I whispered.

He looked at me, puzzled. "Why?"

"Because I don't want this anymore."

"What do you mean? What don't you want?"

"This. You. Us."

"What?" He looked shocked and confused.

"Rafael, I need to go. I'm sorry." I tried to impart some urgency to my voice to encourage him to get out of the car and not to argue with me.

"I don't want you to go."

He reached out to take my hand, but I moved it away from him to my steering wheel. The expression on his face was the same as if I had slapped him. He blinked, his eyes filling with tears, but rather than feeling sympathetic, I just felt angry and tired.

"Rafael, I need to go," I repeated.

I wanted him out of my car so that I could go home. My voice sounded flat and cold, and I hated that, I hated feeling this way, but, at the same time, no part of me wanted to feel sorry for him. He did not deserve my pity. This was all his fault. He had fucked this up.

"What happened? I thought this was what you wanted?"

"It *was* what I wanted. I told you that. But I also told you that I was going to put my feelings in a box, and that I couldn't promise you I'd find them again." I shrugged. "And now they're gone."

He smiled sadly. "So now you're the magician with the disappearing act?"

I nodded. I did not know what else to say. He looked at me for a moment, in silence. Part of me hoped that he was thinking about what he had lost and part of me no longer cared. I was worn out by the drama, by the weeks of waiting and wondering and the torment of unrequited love. Now there was nothing left.

Without anything else to say, Rafael sighed and climbed out of the car.

"I guess I'll see you sometime?"

How does one do a break-up when there is no relationship to end?

I nodded, having no idea if that was something I even wanted. He looked at me, as if there was something more he wanted to say, but then he just turned and walked away. I sat there in my car for a moment, staring out into the night but not seeing anything. I could feel the stress lifting from my body like fog burning off in the afternoon sun.

I had gotten what I thought I had wanted, only to discover I did not want it at all. That realization was liberating. As I saw Rafael recede into the distance, I knew, with greater certainty, that I had done the right thing. He would never have given me the relationship I wanted. I actually felt happy. It was time to go home. As I drove down Franklin, I felt free.

***

When I walked up the stairs to my apartment door, I saw that there was a black bundle of something sitting outside my front door. My first instinct was to sigh, that Rafael had somehow beaten me here and left some kind of gift for me. But then I remembered that Rafael did not have a car, and there was no way he could have gotten here before me unless he magically drove at twice the legal limit. Was it just another unwanted phone book?

As I grew closer, I could make out what it was, although I still had no idea where it came from. It was a bouquet of white roses. I picked them up and looked for a card. There was not one. Puzzled, I stood up and went to put my key in the lock. But as I did so, I noticed that there were pieces of paper stuck to the door. It was dark, but I could tell they were post-its, in the shape of a heart. And on the center post-it, were two letters with a plus sign between them: "J+A." My heart melted.

I took out my phone and called Jack. Suddenly I wanted to see him more than anything.

"Where are you? I thought you weren't back until tomorrow?"

"Surprise! I got back a day early. I'm in my car, just down the street. I'll drive right back. Can I see you? I came straight from the airport."

"Yes. Please. Now?"

I had barely made it into my apartment and was still kneeling on the floor, greeting Miles, when I heard a knock at my door. I stood up and turned around. It was him. He stepped into my apartment, hesitantly, and I reached forward and pulled him to me. With my hand, I turned his face toward mine, to look into his eyes. I ran a finger along the line of his jaw, feeling the softness of his lips, the shape of those gorgeous cheekbones, and then I kissed him.

We had kissed before, but this kiss was different. With this kiss, we knew we were meant for each other, open to each other. The timing, at last, was right. I could see him for who he was. It was as if all the distance and delay had merely made this moment clearer, exploding open into a bright light we were falling into. Here, in the doorway of my apartment, I wanted him. I wanted him desperately. His hand was behind my neck, pulling me closer to him. He grabbed me around the waist, and we were hungry and sloppy and all over each other. We were ravenous for the touch of each other's bodies. It had been too long.

He was tugging at my dress, pulling it up, reaching his hands up my thighs. His hand slipped inside my underwear, inside my body, and he moaned as he felt how wet I was. I reached my hand along the inside of his leg, feeling the heat coming from his crotch, feeling the intensity of his desire for me.

"I want you," I whispered.

"And I want to make love to you," he whispered back, his tongue tracing the line of my ear, my entire body melting on top of his.

"Are you really staying in town for a while?" I asked, realizing, as the words came out of my mouth, how much I wanted that to be the case.

"Yes. I am. With every trip, I knew how much I hated leaving you. I never used to mind the travel that much before, I never really felt the loneliness before until I started spending time with you. After our second date, I started looking for a job that would keep me here. So I could stay here. And get to know you."

"Really?" I leaned back to look at him. "After our second date? Are you serious?"

He nodded and smiled.

"Why didn't you tell me?" I asked.

"Because I didn't know how long it would take, and I didn't want you to wait for me if it took a long time. I wanted to wait to tell you when it was real, when it was happening. So it wouldn't feel like an empty promise."

"And now it's real?"

"Yes." He grinned. "I start next week."

I was floored. I had not seen any of this coming. All I wanted to do was kiss him. My entire body was consumed with desire. I could not think straight. I could not think at all. I just wanted him inside me, I wanted him to fill me up. I wanted to hold him and be held by him. I wanted to feel him against me and inside me. I felt hollow, barren, and empty, with a yearning need only he could satisfy.

Taking my hand in his, he led me into my bedroom. He pressed me against the open door, tilting my head up with one hand, the other hand tracing the line of my jaw, down my neck, his mouth following the trail of his hand, his tongue gently running along my chin, my lips, my neck, my bare shoulder. His other hand slid down my body, grazing my breast, tracing the hardened nipple with his thumb, before it made its way over my hip and between my legs. I gripped the doorframe to stay steady. I could barely stand. My breath was coming out in shallow, rapid bursts. My mind was clouded by my desire.

"Turn around," he whispered to me, and I complied.

He gently lifted up my hair and kissed the back of my neck, little kisses running along my neck and to my shoulders. My knees threatened to buckle as I felt his lips grazing my skin. He began to tug on the zipper of my dress, his mouth following the skin as it was exposed, kisses going down my spine, until the dress was fully unzipped, and then, with delicacy and precision, he slid it off me, letting it fall to the floor.

He turned me back around to face him and just stared. I was still in mybra, panties, and heels.

"You are so beautiful," he said, running one finger along my collarbone and up my neck to my mouth.

I opened my lips and he slipped his finger inside. As I sucked, I could hear him moan, and I reached out with my arm to pull him closer to me so that he was flush against my body. His breathing became shallower, faster, as I licked and kissed and sucked on his finger.

I ran my right hand down the side of his body, along his belt buckle, until I found his erection. His desire for me was massive, and I could feel my wetness soaking my underwear and starting to trickle down my leg. I reached behind and unhooked my bra, letting it fall to the floor. His hands slid around my waist, grabbing hold of my panties, and pulling them down to my knees. They fell the rest of the way on their own, the fingers of his right hand pressing into me. I shivered, every inch of my skin tingling, and I could not stand the anticipation. I could not stand the teasing. I had waited too long already.

I slipped his suit jacket off, first one arm and then the other, throwing it on top of my dress. I grabbed his belt and unhooked the buckle, my fingers fumbling for a second at the button, and then I unzipped him, tugging his pants down. He stood there, at my disposal, and it was a glorious feeling to know that he was mine.

I could see his erection straining against the fabric of his boxer shorts, but I saved that for later. First, I loosened his tie, remembering that first night I saw Rafael and the visions I had for that tie and how I wanted to use it. Now, in this moment, I could not care less. I did not want games. I just wanted Jack's body inside me. I threw the tie on top of the suit jacket and started unbuttoning his shirt. I could not unbutton him fast enough.

A few seconds later, the shirt was on top of the tie. The clothes pile was getting larger, but neither of us was looking at it. We were too busy staring at each other. I was fully naked. All that was left was his boxers. I pulled those down as my mouth ran along his chest and between his legs. I could tell he was holding his breath, only releasing it with one long exhale as I took him into my mouth. He was looking down at me, watching me as I slid him in and out of my mouth, my lips pressing firm, my tongue flicking the smooth skin. His eyes closed, and I could tell he was about to fall over.

I leaned back just enough to shove him onto the bed, and then I climbed on top of him. I put him in my mouth, and the realization hit me that I was here, naked, with Jack, and his desire for me and my desire for him were the only things that mattered. His hands were on my head, tugging on my hair, his body squirming beneath me, his breath quickening, but I did not want him to come so fast. I needed to feel him inside me. I needed him to make love to me.

I lifted my head off him and slid my body up against his until our faces were beside each other. He wrapped his arms around me and pulled me close to him, our bodies touching, his hands running down my back and over my arms, and I had never felt so lusted after or so lustful for another person. I could see his need and desire in his eyes, and I was sure that he could see the same in mine.

"I want you," he whispered, and the pressure of his erection between my thighs was only additional confirmation. His mouth was on my breast, sucking on my nipple, licking my stomach, my arms, my hips. He was all over me, a flurry of tongue and touch. My eyes were closed, my body sinking into the bed, a mess of sensation and stimulus, driven only by my desire. And then he stopped, sat back, and I opened my eyes to see that he was simply staring at me, at my body.

"You are so beautiful," he said, and I blushed.

"Fuck me," I told him, and he did.

He ripped open a condom packet. When he was ready, I reached forward and pulled him back on top of me. He groaned as he slid inside, and I wrapped my arms around him and held him so close that he could not move.

"Wait. Just wait. Give me a minute," I asked.

We lay like that for a minute, feeling each other, feeling the bliss and heat of him inside me, the consummation of so much desire, so much texting—but now, none of that mattered. All of that was behind us. All that mattered was that we were here, together, and that he was inside me, and it felt perfect and blissful, like my body had been shaped to fit around him.

And then I tilted my pelvis up to meet him, and that was the only cue he needed to begin moving. His hands were on my hips, his body lifting and lowering, his pelvis tilting, the feeling of him inside me was almost too much, and I moaned with pleasure.

"Adrian..." he whispered, pulling me up so that the two of us were sitting, his legs wrapped around me, my legs wrapped around him, his arms against my back, and we stared at each other, and I pulled him tighter, closer, deeper into me. He lifted me up and down, so that I slid back and forth over him. He, too, moaned, and then, with a hunger, he rolled me back over onto the bed, getting on top of me, his pace quickening, his breathing accelerating. He was kissing me on my mouth, on my nose, on my throat, and on my breasts, his fingers tugging at my nipples, my legs squeezing around his waist, our bodies completely intertwined.

It was both torturous and delicious. I was losing myself. Every time he slid up, he grazed my clitoris, and I could feel my orgasm hovering on the fringes, but it was not enough pressure to make me come, just enough to tease me excruciatingly. I grabbed hold of his hips and adjusted him, pulling him closer so that the pressure was more consistent, more steady, my tongue fucking his mouth as aggressively as he was fucking me.

The quiver of my orgasm began at my toes, the hint that this wave of sensation was about to come crashing over me.

"Don't stop," I begged, but he did stop, for a moment, to register what was about to happen, and then he picked up speed, his desire fueled by mine.

The quiver crawled up my legs, building in intensity, as our rhythm built, faster and faster, until the wave crashed over me, and I fell into the most incredible orgasm of my life.

"Oh, holy fuck," I cried out, every inch of my body on fire, utterly consumed, and his pace quickened even more as he thrust harder, his moans louder in my ear, and then he exploded inside me with a huge gasp, his body shaking, sweaty, rigid at first, and then he collapsed beside me.

My head rested on his shoulder, our arms wrapped around each other, exhausted, delirious, and happy, in a state of half-asleep bliss, too content to fall asleep, reluctant to let this moment end.

"I want to be with you, Adrian," he whispered.

"I want to be with you, too," I whispered back, and to my surprise, I really did.

And then, as if we had given ourselves permission to move forward together, to begin the next scene, we fell asleep like that. Naked and together.

DAHLIA SCHWEITZER

Dahlia Schweitzer is a writer, teacher, and performer currently residing in Los Angeles.

The author of both erotic novels (LOVERGIRL, QUEEN OF HEARTS, I'VE BEEN A NAUGHTY GIRL) and cultural criticism (for outlets including HYPERALLERGIC and THE JOURNAL OF POPULAR CULTURE), Schweitzer's first academic publication, ANOTHER KIND OF MONSTER: CINDY SHERMAN'S OFFICE KILLER is published by INTELLECT PRESS via THE UNIVERSITY OF CHICAGO PRESS.

In addition to her writing, Schweitzer's critically acclaimed recently re-released album, PLASTIQUE, consists of sexy dance music and spoken-word interludes, designed to enhance the experience of reading her books.

For more information, please visit...

www.thisisdahlia.com